**Highest Praise for Leo J. M**

### *Arch Enemy*

"Utterly compelling! This novel will grab you from the beginning and simply not let go. And Dan Morgan is one of the best heroes to come along in ages."

**—Jeffery Deaver**

### *Twelve Hours*

"Fine writing and real insider knowledge make this a must."

**—Lee Child**

### *Black Skies*

"Smart, savvy, and told with the pace and nuance that only a former spook could bring to the page, *Black Skies* is a tour de force novel of twenty-first-century espionage and a great geopolitical thriller. Maloney is the new master of the modern spy game, and this is first-rate storytelling."

**—Mark Sullivan**

"*Black Skies* is rough, tough, and entertaining. Leo J. Maloney has written a ripping story."

**—Meg Gardiner**

### *Silent Assassin*

"Leo Maloney has done it again. Real life often overshadows fiction and *Silent Assassin* is both: a terrifyingly thrilling story of a man on a clandestine mission to save us all from a madman hell bent on murder, written by a man who knows that world all too well."

**—Michele McPhee**

"From the bloody, ripped-from-the-headlines opening sequence, Silent Assassin grabs you and doesn't let go. *Silent Assassin* has everything a thriller reader wants—nasty villains, twists and turns, and a hero—Cobra—who just plain kicks ass."

**—Ben Coes**

"Dan Morgan, a former Black Ops agent, is called out of retirement and back into the secretive world of politics and deceit to stop a madman."
—*The Stoneham Independent*

***Termination Orders***
"Leo J. Maloney is the new voice to be reckoned with. *Termination Orders* rings with the authenticity that can only come from an insider. This is one outstanding thriller!"
**—John Gilstrap**

"Taut, tense, and terrifying! You'll cross your fingers it's fiction—in this high-powered, action-packed thriller, Leo Maloney proves he clearly knows his stuff."
**—Hank Phillippi Ryan**

"A new must-read action thriller that features a double-crossing CIA and Congress, vengeful foreign agents, a corporate drug ring, the Taliban, and narco-terrorists . . . a you-are-there account of torture, assassination, and double-agents, where 'nothing is as it seems.'"
**—Jon Renaud**

"Leo J. Maloney is a real-life Jason Bourne."
**—Josh Zwylen, *Wicked Local Stoneham***

"A masterly blend of Black Ops intrigue, cleverly interwoven with imaginative sequences of fiction. The reader must guess which accounts are real and which are merely storytelling."
**—Chris Treece, *The Chris Treece Show***

"A deep-ops story presented in an epic style that takes fact mixed with a bit of fiction to create a spy thriller that takes the reader deep into secret spy missions."
**—Cy Hilterman, *Best Sellers World***

"For fans of spy thrillers seeking a bit of realism mixed into their novels, *Termination Orders* will prove to be an excellent and recommended pick."
**—Midwest Book Reviews**

# Books by Leo J. Maloney

**The Dan Morgan Thriller Series**
TERMINATION ORDERS
SILENT ASSASSIN
BLACK SKIES
TWELVE HOURS*
ARCH ENEMY
FOR DUTY AND HONOR*
ROGUE COMMANDER
DARK TERRITORY*
THREAT LEVEL ALPHA
WAR OF SHADOWS
DEEP COVER
THE MORGAN FILES**

**The Alex Morgan Thriller Series**
ANGLE OF ATTACK
HARD TARGET
STORM FRONT

\*e-novellas
\*\* compilation

# Storm Front

*An Alex Morgan Thriller*

## Leo J. Maloney

**LYRICAL UNDERGROUND**
Kensington Publishing Corp.
www.kensingtonbooks.com

LYRICAL PRESS BOOKS are published by
Kensington Publishing Corp.
119 West 40th Street
New York, NY 10018

All Kensington titles, imprints, and distributed lines are available at special quantity discounts for bulk purchases for sales promotion, premiums, fund-raising, educational, or institutional use.

Special book excerpts or customized printings can also be created to fit specific needs. For details, write or phone the office of the Kensington Sales Manager: Kensington Publishing Corp., 119 West 40th Street, New York, NY 10018. Attn. Sales Department. Phone: 1-800-221-2647.

Lyrical Press and Lyrical Press logo Reg. U.S. Pat. & TM Off.

First Electronic Edition: February 2022
ISBN: 978-1-5161-1009-4 (ebook)

First Print Edition: February 2022
ISBN: 978-1-5161-1010-0

Printed in the United States of America

*For my daughter, Katie; my three granddaughters, Katherine, Cecelia, and Grace; and my grandson, Henry*

"A ship in port is safe, but that is not what ships are built for"
—U.S. Navy Rear Admiral Grace Hopper

# Chapter 1

The valves had given her hell. The motorcycle was an eight cylinder, with thirty-two individual valves, and fifteen of them were shot. Of course, with a bike like this there were virtually no spare parts anywhere in the world.

All of the available components were attached to the four Morbidelli 850s in existence. Three of those bikes were in museums, and this one was a temporary resident of Morgan Exotic Motorcycle and Car Repair.

Alex's shop was less than a year old, and six months after it opened, she'd gotten a panicked call from a local collector who had purchased the motorcycle. He had brought it to his garage and had immediately started the bike. The Morbidelli had run for less than five seconds before the engine blew.

After years on display, the engine should have been drained and refilled; then the pistons should have been hand lubricated and hand cranked before starting. It was a rookie but understandable mistake. One of the most valuable motorcycles in the world, the Morbidelli occupied a rare space between a marvel of handmade Italian engineering and a work of art—one that looked sleek and slightly futuristic even though it was as old as she was.

And, of course, Alex had a soft spot for Italian motorcycles.

No one wanted to risk driving a museum piece, but these motorcycles were meant to be on the road. However, if you took them out, you risked losing a priceless and irreplaceable machine. Of course, if you left them in a museum, you risked losing them to slow decay. It was a legitimate debate, but Alex knew what side of the question she came out on.

She turned the key and the bike roared to life. Her ears told her that the engine was firing perfectly, the new valves completely in tune with the originals. This was not a given. It was one thing to find an expert machinist to precisely duplicate the Morbidelli valves. It was another thing to source steel that was an exact match in density and purity.

The simple solution was to replace all of the valves with new ones. But with a machine like this, Alex wanted to keep as much of it original as possible.

Fortunately, she knew someone who could do both. Her friend on the Renard Tech Formula 1 team had not only come through on the valves, but he had sent over the original Morbidelli mold for the valve cover. How he'd gotten it, she had no idea. None of the original tooling for the bike was supposed to have survived; yet there the mold was, on a shelf in her shop.

Alex's thinking on the mold was the same as her thinking about the weapon she always had on her person. Better to have the mold for an essential engine part of a priceless Morbidelli motorcycle and not need it, than need one and not have it.

Alex was tempted to take the motorcycle out herself, but she had a schedule to keep. In fact, she was already behind.

The pressure wasn't from the owner—he was out of town—but from Diana Bloch, who had called a surprise meeting. At Zeta headquarters they didn't like to use the term emergency for something as mundane as a meeting or a briefing, but Alex had the feeling that whatever was going on was edging into that territory.

Still, this delivery was important, certainly the most important one she had made to date in her cover business. And she knew that this might very well be the most valuable bike that would ever be her personal responsibility.

Alex pulled out the ramp that sat under the truck's cargo area, and then she pushed the bike inside. Once it was secure, she closed up the back and headed into the cab.

The truck had been a gift from her father. It was a simple fourteen-footer, but her dad had insisted on giving her a brand-new one. And her mother had designed the tasteful logo that appeared on both sides of the cargo area.

Not every agent at Zeta took his or her cover jobs seriously, but she knew her father took his classic car business very seriously. Certainly, her mother was committed to her own interior design business.

Over the years Alex had absorbed the Morgan philosophy that said anything worth doing was worth overdoing. Otherwise, why bother?

The traffic wasn't bad, and she made the Belmont Hill neighborhood by eleven. If she looked down the long driveways, Alex could get glimpses at the very impressive houses—mansions, really.

Mr. Lacesse's house was among the most impressive in the area. She entered the security code he had given her, and the gate opened.

She drove past the main house and to the large garage. The house appeared empty, which made sense since Lacesse had mentioned that his wife and children were at Martha's Vineyard for the week. He had planned to be at the house to take delivery of the bike but had been called away for business.

Alex was sorry he wasn't there. He had an interesting collection and genuinely understood cars and motorcycles, at least on a historic level. She punched the code he'd given her into the keypad outside the garage, and one of the four large doors opened.

The lights came on automatically to reveal a garage with space for a dozen vehicles. Eight of those slots were filled, three by motorcycles and five by cars. The collection was evenly split between American and foreign models. There was one car—a 1970 Hemi 'Cuda convertible—that she knew her father would love to get his hands on.

Alex unloaded the Morbidelli from the truck and put it in its place. The garage was immaculate, the bay for each car or motorcycle with a small display of original ads, brochures, and memorabilia celebrating the vehicle's life.

Yes, the owner understood and appreciated what he had. And, more importantly, he had promised to start the Morbidelli once a month and also ride it a few times a year on his driveway if nowhere else.

Alex would have liked to spend some more time enjoying the collection, but she had to go. She locked up and headed for her truck. When she turned the key she saw that it was ten minutes to twelve.

That was perfect. If she went straight to Zeta headquarters she'd be there with a few minutes to spare before for the 12:30 briefing.

The gate opened automatically when her truck approached. Alex had put her turn signal on when the ground rumbled and the unmistakable boom of an explosion hit her ears. A split-second later her truck pitched forward.

Her first thought was that it was the house, but a quick glance in her side-view mirror told her that it had been the garage, from which a small mushroom cloud of smoke was now rising.

There was too much flame and dust on the ground to see clearly, but the damage was bad. She realized the garage and its contents were probably a total loss.

*The bike*, she thought.

Her instinct was to leap out of the truck, inspect the damage, and check the house to see if anyone was hurt. But her training kept her in place.

The bomb had been timed to go off shortly after she had been scheduled to arrive, when both she and Mr. Lacesse should have been inside the garage. The fact that he was away and she was early had saved both of them.

But either could have been the target.

He was a wealthy fund manager and could easily have powerful enemies, while she had certainly ticked off more than a few people in her time at Zeta.

The thing to do now was to get back to headquarters and make a report. She could get to the bottom of this there, but that wouldn't happen if she got caught up in a local police investigation.

She almost missed the first gunshot because it was partly obscured by the sound of sirens.

The second bullet hit her windshield. The third hit the side of her truck. Her new truck, she thought angrily.

Alex threw the vehicle into gear and pulled onto the street.

Two more bullets hit her windshield.

That answered her question. Whoever had set the bomb was after her. She hoped they were stationary. The truck was pretty fast for a vehicle of its size, but it wouldn't be a match for a professional hunting team in a good car or SUV.

Alex floored the gas. She'd find out what she was up against soon enough.

\* \* \* \*

Diana Bloch checked her watch. It was just before 9:00 a.m and thus almost time for her call. She buzzed her assistant and said, "Mr. Rand, please make sure I'm not disturbed for thirty minutes."

She opened a window on her computer and waited anxiously. The time difference meant that it was 2:00 p.m in Antarctica. And with her responsibilities at Zeta and her nephew's duty schedule, it was difficult for them to find the odd half-hour to keep in touch.

In fact, this was first time in three months that she had been able to speak to him. She waited less than a minute and then promptly at nine the face of the only family she had in the world appeared on her screen. He was a handsome twenty-two-year-old man with a strong jaw and an impossibly straight nose.

He also had Bloch's sister's hazel eyes. Though Bloch was always pleased to see him, that first view of her sister's eyes staring back at her always gave Bloch a start and a twitch inside of her chest.

"Lieutenant," Bloch said.

"Aunt Diana," Jeffrey said, smiling broadly.

Bloch could never resist his smile and found herself smiling in a way she never did at Zeta headquarters.

"How are you? How is the posting?" she said. The naval base in Antarctica was as remote a posting as a young officer could get, but Bloch was pleased he was there.

Bloch had started in naval intelligence over twenty years ago and now had been at Zeta for several years. That work had taught her that the world was a far more dangerous and unpredictable place than most people ever realized.

Every once in a while the insanity and chaos that was always there showed itself in a major terrorist attack, or the sudden outbreak of war, but most of the time people carried on as if tomorrow would come as it always had.

And usually they were right.

People in the military knew a bit more, but their actual daily work kept them focused on the tasks in front of them even as they were aware of the threats that were always just under the surface.

But for the last few months everyone in the service and in intelligence agencies was on edge. The threats were bigger and came on more suddenly. And Diana Bloch knew personally how close the globe had come to major world-changing disasters in the last year.

In the current environment and at the insane threat level that had become the new norm, Bloch found herself glad that Jeffrey was in the middle of nowhere. Of course, the environment in Antarctica was plenty dangerous, but they were all known dangers—dangers that could be anticipated and planned for.

"It's surprisingly busy here, and I don't mind saying it's a bit chilly out," he said, smiling. "On the plus side, the new pastry chef is killing it."

"Pastry chef?" Bloch asked, surprised.

Jeffrey nodded. "He left a promising career in New York to join up and help us crack codes. He's had us all pulling double duty tweaking environmental control so he can optimize his puff pastry. I'd complain, but the croissants speak for themselves."

"I'm glad that the base has its priorities straight," Bloch said.

"Well, it's not the primary mission, but it is good for morale," Jeffrey said.

"Is there anything you need down there?" Bloch asked.

"Nothing. The base is pretty self-contained," he said.

"I meant..." she began.

"I know what you meant, Aunt Diana, and I appreciate it, but I'm treated well and we are pretty well resourced. We'll have to make do, and I don't want to call attention to myself. I prefer the men dislike me for me, not because my aunt has a direct line to the president and can get a hot tub drop-shipped to Antarctica."

"So you'd like a hot tub then?" Bloch asked.

Jeffrey smiled. "Now that you mention it…"

Before Bloch could respond, a red light flashed on the base station of her desk phone. A second later, her assistant entered the room, his face even more serious than usual.

"Director, we have a situation," he said.

"Jeffrey, hang on, I may have something here," she said.

Her nephew nodded and Bloch looked up at Rand.

When she did, she could see that Rand's expression was stern. Of course, he had six expressions, and all of them were variations of *stern.* This one was stern with a vertical crease in his forehead.

This meant that one of the Zeta agents was in serious trouble.

"Jeffrey, I have an emergency here," she said to her screen.

"Of course, Aunt Diana. We'll talk soon," he said. Then his face disappeared and her screen went blank.

"Who is it, and what have they gotten themselves into?" Bloch said, waiting to find out which member of her other family was in trouble.

# Chapter 2

"There's been an explosion, a very large one in Belmont Hill," Rand said.

Bloch ran through her mental list of agent addresses and ongoing operations. She came up blank.

"Alex Morgan was scheduled to deliver a motorcycle to one of her company's clients there this morning," Rand said.

*So there was a Morgan involved*, Bloch thought. Somehow that figured.

"What do we know?" she asked.

"Not much. Fire and police are on the way. Shepard's people are monitoring police and rescue communications and working on tying into traffic cameras," Rand said.

"Do we know if Alex is alive?" she asked.

He had only gotten halfway through his headshake when his phone beeped. He checked it quickly and said, "We've got some movement on her phone's GPS."

"Have Spartan put together a TACH team and get them on the road. And have Shepard meet me in the war room," Bloch said as she got to her feet.

\* \* \* \*

The bullets that hit the passenger-side window and then the windshield had come from the right. Alex turned hard left, wanting to put the cargo area between her and the shooter.

Even as she made the turn, she heard another bullet hit the passenger-side window.

*That's all new glass*, Alex thought.

That shot told her she was dealing with at least a two-vehicle hunting team—and one of them was the black SUV in front of her. It was stopped in the middle of the road, the passenger door was open, and she could see the gunman aiming his weapon.

She only caught a quick glimpse of the gun before she saw the flash of the suppressor and then a small pit appeared in the windshield directly in front of her face.

If not for the bulletproof glass that her father had insisted on, she'd be dead or dying by now. From the size of the pit in the glass, she guessed it was 9mm. From the brief glance she'd gotten of the rifle, it looked like a Ruger 9mm bolt-action.

That accuracy of the shot told her that her would-be assassin was a real threat. The fact this hunting team hadn't just sprayed her with automatic fire from AK-47s told her something else.

Despite the showy explosion, these were serious people who didn't want to call more attention to themselves than necessary. The single-shot bolt-action would be relatively quiet—especially with a suppressor. It was also pretty accurate for a weapon of its type. Certainly, the shooter had managed an accurate head shot from over one hundred yards.

The explosion and the second car had caught Alex by surprise. The fact that her windshield had stood up to a precision 9mm round would be a surprise for them.

Alex floored the gas pedal, aiming her truck directly at the SUV. She actually saw the instant when the gunman registered the fact that she was still alive and her truck was barreling toward his vehicle.

His look of shock made her smile. Then she watched him dive back into the car. By now, she could see the alarm on the driver's face as he computed his options—none of which were good.

The only choice he had was to throw the SUV into reverse. It wouldn't work, of course. They were at a stop and Alex was nearly on top of them while going almost forty miles per hour.

She considered and then rejected the idea of hitting them head-on. If this SUV were the only car they had, she would have done it, but it was too risky with another car behind her. Even if she took the one in front of her out, the one behind would still be a threat.

As if to remind her of that other car's presence, Alex heard the ping of bullets tearing through the back door of the truck and then getting stopped by the steel plating that surrounded the entire cab.

In addition to the glass, her father and Lincoln Shepard had armored the truck, but just the cab. Putting armor under the skin of the entire cargo area was impractical. You could do it, but the cost in weight would be absurd. However, the armor around the driver's compartment would keep her perfectly safe as long as she stayed inside the cab—and as long as the hunting team didn't have any heavier weapons.

And as long as her truck was still operational.

That was one reason she would avoid a head-on collision, which would risk the radiator that sat in the front of the engine. She remembered watching a demolition derby once with her father. He had explained that the reason that the cars launched their attacks in reverse was that it allowed them to do maximum damage to the other vehicles while protecting their own radiators.

Here, as she loomed over the SUV—which was now going maybe ten miles an hour in reverse—Alex cut the wheel to the right at the last second and accelerated.

This drove the driver's-side front corner of her truck into the center-right of the SUV's front end. It crushed the car's radiator, as well as most of the front end—while putting the SUV into a sudden counterclockwise rotation that announced itself with the ugly screeching and cracking sound of buckling and tearing metal.

Alex's truck blew past the SUV, tossing it to the side as she drove past the wreckage.

She allowed herself a moment of satisfaction, and then she heard the ping of more bullets. Despite the armor that she knew was protecting her, the sound behind her was unnerving. She preferred threats that were clearly visible and in front of her.

Then, as if the universe had heard her thoughts, a third black SUV made a turn onto her street in front of her and started racing her way.

*That is just not fair*, Alex thought.

* * * *

Bloch raced into the war room, where Shepard was opening up a laptop as he sat at the conference table. That done, he hit a button on the star-shaped speakerphone in front of him.

"Are you okay, Alex?" he asked, and Bloch could hear the concern in his voice.

"I am," Alex said, her voice tense.

"Alex, help is on the way," Bloch said.

"I appreciate the effort, Director," Alex replied. "But even if Spartan deployed at the instant of the first blast, she's twenty minutes out. I don't think my new friends will wait that long."

Then the sound of a barrage of automatic weapons fire hitting something solid came through the speaker.

"Still here," Alex said. "On the other hand, they might run out of ammo soon. Their trigger discipline has gone to hell."

"How's the rig holding up, Alex?" Shepard asked.

"It's taking a beating, but nothing has gotten through yet," she said.

"What kind of tactical options does the truck have?" Bloch asked Shepard.

"Passive only—armor plating, bulletproof glass," Shepard said.

Bloch glared at him as the sound of more bullet strikes came through the phone. He put his hands up and said, "What? It's a work truck. It wasn't supposed to have anything, but Dan insisted."

Bloch kept up the glare for another second, though she knew it was unfair. Most agents' personal vehicles didn't even have armor.

"Any idea who you're dealing with, Alex?" Bloch said.

"Nobody I know. And definitely no one from the shop. Most of my customers are pretty happy," Alex said, her voice sounding strained.

*How is that appalling sense of humor hereditary?* Bloch thought.

"They drive black SUVs, they're very professional, and they seem international," Alex said.

Alex didn't have to say any more. *Ares*, Bloch thought. They were the answer to most of the troubling questions that Zeta faced lately.

It also made sense that they would be after Alex. She'd hurt them quite a bit since she had started at the agency.

"There was a three-car hunting team," Alex said. "I disabled one of the vehicles."

Shepard pointed to a map on his laptop. It showed Alex's car as a red dot. It showed the two TACH team cars as blue. They were still easily fifteen minutes out.

"Alex, we can get local police to you quickly," she said. The police would have their hands full at the explosion site, but they were undoubtedly already getting calls about the gunshots. That section of Belmont Hill was literally all mansions that were set back a good distance from the road, but someone must have seen or heard something by now. And there would be other cars on the road. Shepard could hurry that process along and direct the police to precisely where Alex and the Ares team were.

"Negative!" Alex said. "Calling in local police will just get them killed."

That was likely true. However, there was a small part of Bloch—of which she wasn't particularly proud—that thought local PD might distract the hunting team long enough for her agent to get away.

"Make your way east," Shepard said. "If you can get to Northeast Highway—"

"I'll never make it," Alex said. Bloch could hear the screech of tires and more gunshots. "Armor or no armor, they are tearing up the truck pretty good. It's just a matter of time before they hit something vital, or shred the run-flat tires. Find me somewhere open and nonresidential where I can face them."

"On it," Shepard said. Then, a second later he said, "Head east and in three blocks there's a school."

"A school!" both Bloch and Alex said simultaneously.

"You can come in on the far side of their sports field," Shepard said. He took one look at Bloch's face and said, "Okay, head west and you'll hit Green Street Field. It's a park. If you come in on Madison from the north—"

"I know where it is," Alex said.

A loud thud came through the speakerphone and Alex said, "We may have one less car..." There was a few seconds of unintelligible muttering and then Alex continued, "No such luck. Still two cars left."

"What have you got on you?" Bloch asked.

"I've got my daily carry," Alex replied.

"That's it?" Bloch said.

"Yeah, but Shepard hid a ton of clips in the bottom of my seat," Alex said.

"Okay, you have ammunition, but all you have is your one nine-millimeter against two teams with fully automatic weapons," Bloch said, unable to keep the disgust out of her voice.

"I think I have a road flare in the back," Alex said.

"There is something else..." Shepard offered.

"What you did you and my father do?" Alex asked.

"I almost forgot. You said no explosives, but your father thought smoke grenades might come in handy," Shepard said.

"Oh, that actually wasn't a bad idea. Of course, you could have *asked*," Alex said, her voice sounding both pleased and annoyed.

Bloch had known Dan Morgan well enough to know that feeling very well.

"Same place as the clips under your seat, but these are under the passenger seat," Shepard said.

"That should even things up," Alex said. At first, Bloch thought Alex must be kidding, but there was no humor or irony in her tone.

Somehow that worried Bloch even more.

# Chapter 3

Alex saw the park up ahead. Though she thought there was a ball field on the far end, the part she *could* see was open field with patches of trees here and there. That would do very nicely.

She was glad to see that there was no one around. That would change soon, as it got closer to lunchtime. For some reason, there hadn't been any gunfire into her truck for almost thirty seconds.

*Reloading*, she thought. It was only a few more seconds before she heard the reports of more automatic fire behind her. There was the standard ping of bullets hitting steel but many more of the dull thuds of bullets making contact with her tires. The run-flats would hold up to a few bullets each, but they still could be torn apart.

Once that happened she would be a sitting duck in an armored truck that couldn't move, but could still burn...or explode.

Alex scooped up four clips from the spring-loaded tray under her seat and slipped them into the breast pockets of her leather motorcycle jacket. Then she grabbed four of the round smoke grenades and put them in her side pockets.

That done, she took out the last two grenades. One at a time, she pulled the pins and carefully set them into the drink holders, their round shape holding the release lever tight to the body of the grenades and keeping them from detonating.

Alex saw a patch of trees just up ahead in the park and cut the wheel hard to the left. The truck jumped the curb easily and headed straight for the trees. She kept them on her right and slowed to less than twenty miles an hour.

When she was close, Alex cut the wheel hard to the right, putting the truck onto a collision course with a large tree. Then she opened her door and leapt clear, taking two long steps before she rolled to a stop just as she heard the loud crash of the truck smashing into the tree.

The angle of the truck would hide her from the Ares team for a few seconds, so she quickly made her way around the trees and took cover behind another large one. The cab of her truck was already filling with smoke as the two black SUVs pulled up to the curb.

With luck, they would think they had hit her and she'd crashed. Then all she needed them to do was come out to investigate. Her cover position was good and her small, wooded area was already filling with smoke, making it nearly impossible to see her.

In fact, if the smoke grew thick enough she might be able to escape on foot, run to the far side of the park, and make her way to Zeta headquarters.

Of course, that would leave four Ares operatives loose in her city—four gunmen who had tried and almost succeeded in killing a Zeta agent. If she left them alive, who would be next?

Plus, they had made a wreck of her new truck. And destroyed one of the four Morbidelli 850s in the world—a bike that she had spent six months working on.

No, this ended here.

Of course, it was four against one, but Alex had an advantage: They likely thought she was dead or injured. And they wouldn't be able to wait long before they investigated.

The doors on one of the SUVs opened, and two men stepped out. Unfortunately, they were too far to hit with her Smith & Wesson. And while she was sorely tempted to take the shots anyway, that would give away her position and the fact that she was still functional.

No, she'd wait until they got closer. If she could take out these two, that would halve the odds against her.

But rather than walk toward the truck, they disappeared behind the SUV for a few seconds and came out with an RPG. As soon as that registered, one of the men lifted, aimed, and fired the weapon at her truck.

Alex barely had time to flatten herself against the tree and cover her ears. She heard the explosion and then felt the blast wave shake her tree and blow past her. There was now even more smoke in the air around her and Alex didn't wait, she stepped out from behind the tree and took a position closer to the burning hulk of her truck. She saw the two dark-suited figures approach the vehicle.

Even with the RPG hit they would still need to see her body for their mission to be a success. They were soon in range, but Alex forced herself to wait a few seconds more. She had to assume they were wearing body armor, so she would need to make head shots. And she couldn't miss: If they didn't go down, they could rush her, and in that scenario she'd be lucky to get one of them before they finished her.

Struck with inspiration, she pulled out one of the grenades in her pocket, pulled the pin and released the lever. The grenades were on a four-second fuse so she waited a second before she tossed it just to the right and behind them.

These men were trained killers, but instincts were instincts, and they turned their heads when they heard the sound of the grenade hitting the ground.

As it hit, Alex stepped away from her cover and starting firing, letting loose with two shots on the gunman on the left. To his credit, the gunman on the right started bringing his gun around before he had fully turned his head. It was a good effort but wasn't nearly good enough.

As the man on the left fell, she put two rounds into the center of the forehead of the one on the right.

Before he hit the ground, Alex took off at a dead run, curving behind the second SUV and the two men sitting inside. They would be getting antsy, and she would have waited them out if this wasn't a public place.

The white smoke from the grenades and the gray smoke from her burning truck were filling the air and attracting attention. One of the men in the SUV briefly shouted at four passersby to leave the area.

When they started to protest, the Ares operative lowered his window more and fired into the air. The four people took off at a run.

The smoke gave her cover to swing around to the rear of the SUV. She crouched and took a position behind it, weighing her options.

She loaded a fresh clip and felt the weight of the three remaining grenades.

Without hesitating, she took one out, pulled the pin, and tossed it to the sidewalk in front of the SUV.

The same trick had distracted the other two; there was no reason it wouldn't work a second time.

The grenade popped and started spewing smoke. Keeping her head down, Alex reached up with one hand and hit the button that would open the SUV's rear window. She pulled the pin on another grenade, let the glass open a few inches, and then tossed the grenade inside.

As soon as it went off, Alex lifted her weapon above her head to point it inside the vehicle and started shooting.

Keeping her head under cover, she was firing blind, but she had little trouble estimating the two men's positions and emptied her clip into the car.

The Ares operatives didn't even get off a shot, and Alex knew it was over.

People were starting to gather, and Alex could hear sirens coming closer.

She simply stood up, holstered her weapon, and started walking. When she'd put some distance between herself and the park she tapped her ear comm and said, "Shepard, you there?"

"Are you?" he said, sounding surprised.

"I am. The targets have been neutralized," she said.

Bloch's voice broke in. "Are you hurt?"

"No. I'm fine, but if you could give Spartan my position, I could use a ride."

# Chapter 4

Alex was grateful that Bloch didn't insist on seeing her right away. She was able to shower out the smell of smoke from the grenades, as well as the more pungent smell of the smoke from her burning truck.

She felt like a new person in her gray workout sweats. She was also pleased to see that except for a superficial bruise on her shoulder that she got when she rolled out of her truck, she didn't have a scratch on her. Which is not something she could say about the men sent to kill her.

If nothing else, their demise would send a very strong message to Ares command, whoever they were. And besides the psychological value of casualties like that, Ares was now down four highly trained operatives.

And that wasn't counting the losses that Zeta had dealt to them in the last few months. No matter how big your organization, losing four of your people in one day would hurt—certainly it would hurt Zeta. Even if Ares didn't care about the operatives individually, the organization would be less effective with fewer people.

Their tendency to commit suicide when caught meant that Ares agents were highly committed to their cause—whatever the hell that was. And though it was unlikely that Ares would run out of bad guys, Alex could hope. Certainly she would do whatever she could to hurry that process along.

When she was ushered into Bloch's office, the director gestured for Alex to sit in one of the chairs opposite her desk while she finished a call.

"Alex, I'm glad you're okay," Bloch said, looking her over. "No injuries?"

"None. Physically I'm fine, but I'm pretty angry, ma'am," Alex said.

"That we share," Bloch replied, flashing a grim smile. "This was an attack in our home city on one of our own. It feels personal," Bloch said.

"It certainly does to me," Alex replied. "And they came for me at my work, possibly endangering one of my clients."

Bloch nodded with understanding, if not sympathy. "I understand you worked for some time on that motorcycle—a rare one, I'm told. Lincoln Shepard was quite upset."

"Yes, six months of my life. And it was a hand-built Italian masterpiece. I don't mind saying that I'm angry, and I'm ready to do some hunting, Director. Any sign of the two operatives from the first car I disabled?"

"I just heard now from a source in the FBI. Local PD picked up one body at the scene. He was injured in a car crash, though his injuries didn't appear to be life-threatening. I suspect an autopsy will show the man died of cyanide poisoning. The other agent has disappeared."

Alex didn't like the sound of that.

"If he's in the city…" Alex began.

"Shepard's team will find him using their computers long before a hundred agents scouring the city could. I have something else I need to put you on. We have a very credible report from Karen O'Neal's threat identification system. A major incident is likely to occur in less than a month in the Coral Sea. I'd like to get you there and establish your cover as soon as possible."

"I can head back to my apartment and be packed in an hour," Alex said.

"I don't want you to go back to your place. If they knew your work schedule, Ares definitely knows where you live. I don't want to make it too easy for them. You can leave for your next assignment from here—this evening, in fact."

That surprised Alex. She'd never been assigned a mission and left on the same day before. On a complicated assignment there was almost always a day or two of briefings, some specialized training, and time for research and mental preparation if the assignment involved a complex cover.

Bloch studied her, and Alex was certain that the director had read her mind. Then, as if to prove the point, she said, "In this case, your training will be part of your cover. Have you ever been on a cruise, Alex?"

"No," she said. Her parents had talked about taking one together for years. And now that they were on their long-planned trip around the world, Alex figured one or more cruises would likely be part of that. However, the Morgans had never taken a cruise as a family, and since Alex had started at Zeta she hadn't had anything even remotely resembling a vacation.

"That's fine. Do you get seasick?" Bloch asked.

"Never," Alex said.

"Then it's settled. I'm putting you on the crew of a cruise ship in the Coral Sea," Bloch said.

Alex had to think about where that was for a few seconds. "That's north of Australia."

"And south of Papua New Guinea. Karen O'Neal's threat assessment system has identified the cruise line as a potential target. There has been pirate activity in the area recently, but O'Neal's data points to something else, something much bigger. I'm putting you on the crew of an American-flagged vessel that sails out of Brisbane and tours the gulf. Even if your ship doesn't get hit, you'll be on hand if something happens in the area."

Taking a deep breath before she spoke, Alex said, "Ma'am, Zeta was just attacked locally. I think I could do more good here."

Bloch raised an eyebrow. "You do?"

"Yes, and while I appreciate your concern, I don't need to be removed from danger and sent on vacation. I would rather stay at HQ and solve the problem—for both personal and professional reasons."

Bloch stood up as she spoke. "Alex, I understand why you would want to do that, but it will absolutely not happen. Whatever you're thinking, I'm not sending you on this mission to get you out of danger; I'm sending you because it's where I need you. We're in the business of international security, not personal vendettas."

By the time she was done, Alex could see that Bloch was actually angry. "Yes, ma'am," she said. "I apologize for second-guessing you."

"And for your information, you won't be alone on this mission. Alicia Schmitt will also be on board. She'll be under cover as a consultant from Renard Tech., which has installed a new navigation system on board the ship."

"I know she was in the Navy, but it's been years. Will she be able to consult on a cutting edge system?" Alex asked.

"Yes, since she holds two patents for the underlying technology," Bloch said.

"What will my role be on the ship?" Alex asked.

"I want you and Schmitt to cover different ground. In fact, there's a good chance you will rarely, if ever, run into one another. I understand you have some food service experience?"

"Yes, one summer in high school," Alex said, not liking where this was going.

"Good, that will help, but the cruise line has its own training program. I understand you'll be serving drinks by one of the pools. Not exactly a vacation, but you'll be in a central passenger area most of the time."

"Director, wouldn't I do more good in, say, security?"

"You'd certainly be a more attractive target if there's trouble on board. And, frankly, I think you've had enough of that for now."

Everything Bloch said was true, Alex knew, but it still felt like she'd be wasted on this mission. She could see the impatience on the director's face when Bloch said, "Your flight to Brisbane leaves at six. You can get yourself ready until then."

Alex knew when she was being dismissed. Ten minutes ago, she'd been proud of the fact that she had survived an attack from a six-person, highly trained hunting team, taking all but one of them out with her hand weapon and some smoke bombs. Now she was going back to waitressing. Intellectually, she knew it wasn't a punishment, but at the moment it definitely felt like one.

* * * *

As soon as Alex left her office, Bloch buzzed Rand who said, "They are waiting outside."

"Send them in," Bloch said.

Lincoln Shepard and Spartan stepped into her office, and Bloch gestured for them to take two of the chairs by the coffee table on the far side of her office. She took a seat opposite them.

"You both saw Alex?" she asked.

"She looked okay and said she was fine," Shepard said.

"Yes, not a scratch on her. We'll chalk that up to her skills, with a good dose of Morgan luck. All of our agents are highly skilled, but not all of them have that luck. And like any other resource, luck will eventually run out. Ares came for one of our own practically on our doorstep. And yet we know almost nothing about them. However, right now, we know one of the operatives is likely still nearby and possibly injured. I want him; I want to interrogate him. And I want to get to him before he slips away, kills himself, or gets apprehended by local PD or the FBI. I want him on these premises, and I want to talk to him myself," Bloch said.

The two agents in front of her were looking at her wide-eyed, and Bloch realized her anger had become more and more visible as she had spoken. That was fine; once they got the Ares assassin in one of her interrogation rooms she'd show him more of that anger.

For a moment, she allowed herself to imagine how Dan Morgan would interrogate one of the men who had tried to kill his daughter.

"Are we talking about revenge?" Spartan asked. There was no judgment in her tone, just a genuine curiosity. Bloch knew that both Spartan and Shepard were close to Alex, and she suspected that they (as well as most of the team) would be very comfortable with a simple payback mission.

"Of course not," Bloch said sternly. "That is not our business, but while we've racked up a high body count of Ares operatives, we need one alive if we're ever going to take the fight to them. On that score, is your project complete, Mr. Shepard?"

"Yes, it is," he said, taking a handful of normal-looking .45 caliber rounds out of the pocket of his hoodie. He spread them out on the coffee table.

Bloch picked up one of the bullets. "Looks normal to me," she said.

Spartan looked at the rounds, then at Bloch. "What am I missing?"

"We've had a real problem with Ares agents committing suicide before we can take them into custody. They've always been able to activate cyanide capsules in their teeth before we could stop them."

Shepard picked up the story from there. "The director wanted something that would disable an operative and almost instantly render them unconscious. At first the model for the project was the kind of tranquilizer darts they use in zoos and animal control. But they only work at very close range and have terrible ballistic characteristics. The director wanted something that would function as normal ammunition."

Spartan examined one closely and said, "These will do more damage than a tranquilizer dart."

"Even more than a regular round," Shepard said. "To get a fast delivery of the neurotoxin, the bullets fragment on impact. It will knock the subject out quickly, certainly before they can activate their suicide tooth, but if you hit anything vital you'll want to get your target medical attention quickly."

"This isn't revenge," Bloch said. "But it is justice, and sometimes justice is harsh. Certainly, given the death and mayhem Ares has caused—which is only a fraction of what they've tried to do—it seems fair enough."

Spartan picked up one of the rounds. "After what they tried on Alex today, I'd say more than fair."

"My team is doing an all-out electronic search," Shepard said. "Every hospital, every hotel, every flight, every traffic camera. We're monitoring everything, including local, state, and federal law enforcement communications. We're also trying to track the vehicles they left behind to see if we get any leads."

"Spartan," Bloch said. "I'd like you to get as many TACH teams together as you can. Have them hit the road and spread out. If Shepard finds something, I want to have people as close as possible to the location."

"How much of the new ammunition can we have?" she asked.

"As much as you can carry," Shepard said. "But I'd avoid firing it on full auto. A single hit will knock out a normal-sized man. Two might kill him. Even if the damage from the round isn't fatal, a double dose of the knockout agent might be."

"Noted," Spartan said, getting up. "Director, we'll be on the road in twenty minutes."

Her agents hurried out to do their jobs and Bloch felt marginally better that they were doing something other than waiting for Ares to strike again.

And she was hopeful they would take an Ares agent alive. She'd meant what she'd said to Alex. They weren't in the revenge business, but Ares had just tried to kill one of her people.

And while she would take no pleasure in hurting them back, she'd allow herself to take *satisfaction* in a job well done.

# Chapter 5

Dan Morgan looked over at Peter Conley and shook his head. "A spy novel, really?"

In the next beach chair over, Morgan's partner was reading another one of his thrillers. "Don't you get enough of that at, you know, work?" Morgan said.

"These are more fun than the real thing. Plus, nobody shoots at you while you're reading them," Conley said.

"It's your Peter Pan complex," Morgan said.

"That I won't grow up? Now you sound like Dani," Conley said.

"No, not *that* one. Your *other* Peter Pan complex," Morgan said. "The one where you love stories about yourself."

"Peter Pan does that?" Conley asked.

"You speak seven languages and can pilot an F-fifteen, but there are large gaps in your education."

"You don't learn things like that until you have kids, and Dani and I aren't ready for that yet," Conley said.

Morgan felt like he'd been punched in the stomach and actually sputtered out his last sip of iced tea.

"You okay, Dan?" Conley asked.

"What did you just say to me?" Morgan said.

"I said that Dani and I aren't ready for kids," Conley replied.

"I got that part, but I'm stuck on the fact that you mentioned yourself, Dani, and kids in the same sentence," Morgan said.

"So you're the only one in our business who can have a family?"

"Not at all, it's just that you were always the one who said he never would," Morgan said.

"Have you noticed anything different about my situation with Dani?" Conley asked.

"You've been dating, or seeing her, or whatever you two are doing, for longer than a month. I think that's a first for you."

"And how many times have I gone on a couples' vacation with you and Jenny?"

"Including this one?" Dan said, "That would be once."

"So if you're asking me what's going on, I can honestly tell you I have no idea. I'm in uncharted territory," Conley said.

Morgan should not have been surprised. His friend had been different with Dani, but Morgan assumed it was a phase. Conley had been through so many phases in his life. He'd always thought that was why the man had learned so many languages—as well as so many other skills from flying to competition-level poker.

Peter Conley went deep into a subject or an interest, and then moved on. He'd been the same with women—the only difference was that those phases had been much shorter in duration.

"Dan," Jenny's voice called out behind them. Both men turned to see Jenny and Dani waving from the top of the path down to the lake. Even from a distance, Dan could see that the women were wearing different clothes than they had worn when they left. That meant it had been a good day of shopping.

The fact was that it had been a good day, period. He'd been to Geneva at least a dozen times—and some of those times were with Conley—but all of those trips were for work. He'd never spent any time on the lake itself.

The Swiss Alps surrounding the lake were impressive. And because it was clear, he could see the snowcapped peak of Mont Blanc in the background. Even though he'd seen that mountain before, he'd never noticed it. He enjoyed the remoteness of their current spot, and the air was cool and crisp.

He was glad Jenny had talked him into the trip. They had discussed it for years, but he'd always found a reason to put it off. He shouldn't have been surprised that he was enjoying it; Jenny was right about most things.

The surprise had been Peter and Dani coming along. The Morgans were weeks into their trip when they'd made a brief detour back to the United States when they thought Alex might be in trouble.

They'd picked up the stragglers then, when they were in Nevada. After that, the couples had gone to Texas for a quick stop. That turned into another stop in Barcelona, and now they were in Switzerland.

The women laughed and pointed at them.

"I don't like the sound of that," Conley said, but he said it with a smile.

"We'll drop this stuff off," Jenny said, holding up her bags. "Then we'll come down to see you."

"This is good for Dani. She likes Jenny and your wife makes her feel normal, like a regular American."

"They do look like a couple of tourists," Morgan said. That was no small thing. Dani had grown up in Communist China, where the government had imprisoned and then killed her parents for practicing their religion.

Then Dani had joined the Chinese intelligence service and had risen very high in the system that had destroyed her family. When she had met Conley in the Philippines less than a year ago, she was ready to defect.

Peter had helped her and whatever had started between them in Manila was still going on most of a year later. When you spent your whole life in a system like China's you were always looking over your shoulder—even if you were in the inner circle. Maybe especially if you were in the inner circle.

When you were just playing your part until you could escape that system, every day carried enough pressure that it would break most people. But Dani hadn't broken, and when it was over she had found some peace and purpose in America and at Zeta. And it looked like she had found something else with Peter.

Conley was good for Dani, and Morgan could see that she was good for him.

Jenny and Dani started back down the path from their rented lake house. About halfway, Jenny stopped to answer her phone.

The phone had been a compromise that Dan was willing to make. He hadn't wanted to bring one along, but Jenny had insisted, and he was glad she had. A few weeks ago, it had meant that they were able to get a message from Zeta that Alex was in trouble and on the run.

Now, Jenny carried a secure Zeta-issued phone and Morgan was happy to have it. He wasn't happy, however, with the look on her face. She was on the phone for a solid five minutes and Morgan waited impatiently for her to hang up.

When it finally happened, her face was set, which told Dan that what they had to talk about was serious but not a disaster. That was something…

"That was Diana Bloch," Jenny said, as if his wife talking to the head of the most secret international intelligence organization in the world was perfectly normal. To be fair, it had been happening fairly often lately.

"Alex is fine, but there was an incident," his wife said.

Dan felt his internal temperature rising. Jenny continued, "There was an explosion at the home of one of Alex's motorcycle clients. It happened right after Alex had left, so she wasn't hurt. However, some men did chase her on the road, but she escaped and made it to Zeta."

Morgan could easily fill in the blanks himself. Clearly, his daughter was all right, but he suspected that the men who had been "chasing" her were not. Just because Diana Bloch talked to Jenny more often than she talked to Morgan himself, that didn't mean that the director told his wife everything.

"Alex was the target in the explosion," Morgan said. It wasn't a question.

"Diana didn't even let Alex go home, she's been sent on a mission overseas," Jenny said.

"That tells me there's still a danger. It's a good idea to put a little distance between Alex and whoever was after her," Morgan said, though he had a pretty good idea of who that might be.

"More than a little distance," Jenny said. "She'll be working on a cruise ship in the Coral Sea."

"That has to be at least nine thousand miles of distance," Morgan said. "She'll be safe."

"From whoever was after her in Boston, maybe, but Karen O'Neal's threat assessment system has flagged that area, and that ship as a potential target," Jenny said.

That almost made Morgan smile. His wife had become much more involved in the goings-on at Zeta since Alex had started working there. For an interior designer, Jenny had an amazing grasp of how the organization worked.

"That is Alex's job now, to stop threats before they happen and deal with them if they do. We're still getting false positives on the system; it could be nothing."

"Diana is also sending Alicia Schmitt," Jenny said.

That did change things. One agent was a precaution. Two meant there was a good chance there would be trouble.

"I think we should make a little detour," Jenny added.

"A nine-thousand-mile detour?" Morgan asked. "No, from here it would be ten thousand. I know it's hard, Jenny, but we have to trust that Alex knows what she's doing,"

Jenny simply stared at him.

"You had a long talk with me when Alex started this work," he added. "You told me I couldn't hover, that I had to let go, that she'd never be her own person if I was always backstopping her."

"You went to help her in Nevada," Jenny said simply. "We all did."

"You know that was different. She was being hunted by every local, state, and federal agency in the United States. This is Alex simply doing her job."

"I don't like it, Dan. I have a feeling that she'll need us," Jenny said.

*Feeling*, that was the key word. His wife had had an Irish grandmother who read tea leaves and made uncanny predictions. He'd teased Jenny many times about her own "gift," but he'd learned through experience to trust her feelings.

Morgan let out a sigh. This discussion had been over before it started. "So I guess we're canceling dinner?"

Jenny brightened. "Not at all," she said. "Alex will have two weeks of training before her first cruise. At dinner, we can talk to Peter and Dani about the best way to proceed."

Morgan's face gave away his surprise. His wife shrugged and said, "Do you think Peter would let us go without him?"

She was right, of course. At tonight's dinner there would be three highly trained deep cover operatives, with fifty years' experience between them... and his interior decorator wife.

And Morgan knew who would be running the show.

\* \* \* \*

Alex Morgan could barely keep her eyes open. The central staff corridor that ran the length of the ship loomed long in front of her. It was surprisingly crowded, given that it was nearly two in the morning.

The corridor was called I-95. When Alex first boarded the *Glory*, she'd thought I-95 was a reference to the highway that ran up and down the East Coast of the US, but she'd learned it was named after the work visa that allowed the international crew to work on the US-flagged ship.

But right now the nearly endless highway seemed like a better metaphor. She wanted to jog because that would get her to her room and her bunk quicker. The problem was that simply walking required a massive physical effort.

Alex had gone without sleep on missions before, but not for this long. Eleven days of this schedule was taking its toll. Her father had once talked about the two things he hated most in army boot camp. The first was a drill sergeant that he'd clashed with over and over again. Later, her mother had explained that Dan Morgan had gotten into a physical fight with that superior officer. In fact, that was where her dad had first injured his knee. The second issue was the lack of sleep. A few days of significant sleep deprivation was one thing; after a week it qualified as torture.

When she'd first started training on the ship, her instructor laid out the program for the first week and Alex had asked how the schedule was possible, given the fact that the law prevented the cruise line for working them for more than eleven hours a day.

There was dead silence in the room, and then the instructor let out a loud, raucous laugh.

The rest of the new hires had looked at her in wonder—perplexed that she would even ask such a question. Though it was an American cruise line, most of the staff and crew were from foreign countries. In fact, she was the only American she'd met in the company's "restaurant college."

Alex checked her watch. If she got to the room quickly, she'd be in bed and asleep by 2:30. Then she'd get in a full three-and-a-half hours before the alarm sounded at 6:00 am.

There were times in the last week when she'd only gotten three hours, so that extra half hour seemed like a luxury. She swiped her card at the lock on the door and was quickly inside.

She was relieved to see that Sorina wasn't in yet. With luck, Alex would be asleep before her Romanian roommate stumbled in. That was better for all concerned.

It was 2:25. Alex briefly considered showering but realized that she was just too tired. She settled for splashing water on her face and brushing her teeth. She turned off the room light, leaving the bathroom light on for Sorina. Alex was in bed by 2:28, grateful for the extra two minutes.

She had just closed her eyes when she heard a thud against the cabin door. Then there was some fumbling with the handle, followed by loud cursing in Romanian.

All of that told Alex that Sorina had been to the crew bar before heading back to the cabin. That was impressive in its own way. Sorina had ducked out on the team's cleaning project so she'd had a full hour of drinking.

There was more fumbling at the door and more cursing. Alex didn't speak any Romanian, but some of the curses were close enough to their Russian equivalents that she got the gist well enough to understand that what Sorina was suggesting was impossible—even if doors had parents.

Finally, the door swung open and Sorina lumbered in, but not before she flipped on the room light.

Alex squeezed her eyes tighter and said, "Sorina, I asked you not to do that. I left the bathroom light on for you."

"What is problem? Too bright in here for American princess?" Sorina said. Even if the young woman hadn't slurred her words, the smell of beer would have told Alex that her roommate was drunk...again.

The fact that Sorina managed to get in an hour or two of drinking after their sixteen-plus-hour days would have been impressive if it wasn't so exhausting on nights like this.

Among other things, Sorina seemed to dislike Alex for simply being American.

"Just put out the light so I can go to sleep," Alex said, willing herself not to get angry, which would cost her more sleep.

"I am not one of your subjects, my American princess," Sorina said. Her tone was belligerent. Alex had heard her mumbling to other workers about some boyfriend that worked for the cruise line. Sorina had signed up so she could work on his ship when she was finished with her training. However, Sorina was frustrated because she hadn't seen him in months.

But Alex had learned that for Sorina there was very little distance between frustration and belligerence—especially when she had been drinking.

Alex felt her own heat rising and said, "I don't have to be a princess for you to show a little decency."

An instant later, Alex felt the sheet and thin blanket of her bed get yanked off of her. Alex's eyes opened and she was suddenly alert.

"Perhaps you want to teach me some of your famous American decency," Sorina said.

By the time Alex's eyes were fully adjusted to the harsh room light, she was on her feet, and she was in a ready position for a fight. She'd planted her right foot back and her hands were in front of her.

For better or worse, her training had insured that she would be ready to defend herself when threatened. The problem was, in this instance it was definitely *for worse*. She was now facing off against a drunk, angry Romanian woman who had a full three inches on Alex's own five-foot-seven-inch height.

Alex couldn't afford a fight with this woman, even if Alex won.

She did, however, allow herself to enjoy the momentary look of surprise on Sorina's face. In Alex's experience, female bullies used weapons other than physical intimidation. Largely, she assumed, that was because women often didn't have the physical size and strength to back up their bullying nature.

But Sorina had the size and the bad temper to use all of a bully's tools: insults, whisper campaigns, and physical intimidation.

When they had first met, Alex had been impressed by the twenty-one-year-old's stature and sheer physical beauty. She had a remarkable figure, absurdly high cheekbones, and long, shining hair that was nearly black. Sorina could have been a runway model.

However, that beauty was now impossible to see through Sorina's drunken sneer. "Delicate American flower is not a mouse after all," Sorina said.

Normally, Alex would be amused by the butchered metaphor, but somehow it just made her angry.

"No, I'm not a mouse," Alex said, standing firm and putting all of her rage into her eyes.

That made Sorina smile. "Are you ready for this, you stupid American?"

"I'm ready for a little basic respect, a little basic decency, if it's not too much trouble," Alex said. She didn't like the look in Sorina's eye. The woman was working herself up to violence.

And while Alex wasn't worried about getting beaten by the Romanian, she literally could not afford a fight, even if she won. If there was a physical conflict on board, both parties were summarily fired and sent home.

Sorina knew this, but didn't appear to be concerned. Alex had to be. She couldn't succeed in her mission to protect a ship if she got sent back to the States while she was still in training. And even if Alex didn't care about how it would look back at Zeta, people might die if she wasn't where she was needed.

Alex would have to be very careful. Even if she didn't defend herself and took a beating, she still risked getting sent home for fighting.

"So only you stupid American princesses have decency. Maybe you want to teach me some?" Sorina said, bringing her face close to Alex's.

Alex had to force down the heat that was rising up in her chest. Extreme anger when provoked was the Morgan curse—one of them, anyway. She had to fight it.

She took a deep breath, relaxed her ready posture, and said, "No, I just want to sleep."

"That is a good choice, princess. You may be stupid, but you are not an idiot," Sorina said.

Alex had to fight down another impulse—this time to laugh—but she knew it wouldn't help, and she presumed the saying meant something less silly in Romanian.

For a second, Sorina studied her, deciding what to do. Then the woman backed off and turned to go to the bathroom.

"Stupid American," she said, as she closed the door.

Alex turned out the light, gathered her sheet and blanket and got back into bed.

It was nearly three a.m. She'd be lucky to get three hours' sleep if she fell asleep right away. Unfortunately, the adrenaline racing through her body would make that impossible.

Fifteen minutes later, Sorina was snoring in her top bunk and Alex was staring at the clock. If she forced herself to relax, maybe she could get two hours or so of sleep before six o'clock came.

# Chapter 6

"Thank you for coming and congratulations," Ms. Ambong said. The middle-aged Malaysian woman gave the group one of her rare smiles.

"There is no statue, or diploma, but you all have accomplished something very real here," the woman continued.

That was true and Alex felt a genuine sense of pride at the end of her two-week training course, which the staff referred to as Restaurant College.

Alex thought she had worked hard during her one summer of waitressing in high school, but it had been nothing like this. In fact, few things in her life had been as grueling and exhausting—and that included her survival training at Zeta.

There had been long hours, little sleep, and endless lectures about work procedures and customer service—plus a crash course in maritime law and safety.

Again, it reminded Alex of her father's stories about boot camp. And while Alex didn't get into a fistfight with her superior officer, she'd come close more than once with Sorina, who was now sitting a few rows over in the ship's theater that had been taken over for this last meeting.

Sorina had signed up with the cruise line to join a boyfriend. Maybe now that they were all shipping out tomorrow the woman would relax. The training had been hard and had put everyone on edge. There was no doubt that Sorina was a miserable roommate, but they had only one more night together.

Alex could put up with her for a few more hours. In fact, after a short reception in one of the customer lounges, Alex and most of the others would be exploring Brisbane. Though they had been in port there for two weeks, Alex hadn't stepped foot on land since she'd boarded the ship.

She was actually looking forward to seeing a little of Brisbane, though from what she understood of the planned activities, they were mostly a tour of a few local bars and a beach at Port Brisbane.

Still, it would be good to get off the ship, which had started to close in—though it was several hundred feet long and had been largely empty for the training period.

Ms. Ambong called out each of the training class by name. When someone's name was called, they got up, shook Ms. Ambong's hand, and then sat down again. People in Alex's class were from all over the world: the Philippines, Malaysia, Brazil, and a number from across Eastern Europe.

Yet of the fifty restaurant and serving staff in her class, Alex was the only American. Because of that, most of the others regarded her as a curiosity. And more than one of her peers had expressed real concern about whether or not she would be up to the challenges of the schedule. Most of them had meant well, but the message behind the concern was that as an American she was too delicate to last through training.

Alex wasn't sure if Sorina actually felt the same way or if her hostility was something personal. Either way, in twenty-four hours it wouldn't matter. The class would split up and head for any of half-a-dozen ships and Alex would likely never see Sorina again.

"Alex McGrath," Ms. Ambong called and Alex got up. Whenever she could, she followed one of the first pieces of advice her father had ever given her: Keep your first name when you were undercover. It helped you feel comfortable as your character. It also prevented the kind of slipups that could get you killed: Looking up when someone called out your real name, or failing to do so when someone called out your assumed name.

Alex shook Ms. Ambong's hand and said a quiet "thank you."

As she took her seat again, Alex felt a rush of pride at completing the training—partly because Sorina had told her she would fail pretty much every morning and most nights.

When the short ceremony was over, Alex thought about what she would do. Before today, she swore that the first order of business would be to go back to her cabin and sleep for a good fourteen hours.

But she found that she didn't want to do that.

"Alex, we're going to meet up in the captain's lounge for a drink and then head into port," said Ola, one of the Polish girls who had been very nice to her.

"I don't think our princess wants to do that. She needs her rest," Sorina's voice said behind her.

Alex didn't bother to turn around. She could picture Sorina's sneer very well in her mind.

Nodding to Ola, Alex said, "Thank you, that sounds nice."

At the lounge, Sorina actually approached her and said, "You should be careful. Port is not a safe place for stupid Americans."

The threat in the woman's tone wasn't subtle. Fighting on board would get both parties sent home, and would end Alex's mission instantly. Port was another thing entirely.

"I'll have to be careful then, Sorina," Alex said, giving Sorina a wide smile.

\* \* \* \*

Dan Morgan entered the suite and said, "Jenny, I'm back."

"Everything okay, Dan?" Jenny called from the living room.

"Sure," he said. He was glad Jenny couldn't see him from where she was down the short hallway. It would be better if he could duck into the bathroom—

"Dan!" Jenny called out from the hallway, just as he reached for the bathroom door handle.

He decided to brass it out and turned to give her a tight smile. "Hey Jenny."

She scanned him quickly, and then her eyes settled on the blood on his polo shirt.

"I've been teaching Dani poker and we were about to go to the beach. What did you do today?" she said accusingly.

"Well, I told you Peter and I had to meet with—"

"A friend," she said. "You said you had to meet with a friend." Then her eyes focused on his right hand and the scrapes on his knuckles.

"He is really more of a *work* friend," Morgan said.

"You shouldn't come home covered in the blood of *any* kind of friend," she said.

"This really was no big deal. There are protocols for these meetings..." he began.

Jenny held up her hand and said, "Did you have to hurt your friend?"

"No, not really," Dan said, relieved that he could tell her the complete truth about that. There was a time that Dan had tried very hard to keep his work—and the parts of himself he needed to call up to do his work—from his wife.

That had worked for more than fifteen years. Then, he had to leave his real job to have the life that he and Jenny wanted. That lasted for a few years and then that work came looking for him and had almost destroyed his family.

To save his family, Morgan had needed to reveal the side of himself that he'd tried too hard to hide, and they had all survived. Since then—especially since Dan and then Alex had joined Zeta—Jenny had seen much more of him and his work than Dan would have liked.

However, the result was that they were now stronger together than ever.

"Did your *friend* tell you what you needed to know?" she asked.

"He told us what he knew and gave us another lead to follow. If you and Dani are okay, Peter and I will head out again and meet you for dinner," he said.

"Sure, but leave time so that you can change into something that isn't a mess. It's just the hotel restaurant—and I don't think they have a dress policy—but who wants to play into the stereotype of Americans who show up for dinner covered in blood."

"Will do," Morgan said. He kissed his wife and cleaned up while she left to rejoin Dani in the living room of their suite. Overall, Jenny was taking this very well. And she had given him an idea. He called Conley and told him to dress for dinner, but to bring his weapon since they might not be coming back to their suites before their reservation.

"But Dan, what if we have to…" Conley had protested.

"Don't worry, I have a plan," Morgan said. *Plan* was a strong word for what Morgan had, but he did have an idea that would help with their next meeting.

Conley showed up dressed like Morgan, in slacks, a button shirt, and a sport jacket. When the men entered the living room of the Morgan suite, Jenny and Dani were playing cards at the small round table by the windows.

Since they had reached Indonesia, the idea that this was still just a vacation was gone. The four of them had given up the carefully planned itinerary, the rented houses, the shopping trips, and the days at the beach.

Instead, they'd passed the time while learning what they could about what might be coming to this part of the world.

When the men entered, both women looked at them in surprise. "In case our errand runs long," Dan said. "We'll meet you at the restaurant."

Dani raised an eyebrow, to which Conley shrugged and gestured to Morgan. Jenny got up to say goodbye, while Conley and Dani huddled together. He heard them whispering, then kissing, then whispering again.

There was something going on between them, something Morgan had never seen happen with his friend and a woman before.

He knew that Dani wanted to go with them, and she could have helped, but she had agreed to stay with Jenny. There were still terrorist attacks in Jakarta, though the targets had mostly switched from Western tourists to police.

Having someone with Dani's training and abilities with Jenny helped Morgan focus on his work. And the fact was that Indonesia was still fairly sexist by Western standards—especially among the underworld elements they would be visiting. Having Dani with them would simply bring more attention to their movements.

Jenny pulled Morgan to her and kissed him. "Remember, you're doing this for Alex," Jenny said. "So don't hurt anyone...unless you have to."

"I'll make sure our meeting is quick and painless," Morgan said.

"Good, but make sure to take care of *yourself*," Jenny said.

"Always," he replied, and then she kissed him again.

Morgan and Peter took one of the blue Indonesian cabs to the address their contact had given them.

Before they had gotten into the cab, the driver had looked them over, studying their clothes, and said, "Perhaps somewhere else? That is no place for you."

"Thank you, but we'll be fine," Conley said.

The traffic was awful. Morgan had forgotten just how terrible the Jakarta traffic could be. For that reason, on their previous visits, he and Conley had traveled exclusively by motorcycle. Bikes gave them the option of hasty exits from unpleasant situations—an option they had made use of more than once.

You never wanted to be the subject of a chase in heavy traffic if your pursuers were armed and ill-tempered. Those chases tended to be short and end badly.

It took them nearly an hour to get the few miles to Kampung Ambon, one of the more notorious slums in Jakarta. It was full of two-story shanties, where corrugated metal was the most common roofing material and bedsheets served as replacements for broken windows.

There was trash pouring out onto the street, and Morgan detected the familiar smell of Indonesian cooking. He also recognized the smell of fried bananas and chili, which he always associated with Jakarta. And underneath it all was the unpleasant smell of burning garbage.

As depressing as it was, the neighborhood was bustling with activity. People rushed back and forth, children played on the sidewalk, and shopkeepers stood outside their shops and stalls. There was a lot of life here and Morgan thought there was something hopeful about the movement—the life—in the midst of the decay and squalor.

The agents had the cab drop them off a block before the warehouse, and they walked the rest of the way. Their pressed slacks, jackets, and purposeful strides told people they didn't belong in the area. And of course they would be recognized as Americans, or at least as Westerners.

On a normal mission, Morgan and Conley would avoid calling attention to themselves. On this one, attention was essential, and would move things along.

They certainly received enough strange looks as they walked to the address. They passed two groups of young men who called out, "Hey *bule*," to them.

Technically, it was an insult, since *bule* meant "albino" in Indonesian, but it was a relatively friendly jibe since it was a designation given to most foreigners and all white Westerners.

As Morgan and Conley got closer, the looks turned anxious, which told Morgan they were on the right track. Finally, there were three twelve- or thirteen-year-old boys who saw the agents approach and instantly took off running.

"Spotters," Conley said.

"At least they'll be ready for us," Morgan said. That would save time.

Sure enough, when Morgan and Conley reached the doors of the warehouse there were three men waiting outside. The tallest of the men stepped forward and held out a hand—telling Morgan and Conley to stop.

"You are Americans?" the leader said in accented but clear English.

Morgan noted that the three men looked serious but not particularly smart. They also didn't try to hide the bulges under their loose shirts, which told Morgan that they wanted people to know they were armed. The man who had spoken was obviously the trio's leader.

If that wasn't already clear, the man had long thumbnails. It was a status thing in this country. Originally, it had meant that a man did work that was more important than manual labor. However, nowadays, it was often used in gangs and terrorist groups to separate management from staff.

"Yes, we're Americans," Morgan said.

"What do you want?" the man replied.

"Drugs. We'd like a lot of drugs," Morgan said.

It took a second for the man to process that statement and then he said, "There is nothing for you here."

Morgan reached into his front pocket and said, "Hang on, and let me show you something."

All three men tensed and Morgan said, "I'll do it slowly." Then, with exaggerated slowness, Morgan pulled out a wad of colorful bills: Indonesian rupiah.

"We brought a lot of money. And as I said, we'd like some drugs," Morgan said conversationally.

The lead guard was uncomfortable, looking at the cash and then up and down the street. He ran security for a drug operation that was part of a larger terrorist organization, and he clearly didn't want any more attention out in the open.

"Put that away. Come inside and we can talk," the man said.

*Now we're getting somewhere*, Morgan thought.

# Chapter 7

The young Australian men in the first Brisbane bar were very taken with Alex's group, which was made up of women from all over the world. On board ship, Alex was something of a novelty as an American. And she had spent a fair amount of time fending off advances from male trainees the few times she had gone to the crew bar.

Here, however, she looked like just another local to the young Australian men, and that suited Alex just fine. They were much more interested in the Filipino, Brazilian, and Polynesian women. They were also very interested in the Eastern European trainees, especially Sorina.

That wasn't a surprise. She was extremely beautiful with her long black hair. But while Sorina loved to be the center of attention among women, she did nothing to encourage the young men, citing the boyfriend she would be seeing shortly.

Whatever her other faults, Alex guessed that Sorina's loyalty to her beau counted for something. And she'd seemed to have lost interest in Alex, which was another plus. After a couple of hours, they hit a second bar near the port.

Sorina was now good and truly drunk. She vacillated between maudlin exclamations about how much she'd missed her beau to bragging in great and enthusiastic detail about what she was going to do to him when they were reunited.

It was way too much information, and Alex wasn't sure that it was possible in a single night. And even if it were, it didn't all sound like a good idea.

There was talk of visiting a local beach for a bonfire, and Alex thought that actually might be a good idea. She'd never been to Australia before, and it would be nice to see a real beach while she was there.

But first Alex wanted some air. She headed outside into the late-afternoon sun. It was quiet compared to the bar, and the air was both fresh and dry, while the sky was clear and cloudless.

Alex decided that she liked Australia and might like to visit Brisbane again when the mission was over. From what little she'd seen, the city was clean and looked new. She also liked that it had a river snaking through it and pedestrians everywhere.

She also liked that the plants were different. She didn't recognize most of the trees and particularly liked the large, red flowering ones that were almost everywhere.

Alex barely had time to enjoy her surroundings before she heard a familiar, belligerent voice behind her.

"What's wrong, princess, too much excitement for you in there?"

Alex turned to see her roommate approach her. Sorina was wearing a drunken scowl that Alex knew too well.

"What do you want, Sorina?" Alex said, unable to keep the impatience out of her voice.

"I just wanted to see what you stupid American princesses do when you go outside," Sorina said, taking a step forward. Alex held her position and said, "You know, Sorina, I've been nothing but polite to you, and you've been a beast since we met. Why don't you go back into the bar, and after tomorrow we don't have to see each other again."

Sorina started in surprise and said, "The rabbit has a spine."

"All rabbits have spines," Alex said.

There it was again, genuine surprise on the woman's face, which was followed by what Alex could see was rising anger. Sorina hadn't expected pushback.

If she didn't walk away soon, Sorina was about to get even more surprises.

"What did you do in America, princess?" Sorina asked.

"None of your business," Alex replied.

Then, as if Alex hadn't spoken, Sorina said, "I was in the Romanian military. I learned some things there that I will show you now."

Alex scanned the area around them. There was a fence and a marina behind them, a parking lot on one side, and the street on the other. But there wasn't a single person nearby.

That suited Alex just fine.

"Looking for help, princess?" Sorina said, taking another step toward Alex.

"Not at all," Alex said, standing her ground. "Just making sure there are no witnesses."

Alex enjoyed the moment of doubt on Sorina's face. It passed quickly. "Stupid Americans," the Romanian said, taking another step.

* * * *

The two guards entered the warehouse first, then the leader ushered Morgan and Conley in front of him.

Morgan didn't like the low light in the entryway and was relieved when they stepped into the more brightly lit warehouse floor. As they did, Conley handed him a stick of gum and Morgan quickly unwrapped it and put it in his mouth.

Both agents started chewing and got dirty looks from the lead guard. Chewing gum in public was considered rude in this country, and would solidify the perception of the two Zeta agents as ignorant, rich, albino, foreigners.

The lead guard called another man over, and the new guy gave Morgan and then Conley one of the worst weapons pat downs Morgan had ever experienced. The guard ran his hands up and down the sides of Morgan's torso and gave his chest a couple of perfunctory pokes—all while Morgan made a point of loudly chewing his gum.

Of course, the guard missed the Walther that Morgan had holstered in the small of his back—and the one in his ankle holster.

Then the man went on to miss the Glock that Conley was wearing at his own lower back.

*So far so good*, Morgan thought.

These didn't seem to be particularly important or busy terrorists, and from the look of the warehouse they were running a business that was at least partly legitimate. There were rows of pallets and a few open racks of samples that told Morgan that they were warehousing pretty good knockoffs of designer clothes for women in the West.

There was also a half-dozen workers who kept their heads down and went about their work. Morgan suspected they were just that, workers. That meant that the guards and management of the operation were likely the only members of the terrorist cell.

From what Zeta was able to quickly piece together, this operation did a pretty large heroin and a minor gun business that funded another terror group in East Timor. Thus, they weren't an immediate threat to the locals in Jakarta.

The three guards led the two agents up to an office on the second floor that had a large window that overlooked the warehouse floor. However, the blinds were drawn and covered the window entirely.

Inside the office, a man sat at a large desk, smoking a cigarette. He looked up at the two agents and their two escorts.

The man stood up and said, "*Selmat sore*." He didn't, Morgan noted, offer his hand to shake. He also noted that this man was clearly in charge. Besides the office, his thumbnails were longer that the lead guard's.

*Fair enough*, Morgan thought as he chewed his gum more vigorously.

"I am Arief," the man said. Morgan knew the name. It was Arabic, not Indonesian, and meant *honest*.

"I'm Mr. Smith; this is Mr. Jones," Morgan said.

There was some cross talk among the Indonesian men. Morgan didn't understand most of it, though the word *bule* came up more than once. By the tone it was clear that these men didn't think he and Conley were the good, or even amusing, sort of albino foreigners.

"My men tell me you are in the market for…"

"Drugs. Heroin, if you have enough on hand. We're in the city on business and have some entertaining to do," Morgan said.

As he spoke, the lead guard made his way behind Conley.

Morgan's partner allowed it. Clearly, they were going to let this interaction play out, and it would help if the terrorists thought they had the upper hand.

"You have made a mistake," Arief said.

"We were told you had a lot of drugs here," Morgan said.

In his peripheral vision Morgan saw a series of quick movements that ended with the lead guard standing behind Conley with one arm around his throat. Holding him in the crude headlock with one hand, the guard's other hand had a gun pointed to Conley's temple.

Arief pulled back his own jacket to show a gun tucked under his belt. Then other two junior guards drew knives.

*Okay*, Morgan thought. Only two of the four had guns. And the boss was showing off his power—and how little he thought of Morgan and Conley—by not even drawing his weapon.

And the two junior men weren't even trusted with guns—despite the fact that there were in the gun business.

"There's no need for that," Morgan said as the lead guard pushed the barrel of his pistol into Conley's scalp.

His partner was being a good sport about it, but Morgan didn't intend to let this continue for much longer. There was always the risk that the guard or Arief would get trigger-happy, or nervous, or simply make a deadly mistake. And right then, the person most likely to suffer first in any of those scenarios was Peter Conley.

"Why don't you hand over the money you brought," Arief said, holding out a hand.

"I don't like to do business with a gun to my partner's head," Morgan said.

"We are not doing business," Arief said. "We are taking your money. Then we will ask you some questions about how you learned about our operation. After that... I wouldn't worry too much about what will happen after that. I would take a lesson from your friend and cooperate."

Morgan looked over at the lead guard, who still pressing his pistol into Conley's scalp.

"There's not a lot of incentive for me to cooperate. It sounds like you're going to shoot us anyway," Morgan said.

Arief shouted something at the lead guard, who cocked back the hammer of his pistol. That was it, Morgan thought. It would take very little pressure to pull the trigger now. They had to end this phase of the encounter and move on to the next one.

Morgan said, "Okay! You can have the money." He reached into his breast pocket with his left hand and lowered his right to his waist. If he needed to draw, he wanted to be able to do it quickly.

"I just don't want anyone to get hurt," Morgan said.

As Morgan held out the colorful wad of rupiahs, Arief said, "I'm afraid we both know that is inevitable now."

# Chapter 8

As Sorina advanced, Alex stepped backwards. After a few paces, the women were at the corner of the building. Alex turned and took a few quick steps along the side of the structure. Now they wouldn't be seen—or disturbed—by anyone entering or leaving the bar. With the marina fence to one side and the bar on the other, they were now guaranteed at least a few minutes of privacy.

And that would be more time than Alex thought she would need.

"You can't run, princess," Sorina said.

"You really need to make up your mind. Am I a stupid American? A scared rabbit? Or a princess?"

For a second, Sorina seemed confused by the question and then said, "Did I tell you I was in the Romanian military? I'm trained in fighting and I am very good at it."

"Did they train you to do so much talking first?" Alex asked.

"No more talking, princess," Sorina said as she lunged at Alex with both hands out. As an attack, it was very clumsy, even factoring in how much Sorina had been drinking. Alex decided she wasn't impressed by the hand-to-hand training Sorina had received in the military.

The larger woman tried to shove Alex backwards, but because Alex had planted her right foot behind her, it was a simple matter to grab Sorina's wrists, pull the woman forward, and throw her over Alex's hip.

Sorina went flying to the ground. Alex had expected the throw and the fight to end with Sorina face-planting into the dirt. However, remarkably, the woman twisted a shoulder and turned what should have been a fight-ending fall into a surprisingly graceful roll.

The roll finished with Sorina on her knees facing Alex. Then she sprang to her feet and flung herself at Alex, swinging wildly with open hands at Alex's face.

Alex didn't waste time. She blocked the blows outward and then aimed two fast, hard punches to Sorina's stomach. That stopped the woman cold, and Alex was able to grab her right wrist and pull it up behind her.

"Ahhhh…" Sorina said, as Alex twisted her arm up. Alex then swung her left hand around Sorina's throat and used it to pull the woman down to her knees. Alex added a bit more pressure to Sorina's right arm, and the woman cried out again.

"Stop moving or I will break your arm," Alex said calmly.

"Not my face. Not my face," Sorina said, remarkably clearly. "I have to see my—" Then she said a Romanian word that sounded like *ee-you-beet*.

Alex didn't speak Romanian, but it sounded enough like the Russian word for *lover* that Alex had a pretty good idea what she meant.

"Okay, not your face," Alex said, adding a bit more pressure on the arm.

"Ahhhh," Sorina said.

But Alex's own anger was already fading. Sorina had been a miserable roommate, nasty and inconsiderate, to say nothing of her constant insults. Yet there was something in her plaintive "not my face" appeal that had changed things.

Alex still wouldn't trust Sorina for a second, but Alex didn't think she would be any more trouble tonight. Still, it paid to be certain. Keeping pressure on the arm, Alex said, "You and I are done. Do you hear me? Tonight I don't care where you sleep, but it won't be in our cabin. I'll leave a little early tomorrow morning so you can collect your things, but I don't want to see you. And before you get any ideas, know that I can do this again. You may need to tell yourself that I got lucky, or that you were drunk. Fine. Whatever helps you sleep, but know that I can do this again and again. The problem is that it's taking all of my self-control to keep from breaking your arm. If this happens again I won't bother with self-control."

"Okay, prince—" Sorina started, cutting herself off before she finished. *You just can't help yourself,* Alex thought, pulling the arm tighter

"Okay, okay," Sorina said.

Alex waited a long beat and then slowly released the pressure on Sorina's arm and then released her from the headlock. Sorina took a few seconds, collected herself, and then got to her feet. She gave Alex a wary, appraising look and then looked unsure about what to do next. Sorina's expression was somewhere between angry and shocked, but even so, she was annoyingly beautiful.

"You can go back to the bar. I'm going back to the ship," Alex said. Then she turned and headed for the street to find a cab.

Her pleasant high spirits from earlier were gone. And the fight—which she'd been looking forward to—was a letdown. And the post-fight adrenaline crash wasn't helping.

In a matter of seconds, the last two weeks of hard work and little sleep had caught up with her. And the prospect of a full night's undisturbed sleep was *very* appealing.

* * * *

Morgan continued holding out the money as he weighed their options. Because Conley was still in the guard's headlock with a gun pointed to his head, Morgan decided to let his partner make the first move.

He didn't have to wait long.

Arief looked over at his lead guard and had just begun to nod his head when a muffled shot rang out.

Conley's guard's eyes went wide, surprise registering on his face before the pain registered in his body. He opened his mouth and blood dripped out of it. He'd made a series of rookie mistakes. Besides missing the guns that each of the agents were wearing, he hadn't watched Conley's hands. Instead, he'd assumed that because he had the American in a headlock and had a gun to his head, Conley wasn't a threat.

Morgan, on the other hand, *had* been watching and had seen Conley slip his right hand under his sport jacket as soon as the guard had grabbed him. Even moving slowly, it had taken Conley only a few seconds to draw his Glock and point it through his jacket and into the body of the man holding him.

Morgan gave his partner credit: Conley had let the situation play out longer than Morgan would have himself. Before the guard's body had hit the floor, Morgan drew his Walther, aimed it at Arief, and fired into the man's right shoulder.

The shot wouldn't kill him, but it would prevent him from raising his own pistol, which fell under the desk. The impact of the bullet sent him sprawling backwards into his desk chair, which rolled back into the wall.

Morgan decided Arief wasn't an immediate threat and turned his attention to the two guards who were holding their knives in front of them. The blades were curved and several inches long. They were a type of Indonesian knife Morgan had encountered before, and he had no doubt they were sharp.

"You okay, Peter?" Morgan asked, his peripheral vision telling him that his friend was on his feet with his gun trained on the other knife-wielding guard.

"Yeah, but my jacket has a hole in it. It's small enough that we can get away with it for dinner, but I'll have to replace it."

Morgan spared a glance at the lead guard. Conley's bullet had done quite a bit of damage to the man, who was already dead. The entry wound was low in his stomach. The bullet had travelled through the man's entire torso and come out near the top of his shoulder.

Arief was moaning in his chair, and Morgan was relieved to see that he had retreated into his own pain and was struggling to keep his eyes open. That meant he wasn't an immediate threat, unlike the two guards with knives, who glanced at their bosses and then at each other, trying to decide what to do.

Morgan turned his gun toward the ceiling. "It's okay. We don't want to hurt you."

The guards looked at him as if they didn't understand. "Conley, you want to try it in their language?" Morgan said.

"Sure, let me take a few minutes and learn Indonesian," Conley said.

"Right," Morgan said. His partner spoke so many languages that Morgan sometimes forgot he didn't speak all of them.

"Maybe they'll wait while I go get Dani," Conley said.

The guards were sweating, and Morgan didn't like the way they kept glancing at each other.

"Hold on—" he began as the guard closest to him threw himself at Morgan, swinging his curved knife wildly. From the corner of his eye, Morgan saw that Conley's man was doing the same.

Because Conley's gun wasn't pointed up at the ceiling, he managed to get a shot off as the guard leapt at him. Even if the bullet hit the guard, it didn't stop him. His body hit Conley's, and the two men tussled.

Morgan couldn't follow the action any closer because he was dodging the first sweep of his guard's knife. It barely missed his stomach, but because he'd missed, the momentum of the swing put Morgan's man off-balance, and he continued lunging forward.

The guard was now racing toward the wall and Morgan decided to help him, bodychecking the man and making sure he hit the wall hard. Morgan heard the universal "oomph" of the wind being knocked out of someone.

Grasping the man firmly by the shoulders, Morgan tossed him to the floor, pointed his gun at him and said, "Stay down!"

Morgan chanced a look over at Conley. His partner was on his feet, but his guard was clutching a wound in his throat, which was pouring blood.

His own man was still and Morgan turned him over with his foot, keeping the Walther pointed at his head. The guard was deadweight. When he was on his back, Morgan saw why. The curved blade was deep inside his abdomen.

"Dan—" Conley said when he saw movement behind Arief's desk. The terrorist was sitting in his chair and holding his gun shakily in his left hand.

"Don't do it," Morgan said, but Arief was already committed.

Morgan didn't want to shoot the man—again—since they really needed Arief alive for questioning. So just as Arief tried to aim the weapon, Morgan did the only thing he could think to do.

Remarkably, Conley had the same thought at the same time.

Both men lifted one foot and kicked at the metal desk, driving it back toward Arief. The momentum of the desk made the man pitch forward, putting his head just over the barrel of the gun, which went off as it was pointed into his face.

The exit wound made quite a mess on the back wall and Morgan said, "Well, damn."

Conley picked up a laptop and said, "Collect his phone. Maybe Shepard can get something off of it."

Morgan pulled the phone out of the man's pocket and said, "I would rather have questioned him."

"And it would be great if we had an hour or two to search the files and shipping manifests, but it looks like no one gets what they want today," Conley said.

Then his partner pulled at the blinds and peeked outside. "Anyone getting curious?"

"No," Conley said. "I'm guessing they are civilians and they have a lot of practice not noticing what goes on in here."

That was almost certainly true. There would probably be little risk for them if they simply walked out of the office, across the warehouse floor, and out the door.

Morgan quickly scanned the room for anything that Zeta might be able to use to track down this operation's business partners. Before he finished, Conley was already closing up the laptop that sat on Arief's desk.

Crossing the room, Morgan swung open the door to the safe. Besides a few stacks of cash and what looked like someone's lunch, he saw two external hard drives. He grabbed them and slipped one into each of his jacket pockets.

"Good thing they didn't lock that," Conley said.

"I'm not impressed so far by what I've seen of this operation," Morgan said.

"They are definitely not Ares, Dan," Conley said.

"I know, but I was hoping…" Morgan replied.

"You were disappointed that we didn't walk into a facility full of deadly, highly trained killers who have been giving Zeta a run for our money for many months now," Conley said, shrugging.

Morgan shrugged. "I don't always get what I want. And I'm not so sure that Ares are the super-villains we've been thinking they are," Morgan said. Then he added, "Alex took out a team of six when they had the element of surprise."

Conley didn't laugh. He didn't reply at all for a full few seconds and then said, "We'll get them, Dan. Clearly not today, and not in this dump, but we'll get them."

Then Morgan felt it, the rising anger that he'd pushed down so he and Conley could do what they needed to do today. Ares had come for his daughter. They had found her and had come for her while she was making a mundane delivery.

Alex had survived, and it wasn't a miracle either. She'd survived because she was Alex. She was the stray detail they couldn't plan for, and she beat them. She prevailed because she was tough and she was a very good agent.

But Morgan had known a lot of very good agents over the years, good agents who had given their enemies surprise after surprise, and then died at the hands of those same enemies.

Because eventually even good agents could come upon a superior or overwhelming force. In fact, if you did this long enough it was virtually inevitable. Because eventually luck—even Morgan luck—ran out.

Morgan touched one of the hard drives in his pocket. He was hoping for a little of that luck now. If what they'd found here today pointed them in the right direction, Morgan decided he'd show Ares a thing or two about overwhelming force.

He and Conley were getting close; he could feel it.

As if he were reading Dan's mind, Conley repeated, "We will get them."

"First we have to get out of here," Morgan said.

Before the words left his lips, he heard loud voices on the warehouse floor. Conley was closest; he pushed the blinds to one side and peeked out.

"We've got company," Conley said.

"Good," Morgan replied. "I'd like to get some answers in person."

"Wait, it's—" Conley began.

"Local police," Morgan said, looking out the opening in the blinds. "Damn."

"Unlikely they'll know anything that can help us. They are probably just responding to a shots-fired report."

Morgan swapped out the clip in his Walther for a fresh one. "I'm sure we can just explain everything to them."

"Dan, you really want to take out four local cops who are just responding to a report?" Conley asked.

"I'm just thinking about it. I'm not actually doing it. There is a difference, you know," Morgan said.

"Not for you, not usually," Conley replied.

*Fair enough*, Morgan thought. For the purposes of this mission, the local cops were civilians, and Morgan and Conley had never burned civilians if they could help it. But his usual mental calculations were being overwritten by a single thought: *Alex's life is at stake here.*

That was true, but his ability to help her on her mission depended on his and Conley's ability to get the hell out of here with the intel they'd found.

"What's your plan, professor?" Morgan asked. He looked outside again. The four policemen were joined by two others. One was on what looked like a radio, and all of them were looking warily up at the office.

"There," Conley said, pointing up at a skylight above Arief's desk. "Hold this," Conley said, handing him the laptop. "And see if you can find us a distraction," his partner said as he jumped up on the desk and reached for the skylight.

Morgan saw what he needed. There was a sink next to a microwave, which sat on top of a small cabinet. Inside the cabinet there was steel wool and he grabbed a handful. On a small shelf there were a few bottles of liquor. Most of them he didn't recognize, but one he did. The lampen liquor had a high alcohol content—so high that it regularly killed people and was, thus, illegal. That made it perfect for what he had in mind.

He grabbed the largest bowl he could find and dumped the steel wool inside of it.

"You about ready, Dan?" Conley asked.

"One sec," Dan said as he poured the nearly-full bottle of lampen into the bowl with the steel wool. He put the bowl in the microwave, shut the door, and turned it on.

Morgan didn't stay to watch what happened, though he could hear the popping sounds within seconds. He grabbed the laptop from the desk and passed it up to Conley's outstretched hand. It was the only part of his partner that was visible now that he'd climbed up onto the roof and was reaching down.

Conley pulled the laptop up and a second later the hand was back. Morgan grabbed his friend's hand, jumped off the deck and used his free hand to grab the side of the skylight. Both men pulled and Morgan quickly scrambled onto the roof, jumping to his feet.

Morgan heard men knocking on the office door.

"How did you do with that distraction?" Conley said.

Before Morgan could answer there was a loud bang and a flash of orange flame inside the office.

"Pretty good," Morgan replied as the men dashed across the roof. They made for the back of the warehouse, where it connected to another building. At the far end of that roof they took a ladder to the ground in an alley.

A few steps brought them onto a busy sidewalk and they looked for a cab.

Morgan checked his watch and saw they had plenty of time to meet Jenny and Dani. Fortunately, their clothes had come through in pretty good shape.

"If we hurry, I can get this stuff plugged into my computer and Shepard's team can start downloading the data before dinner," Conley said.

Morgan was pleased they would make dinner. And they wouldn't have to change. Other than the bullet hole in the back of Conley's jacket, their clothes weren't any worse for wear.

But something had changed in that warehouse and Morgan only realized that now. They would have dinner with the women and whether or not Jenny and Dani noticed the bullet hole in Conley's jacket, they would sense the change.

The two couples would have a pleasant dinner together, but the final veneer of pretense was now gone. This was work. Whatever Zeta found on the equipment they'd taken, the four of them would now pick a destination in the Coral Sea and wait for the next step.

Though he'd enjoyed the trip—both the part with just him and Jenny and the part with the four of them—he had no trouble shifting to mission mode.

He'd always been able to do that, and it was even easier now since it was to help Alex. The people who had caused so much trouble and death—and who had ordered the attack on Alex—were out there.

Morgan would do whatever he had to in order to stop them. He wished that he could keep Jenny further from it, but the danger to Alex would guarantee that Jenny would want to stay as close as possible to him and whatever threatened their daughter. In her own way, Jenny had already switched over to mission mode.

That was fine with Morgan and made what he would have to do easier. Their trip and the rest of the world could wait.

If it's still there when this is over, Morgan thought grimly.

# Chapter 9

"Director, we have something," Shepard said as he entered her office, carrying his laptop under his arm.

She gestured to one of the seats on the other side of her desk, and he sat, unfolding the laptop in front of him. Bloch saw that he didn't look like himself.

"I understand that Morgan and Conley found a computer that you're analyzing," she said.

"Yes," Shepard said. "And that's promising. We're in the process of tracing all of their shipping manifests and using that to narrow our satellite search for an Ares facility in the Coral Sea. However, we also found something local."

That got Bloch's attention.

Shepard continued: "We've been operating on two working theories. First, that the survivor from the Ares team that attacked Alex was only lightly injured and simply drove himself out of town. We've been looking into rentals and stolen cars for that day, but we've been coming up blank. Our second theory—that he was moderately to seriously injured—is backed up by blood found in the car. For that, we've of course monitored hospitals and walk-in clinics and gone through all records for the seventy-two hours following the incident. However, as you know, we've found nothing. We've also been monitoring veterinary hospitals."

"Veterinary?"

"Yes, veterinarians tend to be good general surgeons—they have to be. Plus, they have all the drugs and equipment in one place. That's where we got a hit. A vet just turned up in a fishing net. He went missing on his boat right after the attack, but the police saw no signs of foul play. It looked like an accident until his body turned up with bullet wounds."

"Okay, so the Ares operative forced the doctor to treat him and then killed him. How do we find him now?"

Shepard swallowed and then continued. "It looks like the Ares man kidnapped a neighbor's nineteen-year-old daughter for leverage. We were on the lookout for the disappearance of family members of doctors and vets, but we didn't check on neighbors."

The young man looked stricken.

"It's all right, Shep," Bloch said. "You and your team can't see around every corner. And you can't think of everything, especially with an enemy that comes up with new tactics daily."

"Yes, but the problem is that the nineteen-year-old girl has also been found dead," Shepard said.

From the look on Shepard's face, it seemed like he had known her, and Bloch had to remind herself that he was not a field agent. He'd been at Zeta for years now—almost from the beginning—but he wasn't used to the kind of horror show that field agents saw regularly. He'd yet to develop the armor that allowed him to see something like that and move on.

Bloch couldn't decide if he was lucky or not.

"They didn't have to kill her. Once the veterinarian had done his job, they didn't have to kill her," Shepard said.

"It's okay to get angry, Shepard. In fact, in a case like this it will help. Get angry, and let's stop them before they do it to anyone else," Bloch said.

"Yes," he said, and took a second before he spoke again. "My team can help there. Once the vet turned up and we connected him to the girl's abduction, we started looking for clues. My assumption was since Alex had taken out the rest of the Ares man's team, he would have to use local assets—ones he could find quickly, and he did. She was grabbed on the street by two MS-thirteen gang members. We found security footage of the abduction and ran facial recognition through the police database. I have names and addresses, as well as the address of the gang's base."

"Do the police have this information?" Bloch asked.

"Not yet," he said. "We have access to more security feeds, including private ones, and they...well, they're slower."

"That is great, Shepard. This is our first lead on Ares... well, ever," Bloch said. Then she put her phone on speaker and dialed.

Spartan answered on the first ring. "Yes, ma'am," she said.

"Is your team ready to go?" Bloch asked.

"Yes," Spartan said in her normal professional tone, but Bloch couldn't help thinking that the woman was insulted by the question. "We have a lead on our Ares operative. Shepard can brief you."

\* \* \* \*

Shepard didn't look okay when Spartan had seen him. He hadn't been sleeping much, though that was nothing new.

She understood what was wrong when he explained that a young woman had been taken as leverage against a veterinarian and then murdered. That explained the photo in his and O'Neal's workstation. Normally, the only decorations on Shepard's side were photos and stickers from video games and movies, as well as action figures, and some items she recognized as movie and video game props.

There were no pictures of family, nothing personal. But today, there had been what looked like a school picture of teenage girl, about eighteen. Spartan guessed it was a high school senior portrait. The young woman had long, curly dark hair and a wide smile. Spartan didn't have to ask why that photo now sat above Shepard's computer monitor.

The photos that he'd sent her of the targets were depressingly familiar. All too often, the gang members weren't scary, muscled villains with facial tattoos. The two that had taken and then murdered the girl looked like skinny teenagers, one with a definite baby face. They looked even younger than their reported nineteen years.

Spartan reminded herself that they had kidnapped and killed an innocent young woman.

The two TACH teams headed south and into Mattapan, one of the oldest neighborhoods in Boston. Spartan had driven through it a few times and knew it was dubbed *Murderpan* by its residents.

It was an interesting combination of quaint history—complete with a working trolley—and urban decay. As they got closer, they passed a row of triple-deckers—three-story, attached houses with colonial columns.

Spartan was glad to see that their destination wasn't one of those. If it came to shooting, she wanted some distance from any civilian neighbors. At the end of the row of triples, there was an intersection, and across the street was their target: a vacant, stand-alone house.

It was in rough shape, having been a crack house before the gang took over. It would no-doubt be disgusting inside, but better to fight in there than risk civilians in the surrounding buildings. Because of its status as a

MS-13 hangout, people on the sidewalk crossed the street to avoid walking in front of it.

Spartan pulled her vehicle over. On the outside, it was a food truck. Inside, it held Spartan and four of her best people. Pulling in behind them was another team in a delivery truck.

She had no doubt that the Zeta people could easily take out the gang's nest, even if they were armed and filled with gang members. It was one thing to be tough when you were attacking other teenagers as a pack, or grabbing young girls off the street, but it was another to be tough when faced with armed and trained opposition.

However, Bloch wanted these two alive for questioning. Even with the knockout rounds, a room-to-room fight would get hairy. It would be much better to wait and simply grab them on the street, stuff them in one of the vans, and get them to Zeta headquarters.

Since their targets were close and ran together most of the time, Spartan and her people simply had to wait for the right time.

Spartan tapped her comm and said, "We're in position."

"I have eyes above you," came Shepard's reply.

Not surprisingly, Shepard had drones in the air. Also not surprisingly, Spartan hadn't seen them.

She didn't have to wait long. Within minutes, Shepard said, "I have two approaching the house from the east."

Lifting her binoculars, Spartan saw the figures. "It's our targets," she said, mildly surprised herself. Finally, some luck.

"Can you get to them before they enter?" Shepard said.

Spartan did a quick assessment. If the light was green, she might chance it, but the light was red. They'd have to wait for the vans to cross the street, and by then the gang members would be almost at the door.

"Negative," Spartan said. "We'll have to wait for them to leave."

Even if it took a few hours, it would be worth it. Once they left, the vans could pace them and then simply stop and force them inside.

Less than twenty minutes later, Shepard said, "There's some movement just north of you. It's almost out of frame. I'm repositioning the drone."

From Spartan's orientation, north meant to her left. As Spartan was turning her head, she saw the flash of movement, a distinctive tail of smoke, and then the headquarters of the local MS-13 chapter exploded in front of them.

Their targets and anyone inside just died. The Ares operative was eliminating loose ends, but that meant he was here.

Spartan scanned with the binoculars. A man in civilian clothing tossed the RPG launcher into a nondescript sedan and got inside.

"I have him," Shepard said. "Proceed with caution. I'm tracking him with drones and traffic cams. *Don't* alert him to your presence."

"Confirmed," Spartan said. "Stay on me," she added for the other team.

They would follow at a distance, far enough away that even an experienced operative wouldn't see the tail. That would be easy enough with Shepard on him. The TACH team could stay completely out of sight while Shepard directed them.

Like their MS-13 targets, now they could grab the actual Ares agent when he was on the sidewalk. It would be a bit more complicated, since if he knew he was cornered, he'd be able to use his cyanide tooth.

That would be tricky, but not impossible to deal with. The important thing was that they were close, very close.

# Chapter 10

Alex had to admit that the *Grandeur* was an impressive ship, so much so that it almost lived up to its name. The vessel had over 4,000 passengers and nearly 2,000 more in crew. It was 900 feet long and nearly 180 feet wide, making it over 200 feet longer than the *Titanic*—with nearly twice as many decks.

It was also significantly bigger and much newer than her training ship. The international mix of the crew was the same, however, but Alex didn't see anyone she knew from her training class as she wandered through this ship's I-95 corridor.

The drab, beige paint of I-95 and the crew areas of the ship were also familiar. Though the passenger areas were new and beautifully appointed, the crew areas could have been on the *Glory*, or—Alex suspected—on any other cruise ship. The scuffs on the walls and the floor and the bundles of wiring on the ceiling also seemed to be universal.

But the guest areas were genuinely amazing, tastefully decorated and modern in bleached wood paneling, shining gold and silver fixtures, and carpets that were what her mother called "beach pastels." The whole effect was that of a high-end seaside resort.

And the lido deck, where Alex knew she'd be working most of the time, was truly something. It was a large outdoor space in the center of the ship whose centerpiece was a large pool, with bars and café-style restaurants surrounding it. There was a smaller pool one deck up and forward, and another one a deck above that.

Alex had just forty-five minutes to explore the ship before she had to report for her official orientation tour and some human resources meetings. And she still had to drop her things off in her cabin.

She'd learned the hard way during her training not to bring a suitcase, since there would very likely be nowhere to put it once it was unpacked. Once she hit the crew area, Alex had to ask directions twice to find her way to her room. Unlike the guest areas, there weren't helpful you-are-here ship and deck maps posted everywhere.

Alex supposed they were unnecessary for crew that knew the ship, but she wondered if she'd be on board long enough to really learn her way around.

Deck four was easy enough to find, but she'd had to go up to deck six to locate a staircase that took her down to the section of deck four, which held her cabin. Once she was in the right section she found her room easily enough.

She opened the door and found herself face-to-face with a pretty Asian woman in her indeterminate twenties. Alex stepped into the room, put down her bags, and held out her hand. "Hi, I'm Alex McGrath, I'm from the US; Boston. I guess we're roommates," she said.

"It's nice to meet you. I'm Rebecca Tsai. I'm from Taiwan," she said in accented, but excellent, English.

"Nice to meet you. Your English is very good—amazing, actually," Alex said.

"For someone from my country?" Rebecca said, her face unreadable.

"Oh my God, did I just insult you? I'm replaying that in my head and it sounds pretty bad," Alex said.

Rebecca smiled. "Not at all. I'm actually proud of my English. I studied in California when I was young," she said. "And your English is also very good, for someone from Boston."

"It's much better than my Mandarin," Alex replied.

"Do you speak any?" Rebecca asked.

"Just a few phrases, but I don't trust them. I learned them from someone I worked with who was dating a family friend. I suspect most of the everyday phrases they taught me were actually pretty terrible words."

Alex laughed when she said that, but she noticed that Rebecca had just glanced down at the floor and Alex's feet for the third time.

"Is there something wrong?" Alex asked.

"Nothing. It's just that...you know what, it's none of my business," Rebecca said.

"What is it?" Alex said.

"You're wearing your shoes inside. In my country..." Rebecca said.

"Not a problem," Alex said, slipping off her sneakers. "My mom had the same rule when I was growing up. I guess I never thought of my last cabin as home, really."

That was definitely true. With Sorina, the cabin was just something she had to endure for two weeks.

Rebecca looked relieved. And it was a small price to pay for peace in the room. If only things with Sorina were that easy.

Alex took a few minutes to put away her clothes and things. It didn't take long. There was a shared dresser with four drawers and a small closet space for hanging clothes, which had room for their uniforms and a few more items each.

Though the ship was much bigger than her training ship, the room was actually a bit smaller, though—blessedly—the bathroom was a little bigger.

Rebecca was very accommodating. Other than the shoes, the only thing she asked for was the bottom bunk, which was fine with Alex. In the few minutes they spent together, Alex had already decided that Rebecca's presence was positive. She was definitely an improvement over the atmosphere Sorina created.

"What are you doing on board?" Alex asked as they were getting ready to go.

"I'm a masseuse. A massage therapist, actually," Rebecca said.

"That sounds nice. I'll be serving drinks on the lido deck," Alex said.

"You will be in the sun, at least," Rebecca said.

As they headed to the stairwell, Rebecca added, "I may have to request a cabin change."

"No!" Alex said automatically. "Was it the shoes? Or the comment about your English…" Alex had a flash of dread as she saw herself as the nightmare roommate that Rebecca had to escape.

The woman smiled politely and said, "It is not you. It's the deck." Rebecca pointed at the deck four sign at the door to the stairwell. "In my country the number four is bad luck. Something like thirteen in yours. I understand that many of your tall buildings don't have a thirteenth floor."

"That's true," Alex said.

"The word for *four* and the word for *death* sound nearly the same in Mandarin," Rebecca said.

"Are you genuinely worried?" Alex said.

Her new roommate looked embarrassed. "Not really, but my family…"

"I understand that. My Irish great-grandmother had these premonitions," she said.

"Did they ever come true?" Rebecca asked.

"More often than you'd think, but mostly they were about family members passing away or the arrival of packages."

"Those are very specific premonitions," Rebecca said.

"And less useful than you'd think," Alex replied. "Look, don't stay if you'd think you'd be uncomfortable, but I wish you would. I had a bad experience with my last roommate—totally her fault, by the way—but I have a feeling that we'll get along well."

Rebecca seemed to really consider that for a few seconds.

"And, when you think about it, it's not really the fourth deck. They don't number the first few engine room and equipment decks. It's only the fourth *cabin* deck, but I think it's actually deck seven. And seven is my lucky number, so I think our luck will even out."

"Then I suppose it's settled," Rebecca said as they reached the deck for their muster station.

Sorting through her luck lately was complicated. Alex had lost the Morbidelli for her client, but she had survived an attack by a highly trained hunting team. At least her roommate situation was looking up. And if the ship was going to be the center of an attack or Ares-generated disaster, Alex could use some good luck.

Fortunately, Alex wasn't superstitious. If the number thirteen or black cats didn't worry her, she wouldn't sweat superstitions from another culture. At the muster station, a group of about twenty had collected and a member of the human resources staff was counting off heads.

"Okay, I'm going to break you up into groups of four," the man said.

*You have got to be kidding me*, Alex thought.

\* \* \* \*

Alicia Schmitt switched on the sensor and checked the numbers on her handheld meter. She checked the position and proximity readings against her reference standards, and they looked good. Actually, they looked very good.

Of course, she'd know more when she checked them against the system console in engineering, but she had no doubt it would perform flawlessly. But since she had half-a-dozen other sensors still to check, that would have to wait.

Schmitt climbed down the access ladder and stepped onto the deck. A man in a white officer's uniform was waiting for her. He had four gold stripes on the epaulets on his shoulders. That identified him as a senior officer. The gold loop next to them told her he was the first officer.

He was in his early to mid-thirties, with short blond hair. He gave her a professional smile and said, "I'm Jack Watson, chief officer," in a clear

Australian accent. He looked up toward the ladder and said, "We have crew that can help you with that."

"Thank you for the offer, but I like to personally check each major component at least once," she said.

"Understood. I'm sorry I didn't come to see you sooner. I know you've been on board for two days," he said.

"Not a problem. I've been pretty busy," she said.

"Myself as well, which is the reason we haven't met yet. The captain asked me to invite you to his table tonight for dinner. We'd both like to chat with you about the new system."

"Of course," Schmitt said. "I'm at your service." That was literally true. She'd already met several times with the chief engineer and different IT personnel. And while normally she wasn't much for socializing, the cruise line and the ship had purchased the Renard Tech system. As their representative, the least she could do was answer the captain's questions.

"I'm fascinated by the system, and Chief Cabato is very high on it. It's the first major, new navigation system since the ECDIS."

Schmitt knew that the *Electronic Chart Display and Information System* had been around for more than 35 years. In that time, it had become not only universal but mandatory.

"Renard Tech is very proud of it," she said.

First Officer Watson seemed uncomfortable and said, "I do have a question about the system's name."

"The TARDIS," she said flatly. It means *Telemetry Adaptive Real-time Dynamic Information System.*"

"Right, I knew that, but were you aware that it is also—"

"Is the name of a ship in a television show," she said. "Yes, Scott Renard has a good sense of humor and an encyclopedic knowledge of—well, of a lot of things."

"Do you work directly with Renard?" Watson asked.

"Not often, but sometimes. We did actually meet about the TARDIS a few times. I contributed to the design."

Watson looked impressed. Scott Renard often got that reaction. As a tech billionaire with many different business interests, he was in the news several times a year. He was also the very visible face of his company and had appeared before Congress more than once. In a world that celebrated reality television stars, it was fair enough that a billionaire inventor, programmer, and CEO who made significant technological contributions would be a celebrity.

"I look forward to dinner," Watson said. "Seven o'clock at the captain's table."

"I will be there," she said.

* * * *

Spartan kept the car the Ares operative was driving at the very edge of her vision. As a result, it would come in and out of sight. Sometimes she would lose him for a block or two and then pick him up again.

She was sure Shepard would be able to track him with the drones and traffic cameras, but she felt better when she could see her target. As good as cameras and drones were, there were always blind spots. And machines could be fooled.

Of course, humans could be fooled as well, but Spartan had some control over that, at least when it came to herself. The key was to train yourself to see what was there, not what you expected to see.

"Spartan," Shepard's voice said over the comm.

"Yes, Shepard," she replied.

"We've done a quick survey of the veterinarian's office. Looks like your target had surgery on his shoulder and perhaps his chest. The key is that he will have very limited use of his right hand, and he will likely be on painkillers."

"Good, so he'll be impaired," Spartan said.

"True, but the trade-off is that his system has been weakened by his injuries," Shepard said. "And painkillers make the neurotoxin in your rounds more dangerous to him. The upshot is that you really should not shoot him more than once."

"Understood," Spartan said.

There was a common misconception about tactical work in general: that TACH specialists always operated in some sort of barely-in-control berserker mode. But like soldiers, the ones that were too excitable weren't very good—and often didn't last long in the business.

Workplace hazards weeded those people out pretty quickly.

Spartan liked Alex Morgan quite a bit, and she owed something to Alex's father, but that made restraint more important here. They needed this Ares operative alive to get what they wanted from him. And if he was going to die, Spartan wanted him to go knowing that he had betrayed his organization under interrogation. And if he didn't die and then ended up in prison somewhere, he would spend most of his days dreading Ares's retaliation for his failure.

"We know where he's going," Shepard said. "He made a short-term house rental less than a mile away. We missed it because he didn't use any of the regular rental services. He found it through some internet classified ad."

"Just give me the address," Spartan said.

Shepard relayed it and she gave her team their instructions. Spartan turned onto the street one block north and sped up. For her plan to work, she needed to get to the Ares operative's destination before he did.

That would be easy enough, since he was going to great pains to obey speed limits and to not run any yellow lights.

Spartan wasn't as careful.

When she pulled over, Shepard told her that the target was a full two minutes behind her. She gave her last instructions and pulled the truck over to the side of the road. Then she started jogging.

Her cover outfit was loose black sweatpants and a sweatshirt with a headband and sunglasses. She also wore a special holster around her waist, with the gun accessible under her sweatshirt in the front.

There were two other joggers on this stretch of sidewalk, so she fit right in.

"He's coming up on your block now," Shepard said through the comm.

Less than thirty seconds later, her target's car passed her and then pulled over to park nearly a full block ahead of her.

The man did a quick check of his surroundings and then got out of his vehicle. It was clear that he had no idea he had been followed—he'd have no reason to.

He was dressed in jeans and a checkered button shirt. His movements were the slow and deliberate motions of someone who was recovering from a trauma. And Spartan was sure that wasn't an act. Managing the RPG that had destroyed the MS-13 nest must have cost him.

Spartan couldn't see where he was wearing his gun, but her money would have put it inside the sling. That would keep it easily accessible, which was very important if he was right-handed and might have to shoot with his left. Extra time to aim would be important.

Of course, Spartan didn't intend to give him *any* time.

She waited until he was almost at his door and she was just a few paces out from his walkway when she yelled, "Look out!"

He may have been a trained and merciless killer, but his reaction was programmed in to most people. He turned his head behind him to look for the source of the shout. He also twisted his body toward her just a little, which gave her a clear shot.

Spartan drew and fired in a single, smooth motion, long before he could even think about going for his own weapon.

Her aim had been perfect, right into his bad shoulder, just above where any body armor would be.

He looked at her in stunned surprise and then dropped to the ground. She was on him in seconds and could see that he was unconscious.

Her people quickly burst out of the food truck with a stretcher.

In less than thirty seconds, he was inside the truck, getting treated by a paramedic.

Spartan checked her watch and did a quick mental calculation. He would be at Zeta headquarters in less than twenty minutes.

# Chapter 11

Alex appreciated having Rebecca's company through the next couple of hours' worth of human resources seminars. There was also a short talk from the manager of the hotel department, under whose umbrella both Alex and Rebecca fell. The two women had to split up, however, when it was time for team meetings because, as a masseuse, Rebecca was part of the hotel amenities department and Alex was food and beverage.

In one of her HR meetings Alex saw an organizational chart of the crew, and it was enormously complicated. It was apparently even more complex than the crew breakdown of a large naval vessel, since there were so many different service departments from technicians, to waitstaff, to dancers, to art auctioneers—which was something Alex was still trying to wrap her head around.

Alex had gotten a glimpse of departmental rivalries since everyone thought their area was the most important one on the ship. She had seen similar rivalries in military, governmental, and intelligence groups. She supposed it was universal, if not inevitable among groups of high-performing people. The *Grandeur*'s crew stuffed into a steel can where people worked together very closely and where just the task of providing thousands of meals a day was staggering.

Her team met on the lido deck for a final pep talk. One of managers greeted them and said, "You'll hear a lot of talk about what division on board is the most important, and I'm here to tell you that without a doubt it is us." When the laughter died down she added, "You can take real pride in that because out of all the services and entertainment that this ship offers, we provide the most actual pleasure to guests."

The presentation was mercifully brief since it was getting close to dinner and people were getting restless. Then the manager said, "One final order of business, in addition to some upgrades during this port call: We've also picked up some new crew. We welcome you. Please, when I call your name, step forward and tell us who you are, where you're from, and why you're here."

Three people introduced themselves before the manager called Alex's name.

Alex stood up and said, "Hi, I'm Alex McGrath. I'm from Boston, Massachusetts in the United States. Before this I worked in a motorcycle shop. I'm here because I've always been fascinated by large ships, and I wanted to travel."

There was polite applause and Alex stepped back. The manager called two more names and then said, "Sorina Popa."

Alex felt like she'd been hit in the chest. It couldn't be...

But Sorina stepped forward and announced, "I'm Sorina Popa. I'm from Romania." This was met by some good-natured cheers from a group in the back. "After school, I was in the Romanian military, and now I'm here because of love. My boyfriend is on board the ship, and after this meeting I will get to see him for the first time in three months."

This was met with sighs and applause, but Alex was having trouble focusing. How was this possible? She and Sorina had never had a friendly conversation, so they had not discussed which ship they would each be assigned to. However, the odds against them getting placed on the same ship were small, and the chances of both of them getting assigned to the lido deck team were miniscule.

It was like a bad joke. Alex was here to save lives, but she'd be working with a woman who had hated her *before* Alex had beaten and embarrassed her outside the Brisbane bar. And if Sorina got physically aggressive again, Alex could get booted from the ship, even if she didn't defend herself.

As Alex and the others filed back inside from the lido deck, she passed the large bar and grill that served the main pool, the Four Corners of the World bar.

Four corners.

Four, which sounded like *death* in Mandarin.

*For crying out loud*, Alex thought.

\* \* \* \*

"He's awake," Dr. Hunt said.

"I'll be right down," Bloch said and hung up the phone.

Less than a minute later Diana Block was standing outside the infirmary. Of course, *infirmary* wasn't the right word for a place that had two full surgical suites, recovery rooms, and five hospital beds with room for more if they were needed. It also held a full lab and diagnostic equipment only found in medium- or even larger-sized hospitals.

Bloch would have liked to think that the facility was just a precaution, but they had needed it often enough that there was no point in kidding herself. Of course, up until now it was for Zeta people who'd been shot or injured. This was the first time they had treated an enemy agent.

Shepard had made a sign that said sick bay and hung it over the door to the entrance, and the name had stuck with the staff. Bloch entered and was greeted by one of the doctors that Zeta kept on call. Dr. Hunt was a handsome man in his forties who had extensive experience treating battlefield trauma cases in the US Army.

"He hasn't spoken yet," Hunt said.

"Can he?" she asked.

"Absolutely. I gave him a stimulant, so he's alert," Hunt said.

He gave Bloch a brief rundown of the patient's injuries and Diana said, "Thank you, Doctor. I will go in alone."

As soon as Bloch entered the small room, the man's eyes tracked her.

The top of the bed was inclined so he was half sitting up. Both feet were strapped to the bottom of the bed, as was his left hand. His right arm and shoulder were heavily bandaged and that wrist was strapped down to his body. Even if he was uninjured, he would be trapped. In his current condition, the only free movement he had was in his neck.

Maybe thirty years old, the man had close-cropped dark hair, vaguely European features, and tanned skin. He could have been from a dozen different places or he might be a mixture of ethnic groups.

"You're awake. Now we can talk. I am Diana—"

"Bloch. I know who you are, Director," he said. When he spoke, it was with a flat, Midwestern accent.

"Yes, you do seem to know something about us. Tell me about you. Tell me about Ares," she said.

He was silent, his face a mask.

"Do you recognize the word?"

"I know Ares is Greek for *spear*, and I know that is what you call us," he said.

His face betrayed no nervousness at all. He was cool and appeared unconcerned to be in the hands of his enemy.

"Is there something else you call yourselves?" she asked.

"We like Ares. It sounds formidable. It is also suggests your end," he said.

"How so?"

"*Zeta* means shield, and shields offer protection from clubs and blades. But a pointed spear had the best chance of piercing it," he said.

"Let's talk about that. Tell me about Ares's plans and about how you intend to *pierce* us," she said.

"I won't tell you anything, no matter what you do to me," he said.

"So far, the only thing we've done to you is to repair your shoulder. By the way, you will never regain full motion in that arm. Maybe fifty or sixty percent if you work at it. Now, I'm going to ask you a series of questions, and you are going to answer them. My first is: What is your name?"

"You can call me John," he said.

"Okay, John, the next ones will be harder. You won't want to answer them, but it is important that you do. While we won't physically abuse you, I did indulge the staff in one area. We didn't replace the cap on your cyanide tooth. Every time your tongue goes to that spot because you just can't help it, I want you to think of Zeta."

John now wouldn't even meet her gaze.

"Would you care to tell me why you are trying to kill my people—besides the fact that we keep getting in the way of Ares's plans for mass murder. Is it because we are the real terrorists and we use the tactics of our enemies? Is it the evils of capitalism? Colonialism? Or is it the fact that we are part of some worldwide conspiracy of tailors to eliminate artificial fibers?"

His face was still an expressionless mask.

Bloch lifted up her tablet and hit the button to turn on the screen. "Before we begin in earnest I want to show you something." She turned the device to him so he could see the picture of the smiling young woman on the screen. "This is Maria Ramirez; she is the reason we have you. She was the neighbor of the veterinarian that you forced to treat you. The children you hired to kidnap and murder her led us to you. I want you to understand that whatever happens to you from this point on is because of her."

There was a flash of recognition in his eyes but no change in his expression.

"You know I won't tell you anything," he said.

"That's where you're wrong," she replied. "You will tell me everything I want to know, and you will be happy to do it. Let me ask you, John: Are you aware of the spear and the shield paradox? It first appeared in a book in China, in the third century BC. It contains the story of a merchant who was trying to sell both a shield and a spear. He claimed the spear could pierce any shield, and the shield could protect against any spear. Hence, the paradox. You probably know the Greek variation that asks the question: What happens when an unstoppable force meets an immovable object?"

"What is *your* solution?" John said.

"My solution is: *We* win. And you will help us." She looked up at one of the cameras above the bed and said, "Please come in, Doctor."

Dr. Hunt entered carrying a small case, which he opened to pull out a syringe.

"This will help you relax. It will also make you very cooperative," Bloch said.

John's eyes flared when he saw the syringe, and Bloch saw the slightest change in his expression. It was the first sign that there was a person in there. When he spoke, his voice was almost as steady as before.

Almost, but not quite.

"It won't matter. Even if you knew everything, you couldn't stop us; you couldn't stop *everything*," he said.

"We'll see about that." Bloch turned to Hunt and said, "Doctor."

Hunt stepped forward, pulled up the hospital gown on the man's good arm and gave the injection.

John's face was a mask again. "It doesn't matter," he said. Then he did something that genuinely unnerved her. He smiled.

After a few seconds, he started to shake.

"Doctor..." Bloch said, but Hunt was already leaning over the patient.

The shakes became full-body tremors, then *violent* full-body tremors. Though he didn't speak or even make a sound, John's body pulled hard against the straps and in every direction.

There were a few seconds of even more extreme convulsions, and then John went still.

Hunt went to work quickly as two nurses ran in with a crash cart. Bloch was sure that the team would do everything they could, and she was equally sure they would fail.

John would die and Zeta would be back to square one in their search for information about their enemy.

# Chapter 12

There was a knock at Alicia Schmitt's door, and she answered to find Jack Watson standing in front of her in his dress whites. Instead of the short-sleeved, white button shirt, he wore a formal white jacket with gold buttons and even more impressive epaulets.

Schmitt had to admit that he was handsome— *extremely* handsome in this uniform. "Ms. Schmitt, if you will allow me to escort you to the captain's table," he said.

"Of course," Schmitt replied.

"And let me say that you look lovely," he said, giving her a sincere smile.

"Thank you," said as she grabbed her bag.

Schmitt was wearing a simple black dress that was appropriate for the captain's table. She knew she looked good, which was important for the part she was about to play.

Though on board as a technical advisor, she was also an ambassador for Renard Tech. As such, she was selling Renard's brand of top-shelf technology. And since the new navigation system was the first sale to a major cruise line, it was also an important client-relations meeting.

As they walked, Schmitt said, "I'm honored that the captain has invited me."

"It was a bit of a surprise. Usually, he doesn't host dinners before a cruise. Part of the reason is that there's so much to do, especially with the upgrades—among them your navigation system," Watson said.

"Then I'm doubly honored," she said.

"He is interested in your background. Note that this will also be a work dinner. He may grill you a bit."

Schmitt flashed her public relations smile and said, "I love to talk about work. It's better than a dinner that's all small talk."

Watson led her to an enclosed area forward on the lido deck. Schmitt gave a passing thought to Alex and decided she'd have to check in with young Morgan when the ship got underway.

The captain was seated at the head of a table that had six other officers sitting with him. They all wore dress whites and stood when Watson and Schmitt entered. Schmitt recognized Captain Richard Garrett from his picture. Somewhere in his late forties, he was tall, fit, with salt-and-pepper hair. He was so good-looking that he could have been featured on an ad or a recruiting poster for the cruise line.

Schmitt stepped forward and extended her hand.

Taking it, Garrett said, "I'm Captain Richard Garrett. It's very nice to meet you, Ms. Schmitt." He spoke with a clear American accent. "You already know our chief engineer, Enrico Cabato," Garrett said.

"Hello, Ms. Schmitt," the chief said in his heavy Italian accent. Schmitt shook his hand and said, "Nice to see you, Chief."

"I also present our head of security, Andre Giotto," the captain said.

"Good to meet you, sir," Schmitt said as she shook his hand.

"And you as well, Ms. Schmitt," Giotto said in a French accent.

She also met two more deck officers who served as ship's navigators. Schmitt was pleased with the group. The surroundings, the clothing, and the mood in the room suggested a social dinner, but the guest list told her this was definitely work.

Every person at the table had a strong professional interest in the new navigation system.

Though she had met a number of naval captains in her military career and a few merchant skippers, she'd never met the captain of a cruise ship. Schmitt was interested to see how he approached his job.

She didn't have to wait long. As soon as the drinks were ordered, he said, "I understand from your bio that you served as a pilot on the USS *George Washington*."

That piqued interest around the table, especially—she noted—in security chief Giotto, who she knew was a civilian light aircraft pilot.

"I did," she said.

"I was in New York on 9/11," he said. "I can tell you that we all appreciated having the *George Washington* nearby after that. It's a Nimitz-class vessel?"

"It is. You know the design?" she asked.

"I do, and I'm fascinated by them. Twenty years between refueling sounds pretty good to us," he said. His smile was disarming. *Very* disarming.

"True, but your lido deck and nightclubs would look pretty good to sailors," she said. "Actually, aside from those things, I think you would recognize most of the systems on an aircraft carrier. Water processing and food service are surprisingly similar. And while the crew of the *GW* is about three times yours, it carries no passengers, so both ships top out at about six thousand souls."

"We do have better amenities, but fewer aircraft and weapons," Jack Watson added to polite laughter around the table.

"And while we could have used the amenities, you don't need the weapons," she said. That was a sore point for some in the cruise business, as well as on merchant ships, but international maritime law, as well as the patchwork of local laws in the various port countries, made it difficult for cruise and merchant ships to carry traditional weapons.

That lack had left a number of merchant vessels vulnerable to Somali pirates, but the solution there had been better patrols by Western navies.

The Zeta file on the *Grandeur* had told her there were some interesting nonlethal and nontraditional weapons on board, but that was a subject that she knew better than to bring up here. Ship's defenses were kept secret for a number of good reasons and even Zeta didn't have a complete picture of what the *Grandeur* carried.

"What did you fly on your ship?" Giotto asked.

"I flew just about everything on board, but my favorite aircraft was the Boeing Growler. It's an electronic warfare jet. I also got a chance to fly one of your Dassault Rafales."

Giotto's eyes went wide with that.

Schmitt continued. "We were on maneuvers with the *Charles de Gaulle* and traded off with your pilots. The Rafale is an amazing aircraft, the most agile plane I've flown. It definitely kept me on my toes."

That was an understatement. All fighters had a center of gravity that favored maneuverability over smoothness of flight, but the French delta-wing craft was downright aerodynamically unstable, which it compensated for with a sophisticated fly-by-wire system. The result was a plane that could maneuver on a dime.

"I was surprised to see Renard Tech get into ships' navigation systems. I thought they are mostly a computer and aerospace company," the captain said.

"There's also the Renard Formula One team. Actually, Scott Renard sees a lot of overlap in all of those areas. Your navigation system requires powerful, real-time computer processors, sophisticated sensors, robust communications, and cutting-edge design. Plus, the system gives you access to the Renard Tech satellites for GPS and communications."

"I do appreciate redundancy," the captain said.

"In aerospace, redundancy isn't just important, it's a necessity," Schmitt said. "That's why in this system, the whale-alert system equipment and the collision-avoidance system all operate independently. And in a pinch, each system can do the job of all the others. The same with the magnetic compass, the electronic compass, the standard GPS system, and the Renard Tech satellite backup GPS system. Each major component has at least one additional backup compared to your previous system. You'll also see that range and accuracy has been improved in each area."

"All of that was in the specs, which I reviewed before the company approved the purchase," Garrett said.

"And I presume the tests you've seen have been satisfactory," Schmitt replied.

"They have. In fact, the system has over-performed the specs," the captain said.

"All of that pleases me, but I can't help but notice that all of the components from the original system, including sensors, processors, and terminals are still operating," Schmitt said.

There was a moment of silence at the table that the captain broke with a chuckle and a smile. "I have a great deal of faith in you, your company, and your equipment so I hope you won't be offended if I maintain further redundancies, at least temporarily."

*Touché*, Schmitt thought.

"I would like to have you coordinate with Mr. Watson to bring each of your new components online one at time. No hurry, of course. You'll be with us for a month, I understand," he said.

Schmitt had intended to spend that month troubleshooting the fully operational system and providing on-site technical support. This was a surprise, but Schmitt suspected that was the captain's intention.

What followed was a pleasant but extremely detailed debriefing for the senior deck officers. They obviously knew the system's capabilities backwards and forwards and their questions drilled pretty deep. That all suited Schmitt fine.

By the time the dinner was over, any preconceptions about the civilian officers were smashed. They were as engaged, as serious, and as knowledgeable as any she'd met in the service.

"The captain liked you," Watson said, as he escorted her back to her cabin.

"I'm glad," she said, meaning it sincerely.

"With new vendors, we never know if we're getting the real deal or a pleasant public relations person," Watson said.

"And I was impressed by the captain," Schmitt said.

"There are quite a few stories about him from his days on merchant ships in the Mediterranean. If only ten percent of them are true, he's had an amazing career."

"I've served in the Med. It can be a rough neighborhood," she said.

"Especially for unarmed cargo ships," Watson replied.

"I thought you all were, frankly, more serious than I expected," she admitted.

"We get that a lot in this line of work from people who served in the armed forces. But think of it this way. In the Navy you maintain very high safety standards while focusing on your primary military mission. For us, safety is the mission. Well, that and the buffets, and the free drinks, and—naturally—the live shows." His grin softened the point, but it was a serious one. "If we lose passengers, they don't come back. And we depend on repeat business."

They reached Schmitt's cabin. "Thank you for the education. Now I can focus on getting the system fully online," she said.

"It will be my job to make that as pleasant—or at least as painless—as possible, Ms. Schmitt."

"I will see you tomorrow on the bridge, Mr. Watson," she said.

"I look forward to it," he replied.

Watson briefly held her gaze before he turned and headed down the corridor.

Schmitt suspected he would ask her to a private dinner before her work was done here, but she would worry about that later. As the captain said, they had plenty of time.

\* \* \* \*

"Hi, Alex," Rebecca said as Alex entered the cabin.

That was new. No scowl. No insults. Not even a cold shoulder. Clearly, Rebecca didn't have much experience being a roommate.

"Hey, Rebecca. How were your meetings?" Alex asked.

"Long," Rebecca replied. "You?"

"Same," she said. "I did have something funny happen. You know the roommate I told you about. Turns out she's on the ship."

"Your *friend* Sorina?"

"Yes, what are the chances of that?" Alex said.

"Given the number of ships in the cruise line, the size of your class, I'd say very small. Of course, it is July," Rebecca said.

"July?" Alex said. "What does that have to do with anything?"

Rebecca shrugged and said, "Bad luck."

"You're kidding, right?" Alex said.

"Not at all," Rebecca said. "In Taiwan we call it *ghost month*. We believe that all of the ghosts of the dead return to earth for the month. That leads to all kinds of bad luck."

"I assume that's because the word *July* sounds like the word for death in your language," Alex said.

"You will think I'm kidding, but I swear to you that is why," Rebecca said.

"One final question. Do *most* of the words in your language sound like the word for *death*?"

"Now that you mention it, more than you'd think. Come on, get ready, we're going to the forward crew bar. It's our last night before real work starts," Rebecca said.

Alex made a point of stretching and yawning and said, "I was thinking of just reading and turning in early."

"Now *you're* kidding," Rebecca said.

"No, I'm just—"

"Scared," Rebecca finished for her.

"Scared? Not at all," Alex said.

"You're afraid we'll run into your friend," Rebecca said.

"No, I'm not," Alex said.

"But you're going to stay in to avoid her?"

"I'll admit that I would rather not run into her right now," Alex said.

"But not in a frightened way?" Rebecca asked.

"More like in a I-don't-want-to-get-fired-because-I-got-into-a-fight-with-an-angry-Romanian way," Alex said.

"In my country we call that scared. I also learned a very important lesson when I was young: if you don't stand up to bullies, they will never leave you alone," Rebecca said.

"Wisdom from your culture?" Alex said.

"No, from the *Brady Bunch*, but I believe it's universal," Rebecca said. "I tell you what— *I* will protect you from the bully."

"First of all, I'm not being bullied. Second, I don't need anyone to protect me. And third, you are five-foot-two and maybe a hundred and ten pounds. How are you going to protect anyone?"

"I am five-foot-two-and-*a-half*. Secondly, I thought you didn't need protection," Rebecca said.

"This is childish. Is your next move to call me chicken?" Alex asked.

"Only if you make me because you are acting like a—"

"All right!" Alex said. "But just to prove that I'm not scared of anything. I'll stay for a few minutes and then leave to go to bed because I really am tired." By the time she was done Alex realized that her face was red and she was breathing heavily.

"Of course. You look exhausted. You can barely keep your eyes open," Rebecca said.

Alex laughed out loud at that.

"How long do you need to get ready?" her roommate asked.

"Ten minutes and then we'll go see my Romanian friend," Alex said.

# Chapter 13

"Director," Lincoln Shepard said when he entered Bloch's office.

Bloch noticed two things about Shepard. One, he wasn't carrying his laptop. And two, he looked terrible. His eyes were sunken and had dark rings around them. He also looked...disheveled.

Though he was wearing his standard uniform—jeans, T-shirt, and hoodie—something was off. For the first time since she had known him, his T-shirt was plain. There was no obscure logo or character from a film or a video game. It was just a simple gray T-shirt under a blue hoodie. And it was wrinkled and hanging out under the hoodie in the back. She also noticed that he'd missed a loop on his belt.

In addition, his normally perfect posture was stooped, which Bloch had never seen before. And his usually neatly combed sandy blond hair was pointing in multiple, different directions.

Bloch had seen Shepard go without sleep before. She'd also seen him under stress—including the time when Alex Morgan and Shepard's partner, Karen O'Neal, had both been kidnapped by terrorists.

But he had never looked like *this*. He had never looked haunted. He sat down in one of the chairs opposite her desk.

"The computer and hard drives that Morgan and Conley picked up seem to be paying off," he said.

"How so?" she asked.

"We now have nearly complete records of the warehouse's operations for ninety days, at least in terms of shipping. Combined with the information we're getting from the Indonesian customs contact you pointed us to, we'll be able to track every shipment sent in that time period. There are challenges, of course, since we have to assume that they never shipped directly to Ares personnel or locations. That means tracking sometimes multiple levels of reshipping, but even that is a linear process. And it helps that we can focus on destinations in and around the Coral Sea. The team is on it; eventually, we'll get a hit."

"Excellent, thank you," Bloch said.

Clearly Shepard wanted to say something else, but he looked like he didn't know how to start. Then for an awful moment it looked like he was going to be sick in her office. After a few seconds, he said, "I watched the video of your interrogation with John."

"Good. What was your assessment? He alluded to multiple threats," she said.

"I believe him. I don't think it was bravado. I think he was serious. That is what I wanted to talk to you about. I think there is something very bad coming, likely more than one very bad something. I don't know if it's the immediate threat in the Coral Sea or if that's just part of it."

"Intuition or analysis?" Bloch said.

"Both," he replied.

"I understand. I'm overdue for a talk with the president, among other parties. I think you are tapping in to something that many of us are feeling. The threats are getting bigger, more deadly, and closer together. Because of that, I'd like you to do something for me. I'd like you to stop blaming yourself for Maria Ramirez's death."

"Director?" Shepard said.

"I've seen you tired before, and this isn't it. You are not a field man, so there are things you never got a chance to learn. One of the most important lessons is that even if you do everything right and ultimately accomplish your mission objectives, sometimes people die."

For several seconds he didn't speak and then he said. "I have been tired and I will admit that once I realized that Maria's death was preventable—"

"That's where you are wrong. Even if you had somehow identified the missing doctor, *and* you had thought to check on his neighbors, *and* you had acted immediately—she would still be dead. Call it a tragedy. Call it bad luck. Call it whatever you like, but you need to understand that there are only three people responsible: John and the two people he hired. And largely thanks to you, all three of them can do no more harm."

"I understand, Director, but I do wish that I...*we* could have done more," he said.

"There is plenty more to do. If I thought it would help I'd be happy to see you punish yourself, but there is something you can do for the team and for Maria Ramirez—you can make sure her death has meaning. She's already led us to her killers; now it's time to find their masters and put a stop to all of this."

"You're right, of course," Shepard said. "I certainly don't want to hurt the mission because I'm too emotionally involved in…well, in recent events."

"It's something we all have to learn when we get out in the field. Knowing our limits and moving on when we need to are necessary to do what we do," Bloch said.

"I really do understand that. And the team can follow up on the shipping and customs leads. If you don't mind I think I could use a small break. Maybe the rest of the day and tomorrow morning," he said.

Bloch had forced him to take time off before, but this was one of the few times he'd asked, and it was the first time ever that he'd asked during an active mission.

"Of course, take whatever you need. As you say, I'm sure your team can follow up," Bloch said.

Shepard collected his computer and left her office. As he did, Bloch was certain of one thing: He didn't mean anything he had just said.

Except for the part about needing rest—though she strongly doubted he would be getting any in the next few days. He had said all the right things and had told her what she needed to hear to end the conversation.

Virtually all field agents she had ever known had faced similar crises very early in their careers. Dealing with their own perceived failures was difficult, especially when those failures were compounded by guilt.

Most got past it, but some never did. The lucky ones simply retired early. The unlucky ones started making mistakes, or started taking absurd risks and ended up dead.

That wasn't an immediate problem here, but one thing was certain: Lincoln Shepard was not okay.

\* \* \* \*

From the look of the forward crew bar, there was no question that the *Grandeur* was an upgrade from her training ship. The bar was the first crew space she had seen that didn't have the drab, industrial feel of an I-95 hallway.

It might not have been as well-appointed as the guest bars, but it was miles above anything on the *Glory*.

Alex was glad Rebecca had dragged her. She might be on board for weeks. She'd be busy with work, and she had to stay mission-ready in case there was trouble. It didn't make sense for her to expend any energy avoiding Sorina.

And now that they weren't living together that should be relatively easy to do. And even if it wasn't, she simply looked at the Romanian woman as a threat to her mission that needed to be handled with finesse rather than force.

Almost as soon as they entered the bar, Alex saw one of the women from her training class, who greeted her with a friendly wave. At the bar, Alex got herself an absurdly inexpensive gin and tonic. She remembered the cheap liquor from her training. It was fair enough, she supposed, given how hard the cruise line worked the staff.

Actually, there were quite a few compensations: gyms, pools, and Jacuzzis were there to make the long hours bearable.

She and Rebecca headed deeper into the bar to look for a table when Alex heard a loud laugh that she recognized—one that caused a chill to run down her spine. Her eyes automatically sought out the source of the laugh and less than a dozen feet away she saw Sorina.

Alex's former roommate seemed very drunk and very happy. The drunk part was not a surprise, but the happy part was new.

The source of that strange turn of events was next to Sorina. Or, more accurately, Sorina had draped herself over and around the source of her joy. The dark-haired man she was attached to had the complexion of someone who lived around the Mediterranean.

He seemed very content to have Sorina's arm tightly wrapped around his waist. That much, Alex understood. Whatever else Alex could say about Sorina, the woman was beautiful.

They made an attractive couple—her with her pale skin and nearly black hair, and him with similarly dark hair but dark skin. The contrast was striking. And though Sorina was perhaps an inch taller than him, he obviously didn't mind supporting her weight.

Alex started to turn away when a voice rang out. "Alex!" Sorina called.

"Alex," Rebecca said, nudging her, and Alex realized that she had been frozen in place. Then Rebecca tugged her forward and Alex said, "Hello, Sorina."

"My sweet one, this is Alex, she is from America," Sorina said to her man.

"Alex, this is the man I told you about, Ramón. He's from Portugal," she said with wonder, as if Portugal was Oz. Or Narnia.

As a point of fact, Sorina had never told Alex about him, though Alex had overheard the woman speaking to others.

Ramón grabbed Alex's hand and shook it. "Ramón Volores. It is very nice to meet you." He smiled as they shook, then his eyes quickly scanning her up and down. That gave her a chill, but fortunately Sorina didn't seem to notice.

Alex introduced the couple to Rebecca, and Ramón looked her over as well.

Then Sorina started tugging on Ramón and said, "I'm sorry we have to go. We need to be alone." Then she actually smiled at Alex and said, "Don't stay out too late, you know you need your sleep."

*What just happened?* Alex thought as she watched them walk away with Sorina keeping her arm wrapped around Ramón tightly.

"She seems nice," Rebecca said.

# Chapter 14

"Hi, I'm Alex McGrath," she said, extending her hand.

The Filipino woman looked like she was surprised to see her. Alex read her name tag, which said *Rosa Aquino, Philippines*.

"Ms. Aquino. I'm Alex McGrath. I'm reporting for—"

"You're late," the woman said firmly.

"I'm on the schedule for a noon-to-six shift, and it's eleven-thirty," Alex said.

The woman looked pained. "I forget that you are new to the cruise line. You're scheduled for twelve to six, which means you come in at ten to complete your side jobs."

"Oh, I didn't know," Alex said.

"Now you do. Ten tomorrow. Also, you can call me Rosa," she said, holding out her hand. Alex shook it.

Rosa checked her watch and said, "Because you were late, I only have a few minutes with you."

As the lido deck headwaiter, Rosa was responsible for all of servers for all three pools and related bars. "You're in the Lagoon. As you can see, it's the biggest of the pools," she said.

That much was obvious. It was large, a giant square in roughly the center of the ship.

"It's also the most family-friendly," Rosa added.

Since it was lunchtime, there were very few people around the pool. However, at least half of those were families with children. It wasn't what Alex had imagined, which was mostly bringing top-shelf cocktails to the very wealthy.

"It will get pretty hectic pretty soon," Rosa said. "You'll also be getting a lot of orders for the grill at the Four Corners bar," she said, pointing to the tiki bar facing the front of the ship (*the bow*, Alex reminded herself). "The kids love the hot dogs and the fries are very good, but you have to get them there quickly so they are crispy," Rosa said.

It was more than four years since her waitressing job at the Minutemen Café, and Alex realized that she would be doing the same work she did the summer after her junior year of high school.

"When you get some seniority we can talk about moving you to the Cove," Rosa said, pointing forward to the bow, where a set of stairs on both sides of the deck led up to another, smaller pool area. "That's adults only; less food, better tips."

That would be nicer and more in line with what she had in mind, but Alex reminded herself that the mission was her priority. Real work wouldn't kill her, and she would likely not be here long enough to worry about moving up to the Cove.

"What about the pool above the Cove?" Alex asked.

Rosa shook her head. "Boring. Over sixty-five. They don't drink much and they don't tip much."

That wouldn't work for her mission at all. Actually, the lagoon was the ideal place. She was literally at the center of the ship and could see the majority of the people on the lido deck, even people who were just walking through on their way somewhere else.

"Okay, let's get you an apron," Rosa said. "You're on in five minutes."

Alex heard a familiar laugh and looked up to the Cove, where she could see Sorina already serving someone.

*Seniority?* she wondered. Alex was tempted to ask Rosa how that had happened, but held her tongue. From the point of view of the mission, it really was better for her to be in the center of action.

Plus, it was better to have a little distance between her and Sorina.

Alex put on her apron and a name tag that read *Alex McGrath* on the top line and *Boston, United States* on the bottom.

"This is your station," Rosa said. "There are four of you and your station includes all of the tables and beach chairs on the port side of the ship."

That placement would give Alex a good vantage point on activity on the lido deck. Of course, it would also keep her close to Sorina.

However, Alex decided that she would just have to deal with her former roommate. She was on a cruise ship. The sky was clear, the weather warm, and the lido deck smelled of the sea and the food from the Four Corners café. She decided it was a good place and she resolved to enjoy it as much as she could while she was there.

"Just make sure all of your tickets say section four," Rosa said.

*Four*, Alex thought. *Perfect*.

\* \* \* \*

Dr. Hunt said, "No surprises from the autopsy."

Bloch looked across the desk and at the doctor's serious face.

"Drug interaction?" she asked.

"Yes, and I should have seen it," he replied. "Interrogation drugs haven't fundamentally changed much since the first truth serums were developed. We use a formula based on sodium thiopental, but all of them are variations of anesthetic. This means that they are susceptible to drug interactions. Anesthesiologists go to great pains to avoid these interactions because they can be deadly. In this case, it was very easy for John to take something that would interact with our drug, stop his heart, and then make reviving him impossible."

"Does this mean we can never use any interrogation drugs against Ares personnel?" Bloch asked. That would reduce their options. As a matter of policy, there were interrogation techniques that Zeta didn't use, but in the face of a mass casualty attack there were principles they might not be able to afford—especially if the normal drugs were off the table.

"No, in the future we can do a more thorough testing of any subject's blood. In any case, the drugs in his system were not the kind of things an Ares operative could be on at all times. I suspect they are a temporary measure used when one of theirs is operating alone and thinks he might be captured," Hunt said.

"That's something. Do you have a medical solution to the problem of their cyanide teeth?" Bloch asked.

"There's nothing I can do about that medically. In fact, the teeth are much thinner and easier for the user to break than the ones the CIA uses. It actually takes some doing to break CIA-issued teeth. The problem here is stopping the teeth from being compromised. My guess is that Ares loses a number of operatives a year from accidental ruptures."

"Thank you, Doctor. Please make sure we have plenty of samples of John's DNA. We've gotten no hits on it, or on his fingerprints. Like the other Ares agents we've been able to examine, he seems to have sprung up from nowhere, but maybe the CIA or some of our international partners will have better luck."

When the doctor left, Bloch was surprised to see Karen O'Neal waiting for her. O'Neal had been with Zeta nearly from the beginning, and Bloch had met with her many times, but she didn't think O'Neal had ever come to Bloch's office alone.

"Director, Lincoln isn't doing well," O'Neal said with her usual directness. The young woman had probably the highest IQ at Zeta—well into category of the truly exceptional. However, O'Neal didn't seem to know how to hide her feelings. And Bloch could see that the young woman was very concerned about Shepard. Besides their work partnership, Bloch knew they were partners at home as well. Though all too often that home was a surprisingly well-appointed apartment they had carved for themselves out of the computer, engineering, and fabrication floors that were collectively known at Zeta as "the basement."

"I have noticed. Do you think he would benefit from some more time off?" Bloch said.

"No!" O'Neal said with surprising sharpness. "I'm sorry, Director, but that would be the wrong approach. Do you know where he is today?"

"I told him to get some rest and come in late," Bloch said.

"He's at the funeral for the girl who was killed, Maria Ramirez," O'Neal said. Then she added, "Though he promised me that he would go to the church only and not interact with the family. He's in pain, Director, and I think he might be in...real trouble."

O'Neal took a moment to gather herself and then said, "A few years before we met, Lincoln had a sister. She died at nineteen, of leukemia."

"Helen," Bloch said, remembering the name from Shepard's file.

"Yes, Helen," O'Neal said. "I know that only because his mother told me. He never talks about her; never, despite the fact that they were very close."

Bloch knew something about grief and suspected that Shepard didn't talk about his sister because they were very close.

"And to be clear, Lincoln talks to me about everything, even things you would think he would keep to himself. In fact, he's even told me—"

Bloch raised her hand to keep O'Neal from finishing that sentence. "I understand. That explains why Ms. Ramirez's murder has hit him so hard."

"Yes, we can understand, but that doesn't tell me how to help him," O'Neal said, looking to Bloch for answers.

Bloch did something she almost never did in front of the staff. She let out a sigh. "There's no playbook for this. When a field agent has this kind of struggle, I can pull them out of action temporarily so they are not a danger to themselves, and then hope for the best. Here, I could give him some involuntary time off, perhaps for both of you. While I would hate to lose you two for any length of time, I'm sure your staff can carry on most of your department's functions."

"I think rest would just make it worse," O'Neal said flatly.

"I'm open to ideas," Bloch said.

"He needs a problem, ma'am, something that will engage him," O'Neal said.

"We have plenty of those, but he'll smell make-work a mile away," Bloch said, regretting her casual tone. O'Neal looked genuinely scared, which was something Bloch had never seen before.

"It needs to be something critical and urgent," O'Neal said.

For a second Bloch didn't know what to say, and the nakedness of the dread on O'Neal's face made Bloch's frustration at her inability to help even worse.

Bloch had nothing, and Lincoln Shepard might not come back from this setback if she didn't come up with something quickly.

And then to her surprise she realized that she did have something— actually, quite a bit more than something. It was genuinely critical. And as for time-sensitivity, Zeta needed it yesterday.

"There is something," Bloch said. "Do you know if Dan Morgan, Peter Conley, and Dani Guo are still in Indonesia?"

"No," O'Neal said. "They are en route to the Coral Sea."

"I need to talk to them," Bloch said. "Let me know when Shepard is in the building."

# Chapter 15

"One melon ball," Alex said, handing the drink to the man on the deck chair.

Taking the glass, he said, "Hi, I'm Eric." He was American, and right then he looked very uncomfortable.

"I saw you last night at the forward crew bar," he said.

*Oh*, Alex thought. She smiled politely but quickly tried to calculate a way out of this situation.

"You're crew?" she asked. If he was, he wasn't allowed in the guest areas, even if he was off duty.

"It's okay, I'm with entertainment," he said.

That was different. Entertainment included singers, dancers, and comedians. They were technically crew, but they were allowed and even encouraged to mingle with the guests, who saw them as mini-celebrities.

"What do you do?" she asked.

"I'm with the Broadway revival show," he said. "Look, I wanted to ask you something."

He was about twenty-five and good-looking, and his attention was flattering. If he were crew, it wasn't against the rules for them to socialize, but that just wouldn't be compatible with her mission.

"I saw you at the bar last night and I wanted to ask you about your friend," he said.

"My friend?" Alex replied.

"The tall girl…" he began.

*Sorina?* Alex thought. "The one who was literally hanging over that guy," she said.

Eric looked like he was about to blush, and then he actually did. "What do you know about her?"

"I know she's from Romania and was in the military for two years before she started with the cruise line," Alex said.

He perked up at that. "We have that in common. I was in the service for four years after high school. Is it serious with that guy?"

Alex gave him a tight smile and said, "I'm afraid so. She followed him here."

"Oh," he said, seeming to deflate. "I know I sound stupid, but I've been on board for a while. I know that there are a lot of very...*short-term* relationships at sea, so I thought I'd ask."

"Look, I can introduce you. She's new on board, and I'm sure she could use a friend," Alex said.

Though, truthfully, Sorina only seemed interested in her Ramón.

Eric jumped to his feet and said, "Okay, thanks." As an afterthought, he said, "Nice to meet you, Alex" and shook her hand.

"You too, Eric," she said.

He looked embarrassed and shuffled off, leaving his untouched melon ball on the table by his chair.

Alex put the drink back on her tray as her phone beeped. The rules said she should not check her phone while she was working, but the special beep told her it was a message from Alicia Schmitt.

She dropped the drink with the dirty glasses, slipped behind a column near the bar, and pulled out her phone.

The message was from Schmitt and contained only three words: **We're being tracked.**

* * * *

When Bloch arrived, Shepard was in the workstation he shared with O'Neal and staring into his monitor. He must have changed after the funeral, because he was wearing his typical jeans and hoodie. He looked neater than he did yesterday, which Bloch chalked up to his attendance at the funeral.

"A word, Mr. Shepard," Bloch said.

The young man turned to her and said, "Of course."

"In private," she replied.

It took him a second to process that, and then he followed her to the small coffee room. Actually, coffee room was too narrow, since the space contained several different coffee machines, as well as cappuccino and espresso equipment and a few other hot beverage dispensers that she didn't recognize.

"Shepard, we have a situation—"

His shoulders slumped even more and he said, "Director, I know that I've been—"

She waved the rest of his sentence away and said, "This isn't about you, Mr. Shepard. We have a situation in the field, and I need to know what you and your team can do about it."

That seemed to wake him up a bit, and she continued, "Do you know where Morgan, Conley, and Guo are right now?"

"They are on their way to a location on the coast of the Coral Sea, heading for the first suspicious shipping destination we pulled off the hard drives Morgan and Conley recovered in Jakarta."

"Have you read the report from the warehouse?" she asked. "Not the technical report, but the mission report."

"No," Shepard said.

"I suggest you do, but suffice it to say that Morgan and Conley did what they do, except even more of it than usual. The only reason they are alive is that they were facing ordinary terrorists. But you and I both know that when they start knocking down doors around the Coral Sea, sooner or later they are going to face highly trained Ares killers on their own turf," Bloch said.

She let that sink in with Shepard and then continued. "For all we know they will end up walking—or more likely—running into an Ares base, possibly even Ares headquarters, and what do you think is going to happen then?"

"Maybe you could order them to call for backup," Shepard said.

"Backup? They will be eight thousand miles away. And we all know that something big is coming. Even if we don't believe what the Ares operative John told us, O'Neal's threat assessment system confirms it. Do you think Dan Morgan will stop after what happened to Alex in our own backyard? When he knows that if he doesn't do something, Alex and Alicia Schmitt might be facing a worse threat alone on a cruise ship with no resources."

"You could order Morgan and—"

"Have you met Dan Morgan? Or Peter Conley, for that matter? And I had hope for Dani Guo, but I see that she's now spent too much time with the both of them. I won't even phrase it as a question, I will tell you what will happen. They will storm whatever facilities they find, they will perform remarkable feats, and then they will die. We can put their names on a plaque in the mess, soon to be followed by Alex Morgan and Alicia Schmitt."

"Director, we're doing everything we can…" Shepard said.

"You are, and I need you and your team to keep doing it, because we need every scrap of information we can get on Ares and where they are operating from. However, that same information is likely to get five of our people killed. What we need—what *they* need—is a weapon."

"A weapon?"

"Dr. Hunt tells me that their cyanide teeth are relatively fragile," she said.

"That's true," he replied. "If one of their operatives bites down too hard they could die on the spot."

"That's what I'm counting on. Now I need you to find a way to help that process along. I need a weapon that will trigger the teeth from a distance."

"How?" he asked.

"That is what I need you to tell me because I have no idea. Lasers? Static electricity? Strong language? But whatever you come up with, I need you to do it quickly, because if we had five prototypes ready to go in your lab right now, it would still take us twenty-four hours to get them to our people."

Bloch actually saw the change in Shepard's eyes. The stricken, haunted look he had worn for the last few days had turned to fear once she laid out the problem and the danger to Zeta's agents, who were also his friends. Then the look turned to something else. It was a look specific to him that said his mind was intensely concentrating on a number of things at once.

All of those things were warring with his grief, and even if they weren't winning, they were gaining ground.

"None of those things would work. Music, maybe…or just sound. Hit the right frequency and a soprano can crack crystal. But this would be different. The synthetic enamel they use is stronger than glass. And even if you could do it, the power requirements would be too much. And that's if you were working at close range. Of course, if you applied…"

His words drifted off, but Bloch could almost feel his thoughts racing and colliding with one another. She let that continue for a full minute and said, "Shepard?"

It was like she'd woken him from a dream and he said, "Director, I'm not saying it's not possible, but we'll have to invent five things that don't exist and modify a few more."

"Then I suggest you get started, Mr. Shepard," Bloch said.

He got up. "I'll have to requisition some new equipment."

"Consider it approved," Bloch said.

Then Shepard was out the door and heading back to his workstation at a jog.

In all of her time at Zeta, or in any leadership role, Bloch didn't think she had ever so cynically and unfairly manipulated one of her people. It would have been shameful if it hadn't been necessary and for Shepard's own good.

Of course, it had helped that every single word she had said to him was true.

\* \* \* \*

If Alex hadn't been hurrying, she might have been able to avoid it, but given the nonstop rush that had been going on for two hours now, hurrying was a necessity. The kitchen was going all out, but they just couldn't keep up with the orders. The waits were getting longer, and the passengers were getting restless.

The BLT and tropical cocktail that were on her tray now had been ordered by a perfectly pleasant woman half an hour ago. She'd been reasonably polite the first time she'd asked after her order, and less polite the second time. Now Alex was determined to get her lunch to her before the fries got cold.

With children running around the pool, the path between the kitchen and her customer had become an obstacle course. She was hyperalert to the kids in front of her. As a result, she was slightly less aware of the threats emerging in her peripheral vision.

By the time she noticed the two ten-or-so-year-olds playing tug-of-war with one of the deck chairs at the edge of the pool, she was almost on top of them. With impeccable timing that could not have been re-created intentionally, one of the kids let go of the chair, leaving the winner of the tug-of-war to fall onto his rear just as Alex was approaching.

As he fell, he let go of the chair, which skidded half-a-dozen feet across the deck to make solid contact with her right shin. As that leg started to buckle, she turned her body so she was able to briefly sit on the chair that had hit her.

Less than a second later, she was standing again and, remarkably, the order was still on her tray. The kids ran off to make mischief somewhere else, and Alex delivered the food to a tight-lipped "thank you" from her customer.

Alex had taken just a few steps when a voice beside her said, "Excuse me." She looked down and saw a man in maybe his mid-twenties. He had short brown hair and Western, but slightly exotic, features and very striking pale blue eyes.

"I don't know if I just witnessed a miracle or an act of superhuman skill," he said.

"Neither," she replied. "More like reflexes born of self-preservation."

"From, I assume, years of advanced training," he said.

"Yes, let's go with that," she replied.

"I'm Devan Martin," he said, in what she recognized as a London accent.

"Alex McGrath," she replied.

He glanced at her name tag and said, "Alex from Boston."

"Devan from London," she said.

"Another unusual skill," he said.

"Not really. I can only recognize London and Cockney. And you sound nothing like Dick Van Dyke."

"Alas, one of Her Majesty's best," he said, smiling.

"Can I get you something?" she asked.

"An old-fashioned," he replied.

"Right away," she said.

As she was turning away, he said, "Nice to meet you, Alex from Boston."

"You too," she said, remembering her cruise line training that stressed over and over that positive interactions with the crew were one of the biggest takeaways for their customers. Of course, there were lines that that interaction could never cross, but most interactions—including light flirting—were just good customer service.

Of course, her cover required her to behave like a real server. And her nature required her to try to excel at anything she was doing, but the mission—her real mission—absolutely had to come first.

And she had that cryptic message from Schmitt on her mind. *We're being tracked*, it had said.

It didn't say who, or why, but that was because Schmitt didn't know herself. Mission protocols meant the team shared whatever information they had, even if it was something that no one fully understood or could act on.

Alex would just have to be ready when the details started to come in. And if Alex had learned anything from her time at Zeta, those details always came in faster and more intensely than you'd like.

As if Schmitt had been monitoring her thoughts, Alex's phone beeped. Ducking into a corner, she opened it to see a short message from Schmitt. Lifeboat 42, 6:15.

# Chapter 16

Lifeboat 42 was a good place to meet. It was near the rear of the *Grandeur* but still on the lido deck. However, at that point on the ship the outdoor portion of the deck was less than a six-foot walkway outside of one of many interior bars and lounges. As a result, it was rarely used by guests and was mostly for the crew to get around while avoiding high-traffic guest areas during the day.

This time of day, most of the guests were at or getting ready for dinner, so there were few enough people around that the crew wouldn't be needing outdoor shortcuts.

Alex approached the large, mahogany bar that told her she was in the right place. At the far end of the bar, she saw the exit door that would take her where she needed to go.

She walked with purpose, but was stopped cold when she saw Alicia Schmitt at the bar with an officer. No, not just an officer, but the ship's first officer. Though she had never met Jack Watson herself, she recognized him from his official photo.

The picture had showed a handsome man, but even from a distance Alex could see that it hadn't done him justice.

However, the real surprise was Schmitt herself. Since the woman had been one of her hand-to-hand and martial arts instructors, Alex knew from bitter experience that she was tough and athletic.

However, the shimmering silver dress showed Alex a side of her colleague that hadn't even occurred to her. From the way First Officer Watson was looking at her and the relatively little space between them, it appeared that he was very comfortable with that side of Alicia Schmitt.

They said a few parting words and then Watson turned and headed toward Alex. She smiled and said, "Sir" as they passed each other. Ahead of her, Alex watched Schmitt disappear through the exit door.

A few seconds later, Alex reached the door and followed her. When they were alone outside, Schmitt said, "Hello, Alex. How are you doing?"

"Well, nothing to report from my side," she said.

"And I can't tell you much more than I did in my text. Someone is about twenty miles out, tracking us."

"What do you know about them?" Alex asked.

"Our radar says the ship doing the tracking is one of a number of small vessels in a group. Could be pirates. Could be pleasure boats. Could be fishermen," Schmitt said.

"Except?" Alex replied.

"Except for the fact that they keep painting us with radar," Schmitt said.

"Painting?" Alex asked.

"They send out a broad signal looking for something, in this case us. We measure the return signal as a digital chirp. The nature of the chirp tells us if they are looking for us or locked on to us," Schmitt said.

"So they're still looking for us?"

Schmitt frowned. "No. A radar lock would be too obvious. Intermittent, short-term painting could be explained in other ways. Even small pleasure craft can have radar nowadays. They turn the system on intermittently to keep a rough idea of where we are."

Given Schmitt's experience in the Navy and as a pilot, Alex had no doubt that the woman's judgment was correct. The only question now was what to do about it.

"Have you told the captain?" Alex asked.

"Yes," she said. "He's not convinced that it's a threat."

Reading Alex's expression, she added, "Most of the crew came up on civilian vessels, either cruise or merchant ships. And civilians evaluate threats differently. For now, we wait. If the other ship locks on to us we'll have some time to take action."

"Can the *Grandeur* defend itself?" Alex asked.

"Yes. Though officially they don't have any weapons on board, they have a number of nonlethal means to repel boarders. In fact, First Officer Watson won't tell me all of the countermeasures they have in the event that, say, a group of determined pirates attempt to board. If it's Ares, and they overwhelm ship's security, then we will earn our pay. Zeta's threat assessment system flagged these waters and this ship as the most likely targets for some kind of attack. Between the crew and us, there are almost no threats we can't deal with."

"Almost?" Alex said.

"If the bad guys have cruise missiles or the equivalent, none of the ship's security protocols and none of our training will help. Anything short of that we can handle," Schmitt said. Then she put a hand on Alex's shoulder and added, "I know the waiting is hard, but remember that everything you learn about your environment will help if it comes down to us. Good luck, Alex," Schmitt said.

"Good luck to you," Alex said and then Schmitt was gone.

Alex waited a minute and then followed Schmitt back inside. Checking her watch, Alex saw that she'd just used twenty minutes of her hour dinner break. In forty minutes she'd have to be back at her station for her seven-to-eleven shift.

She wondered if this was what serving in the Navy during wartime was like: Full days of work while you were on the lookout for threats you could handle while you always knew there was the possibility of a sudden, devastating attack that could come without warning.

Of course, that state also described most of the missions she had been on for Zeta. The difference here was that she was on a ship and there was no question that they were very isolated. In the event of trouble, there was little chance that backup or help of any kind would come in time to make a difference.

And, of course, there was nowhere to go if retreat was your only option—unless you were a very, very good swimmer.

She picked up her pace, realizing that she'd have to put off any further thinking about that sort of thing until later. Right now, she'd be lucky to get a bite to eat and return to her station (*section four*, she reminded herself) by the beginning of her second shift.

\* \* \* \*

"Karen O'Neal," Bloch's assistant said.

This was the second time in twenty-four hours that O'Neal had come to see Bloch by herself. It was also the second time since the woman had joined Zeta.

"Send her in," Bloch said.

O'Neal rushed in and stood in front of Bloch's desk. Before the director could even gesture for her to sit, O'Neal spoke. "Have you seen what Lincoln has done since you spoke to him?"

"I haven't seen him, but I have seen quite a few equipment requisitions: industrial, medical, and some new fabrication machines. There was even some musical equipment. I can't make any sense out of it, but it's all very expensive," Bloch said.

"He's been in the engineering and computer labs, working with the equipment he was able get delivered locally while we wait for the rest. And he's completely shut himself off, except to bark at the staff. He's barely talking to me, and only then it's because I'm a source of algorithms for his multivariable dynamic system computer models." Then the woman looked at Bloch expectantly, as if her points had spoken for themselves.

Bloch looked for emotional cues on O'Neal's face to try to figure out what was expected of her, but, as usual, the young woman was unreadable. "I understand. This is an important project and I think we'll have to be patient with Shepard—"

Before Bloch could finish, O'Neal sat in the chair, though "collapsed into it" would be more accurate. When O'Neal looked at Bloch, her eyes were red and she seemed near tears. "Thank you, Director."

Bloch kept silent. She had no idea what to say, and she was too shocked to see O'Neal like this. The young woman barely showed emotion, significantly less than the rest of the team at Zeta—who were all intelligence professionals who had made careers out of keeping to themselves. Bloch had actually wondered if O'Neal was capable of this sort of display.

Then the director did something she had never done in her tenure at Zeta: She handed a tissue to one of her distraught staff.

"I didn't know how to help him. I couldn't reach him," O'Neal said. Then the tears weren't just threatening to come, they were here. "Director, I thought we might lose him, really lose him. I didn't see how he could come back from the place he was in. He blamed himself…"

"I know, Karen. I saw it. I'm just glad that we had such an urgent need for his…gifts. This work is important. If your team can succeed, it may change everything for us," Bloch said.

O'Neal wiped her eyes, shook her head once, and then spoke as if the last few minutes hadn't happened. Her eyes were still red, but her voice was steady and, for her, normal.

"Lincoln did send me to talk to you about his request for lithium-six deuteride. He says the only source for that quantity would be Los Alamos, and that in answer to their inevitable question, we really need no less than that amount, and we need it right away."

"I'll see what I can do," Bloch said as O'Neal left.

She opened the request from Shepard on her computer and checked the amount of lithium-6.

*Good lord*, she thought. This was going to take some doing.

* * * *

Alex made it back to her station with two minutes to spare. Nevertheless, her supervisor Rosa was waiting for her and clearly impatient.

"Alex, we have a problem with your friend," Rosa said.

"My friend?"

"The tall one, Sorina," Rosa said.

"I wouldn't—"

"I need you to sort this out right now," Rosa said.

"I wouldn't call her my friend," Alex said. "I'm probably not the best person—"

Alex saw Rosa's expression and stopped talking. "Alex, please don't play games with me. I know you were roommates, and we all saw you last night at the crew bar."

"That was really—"

"Alex, come with me," Rosa said. The woman led her to the lido deck kitchen area, then deeper inside near one of the dry goods walk-in pantries. Rosa knocked on the door, which was quickly met with a string of what Alex recognized as loud, Romanian profanity.

Rosa gestured to the door as if to say, *See what I mean?*

"I'm sorry, Rosa, I don't know what's going on here," Alex said.

"She's in there and she won't come out. Everyone is afraid to go in. She's very intimidating, you know. And in this state I think she might be violent," Rosa said.

"I know what you mean, but I'm not sure what you want me to do," Alex said.

"I want you to fix this," Rosa said. "I want you to go in there and talk to your friend. We need access to the pantry, and I need everyone to get back to work."

"I really don't think I'm the one you want to do this," Alex said.

"If you don't, I will have to send your friend home," Rosa said.

That was an angle Alex hadn't considered. It might even solve one of Alex's problems for her.

"If that's what you have to do," Alex said.

"Wow. I thought you were her friend," Rosa said. "Let me explain to you how this works. I'm responsible for all servers on the lido deck, and we can't do our jobs if we can't get into the pantry in the next thirty minutes. So if you don't go in and bring your friend out, I have to do it. And I'm definitely not going to. Now follow me."

Alex sighed and followed Rosa to the pantry door. The headwaiter looked at Alex expectantly. Steeling herself, Alex knocked lightly on the swinging door.

It took less than a second for Sorina to shout, "Go away" and then a string of Romanian words.

"Sorina, it's Alex," she said.

"You go away most of all," Sorina screamed. What followed was an even longer string of Romanian words broken up by "stupid" and "princess."

Rosa raised an eyebrow and pointed inside.

Alex didn't delay the inevitable. She pushed open the swinging door and stepped into the pantry.

# Chapter 17

Alex thought the pantry was in surprisingly good shape. There were a few boxes on the floor, some which had obviously been thrown at the door. Alex assumed that had happened when someone else had tried to enter.

In the middle of the room was Sorina, who had been sitting on the floor with her face in her hands when Alex entered. Hearing Alex, Sorina raised her head, her eyes red-rimmed and leaking blotchy mascara—which had run down her still wet-with-tears-face.

Sorina looked genuinely shocked to see Alex. That much Alex understood; she was just as surprised to be there.

"You?" Sorina said.

"Sorina, we have to get you out of here. If this goes on any longer Rosa will send you home," Alex said.

"I don't care," Sorina said. Then she broke into a burst of fresh sobs.

"Well, I'm stuck in here with you, so I'll get sent home too," Alex said.

That seemed to get through to Sorina. She looked up at Alex and said, "Stupid princess, I don't care what happens to you."

*Fair point*, Alex thought.

She needed another approach and she needed it fast. "Why don't I go find Ramón. Maybe you can talk to him," Alex said.

What burst out of Sorina was not sobs, but wails, and the woman covered her face in her hands again for a solid two minutes. Then a look of sudden anger appeared on the woman's face. "You can find him in his cabin, with Olga, a Ukrainian pig who works in the casino."

"Oh, Sorina, I'm so sorry," Alex said, and Sorina's anger crumbled. She looked like she was going to cry again, but held it together. Alex decided to take a chance. If she was going to wrap this up any time soon, she'd have to take some risks. "Sorina, I'm just going to sit here for a minute."

Alex sat down as close to the Romanian woman as she dared, leaving a couple of feet between them. Then she took a handful of cocktail napkins from an open bin and handed them to Sorina, who wiped her face.

Sorina looked drier, but she'd also smudged her dark eye makeup over a larger area. Sorina gathered herself and said, "I went to his cabin during our dinner break. I was going to surprise him." She took a deep breath and said, "I did. He was in his bed with that..."

"Oh Sorina, that's awful," Alex said.

Sorina looked at her in mild surprise. For a second her face was a mask of warring emotions, and then the Romanian woman lunged for her. Before Alex could react, Sorina had buried her face in Alex's chest and began a series of gentle sobs.

*Well, I didn't see that coming,* Alex thought as she automatically put her arms awkwardly around her former roommate.

"I want to kill her," Sorina said.

"That won't help," Alex said. "She doesn't owe you anything. Plus, I don't think it's her you are mad at," Alex said.

Sorina shrugged and reluctantly agreed. "No, she's just a stupid whore. It's him I want to kill."

"See, that's progress. And I'll help you. We can toss him overboard and no one will know," Alex said.

Sorina looked up at her and said, "Would you really do that for me?"

"Sure," Alex said and smiled.

That made Sorina laugh. "I would but—but—I love him too much." That set off a fresh round of sobs.

When they eventually subsided, Sorina looked up at Alex through her red-rimmed eyes and tear-streaked face. "I'm sorry I hated you for being a stupid American," she said.

"You know, just *American* would be fine," Alex replied.

"Actually, most Americans I've met are not so bad. From now on, I will just hate you for being a princess," Sorina said.

Now it was Alex's turn to laugh. "See, more progress."

"He really hurt me," Sorina said, the naked pain on her face making the words unnecessary.

"I know, I'm sorry," Alex replied, pulling the larger woman in tighter.

"He was my... he took my innocence," Sorina said and buried her face in Alex's chest again.

In that moment, Alex was glad Sorina couldn't see the surprise on her face. "Men," Alex said, as if that explained everything.

"Why do they toy with us? Why don't they love us when we love them?" Sorina said.

"I don't know," Alex said, but she thought, *There are worse things. Sometimes they love us when we love them, and then they die.*

Alex kept that thought to herself since she knew it wouldn't help.

"He didn't deserve what you gave him, what you felt about him. There'll be another man, one who does," she said.

"But I don't want anyone else," Sorina said and began a new fit of sobs.

"I know you think that now, but eventually you will find someone else. There was a guy from the entertainment staff asking about you. An actor," Alex said.

That got no response from Sorina.

"He was very handsome," Alex said. "And tall."

Sorina pulled back from Alex and said, "I don't think he would like me very much if he knew me."

"Just don't call him a stupid American," Alex said.

Sorina was quiet for a few seconds and then said, "Ramón knew I was Romani and didn't care. He said he could overlook it. Do you think your American boy would like me if he knew that?"

"I'm sorry Sorina, I don't know what Romani is," Alex said.

Sorina shook her head. "Stupid Am—" she said and stopped herself. "*Ignorant* American," she corrected. "Romani is what you would call Gypsy. Do you think your American boy would like me if he knew the truth about me—that my mother is Romani."

"Yes," Alex said. "I think pretty much all American boys would think it was hot."

"I don't believe you," Sorina said, studying Alex's face.

"It's true. I guarantee it,"

"Do you have any idea how they treat us in my country?" Sorina said. "You don't know what it's like."

"I don't know what it's like. And I can't speak for all the guys on this ship, but I can speak for American guys," Alex said.

"Even if that's true, how can I even love another man?" Sorina said.

Alex had to think about how to handle this. "I know that Ramón was... special. And he was your first love, but I promise you that when you are ready there will be another man for you."

Sorina studied her face and said, "What happened to your first...love?"

"He died," Alex said.

Sorina's eyes went wide and then she asked, "Was there another?"

"Yes," Alex said. *He died too*, she thought but didn't say. "Sorina, you're very beautiful. There will be plenty of men who want to be with you when you are ready."

Sorina looked like she wanted to believe it was true, but wasn't ready to accept the possibility. Alex helped her up.

"Why don't you go back to your cabin? I'll fix it with Rosa," Alex said, having no idea how she was going to do that.

Rosa appeared just as Sorina headed down the corridor. "Where is she going?" the woman snapped.

"I sent her back to her cabin. She'll be fine tomorrow," Alex said, hoping that would be true.

"She needs to get back here right now or I will have her sent home. I may do that anyway," Rosa said.

"She got some bad news. I'm sure she just needs a night's sleep," Alex said.

"The customers liked her, but I can't have this. She'll have to go," Rosa said.

"Rosa…" Alex started to say, but couldn't think of a single argument she could make. In fact, going home might be just what Sorina needed. But even if that were true, Alex thought it should be Sorina's choice. Alex had no idea what the woman's life was like at home, though Alex now suspected it was more difficult than she would have guessed.

"Sorina is Romani. Do you know what that is?" Alex said, her voice taking on more authority as she spoke.

"No, and I don't care," Rosa said.

"You should. Given what she's faced at home, I would be very careful before you open up the cruise line to any charges of discrimination."

"Discrimination?" Rosa asked, genuinely perplexed.

It did sound absurd, given the makeup of the crew and the fact that from the outside Sorina looked like a very attractive Western girl.

"Yes, and her father is a human rights attorney for the UN. I would make sure you are treating her like you would anyone else," Alex said.

That last part might have been a bit much, but Rosa seemed to accept it.

"Look, she had a very rough time today. If she's not better tomorrow I think she'll leave on her own," Alex said.

"Okay, then I am making her your responsibility," Rosa said. "If you are sure she will be fine, that shouldn't be a problem."

Rosa looked at her expectantly and Alex said, "Sure."

"Now get back to work. I have two servers trying to cover your station and things are backing up. I don't know what we're going to do about Sorina's station," Rosa said, shaking her head.

As they were speaking, Alex's phone emitted the distinctive low volume beep that told her she'd received a text from Schmitt. She couldn't check it while she was standing with Rosa so she raced back to her station.

Before she got there, Alex was accosted by two angry waitresses who shoved order tickets at her. Using the tickets to hide her phone, Alex read the message. It contained just four words: We're being actively tracked.

\* \* \* \*

Schmitt was impressed that the captain wanted to talk on the bridge. That meant he was comfortable having this level of discussion in front of his entire bridge crew. And that further meant he trusted them enough to tell them the truth. Those facts said a lot about Captain Garrett and his bridge crew.

"Ms. Schmitt, thank you for coming," Garrett said.

"Of course," she replied.

"You're certain about the readings you're getting?" he asked.

"Yes, sir. We know that one or more parties have been scanning the area with radar, presumably for us. Now we can confirm that the same party isn't just doing a broad, random search, but their radar is tracking our movements. As you know, this is very mature technology. It's been part of tactical radar systems on naval vessels for decades. And civilian systems currently have most of the capability built in, but the equipment isn't optimized for tactical use. However, Scott Renard is a big believer in the notion that it's better to have a technology and not need it then need it and not have it."

"I agree. What is your analysis of the party that's tracking us?" he asked.

"Most likely pirates. As you know, there has been a large increase in piracy in the Coral Sea," she said.

"But they have only targeted merchant vessels up until now," he said.

"Wisely, authorities react more strongly when a large number of civilians are threatened. Even if we are approached, any pirates might see that the *Grandeur* is a cruise ship and move along," she said.

That was true—if it *were* pirates—but that was far from certain. If it were terrorists, or Ares, then the opposite was true: The more civilians in danger or dead, the better.

"Even if they don't move on," he said. "This ship will likely give them a few surprises. If nothing else, she's faster than she looks and if they are using small craft—even if they are quick—there's a limit to how much fuel they can carry."

"And our radar isn't showing anyone moving in our direction," Schmitt said.

"We will monitor that from here and I presume you will monitor progress on your system," he said.

"Of course," she replied.

"So I will assume the threat is minimal until we see a change," Garrett said.

"I think that's a reasonable course, sir," she said. His position made sense for a civilian captain in Garrett's position. He didn't know what Schmitt knew: that her supersecret intelligence organization had identified the immediate area and possibly the ship as the target of a major terrorist incident.

And unfortunately, Schmitt wasn't authorized to tell him. She'd have to wait until a real threat emerged and report it. To be fair, there was no action he could take until then. Nevertheless, she would have preferred to be honest. It was always better when everyone on a team knew the risks and the stakes.

"Thanks, Ms. Schmitt," he said. Then he turned to his first office and said, "Jack, I'll walk her out."

The captain held the door for her, and they both stepped into the corridor.

"Ms. Schmitt, given the nature of the tactical features on your system, can I assume that it will tell you if the tracking were to become a full weapons lock?" he asked.

Schmitt had to cover her surprise at the question. "Of course," she said.

"Very good," he replied. "Enjoy the rest of your day."

Schmitt felt nothing but relief as she headed back to engineering to monitor the system. Most good captains had the gift of insight, and that ability often kept fishing boats in business and the crews of naval ships alive.

When it came to Captain Garrett, Schmitt hoped that all of the legends about him were true.

# Chapter 18

Dan Morgan didn't like leaving Jenny in the hotel. He understood her desire to stay with him while they tracked down the people who might be a threat to Alex, but as they got closer and closer to their objective, Morgan was less and less comfortable. Things were getting more dangerous.

Jakarta was one thing, but Port Moresby was another.

He and Peter had been to the port a few times over the years, but he'd never fully relaxed even when it was just the two of them. Besides the usual violent crime—which had always been a problem—tribal and clan violence was up this year significantly.

On the one hand, since Port Moresby was the capital of Papua New Guinea, it was probably the safest region. On the other hand, it still had a level of violence that was rare in cities that were not currently at war.

Of course, Dani was with Jenny, and both women were armed, but Morgan still didn't like it. He'd long ago given up on keeping what he did from Jenny, but there were things he just didn't want her to ever see, let alone experience.

The Port Moresby Hilton was nice, but definitely not the best hotel in the city. That status made the hotel even safer, since the risk of kidnapping or attacks on Westerners tended to favor the wealthiest and best-appointed enclaves.

Despite all the crime and unrest, the country was absurdly beautiful. It was one of the many places he and Conley had vowed they would explore properly when they weren't on a mission.

There was remarkable natural beauty, especially along the coast, but none of that was worth putting Jenny at risk for a second more than necessary.

He and Conley took at cab from their hotel to the Airways Hotel, which was the nicest hotel in the city. However, since the meeting was set by the people in the Australian consulate, he didn't have much choice about the location, especially since he and Conley needed their help. This was, after all, their city.

Well, not theirs exactly. Australia had ceased administering Papua New Guinea in 1975. Yet the ties between the two countries were strong, partly because of their history together, and partly because the nations were only ninety miles apart.

Outside, it was warm, maybe eight-five degrees. The country didn't have a dry season, but it did have a *drier* season. That meant it only rained once a day and the humidity was usually under 90 percent.

Morgan and Conley entered the lobby and took seats near the window, as per the arrangement with the Australians. Less than a minute later, Morgan heard footsteps behind them and a voice in an Australian accent that said, "Good day, my American friends."

As the two agents stood and turned they saw the smiling face of a man in his early thirties. "Phil Givens. And you are Mr. Newby," he added, shaking Morgan's hand. "And Mr. Best," he said, shaking Conley's hand.

"Thank you for seeing us, Mr. Givens," Conley said. "We appreciate the assistance."

"Of course, when your office calls, we are always happy to help," Givens said.

By "your office" Morgan knew that the man was referring to the office of whatever highly placed person in the State Department who had set up the exchange as a favor to Diana Bloch.

"Did you bring the material?" Morgan asked.

"I'm afraid not," he said. "My boss wanted to meet you both and give it to you in person," Givens said.

Morgan was quickly on guard. "We are on a deadline. And our office instructed us to keep this low-profile," he said.

"We don't have to go to the consulate. I work out of a satellite trade office. It's closer and *very* low-profile. It's also busy and a bit of a mess, but it's where we have the records you need."

"Lead the way," Morgan said.

"I'll just let our next meeting know we will be a little late," Conley said, taking out his phone.

There was a car waiting outside the hotel. It had Australian diplomatic plates and looked genuine. They waited for a few seconds while Conley sent off a message on his phone. Then left the hotel, and just before they got into the car, Conley told Morgan that Bloch had approved the change of venue for the exchange.

From this point forward, Zeta would use the GPS signals on their phones to monitor their location; if anything went wrong, or if the car deviated from the route, Zeta HQ would know.

Of course, Zeta HQ was several thousand miles away, so even if something went wrong and Zeta knew about it, Morgan and his partner would be on their own. Of course, that was nothing new.

After less than five minutes of driving, they pulled up to a small building that had a large sign that said laundry in English and the equivalent underneath in pidgin or one of the country's 700 local languages.

"We're on the second floor," Givens said from the passenger seat.

Morgan scanned the front of the building. There was a door on the right side that said Trade Office in English only. Conley seemed satisfied, which meant the address checked out.

They stepped inside and walked up a long flight of stairs to the second floor, and then entered a messy, bustling office with six desks arrayed in two rows and a counter in the back. It looked like a DMV office on the day before a three-day weekend.

"I'd say business is booming," Morgan said.

"It is, but we have to keep telling ourselves it's a good thing," Givens said. He led them to the back, then behind the counter, then through a door behind that.

They were now in a small room in which a bored-looking uniformed security guard was sitting at a small table. In front of him was an elevator door. "I'm sorry, gents, but there are no weapons past this point."

Morgan didn't like it, but it was standard enough when you were entering a secure facility. He handed the guard the Walther from his shoulder holster and the backup strapped to his ankle. Conley gave up his Glock, and they entered the waiting elevator. The car went down two floors to what Morgan guessed was a basement level under the ground-floor laundry.

They came out into a small lobby with a well-dressed receptionist who greeted them with a professional hello and then they walked through a bright, open-plan office with four desks manned by serious-looking people working quietly on their computers. Unlike the office above them, there was no noise, no feeling of barely controlled chaos, and no piles of papers everywhere.

Givens led them to the back and to a single, large office with an open door and a nameplate that said, *John Roberts, Section Chief.*

Givens introduced them to Roberts, a well-dressed man in his mid-thirties, and then disappeared.

The desk was neat, but was slightly less immaculate than the ones outside. There were files and reports on the surface as well as a framed photo of a young woman holding a baby.

There was also a coffee mug that said *World's Greatest Dad* sitting on top of a pile of papers. On the shelf behind him was a card that said, *Happy Father's Day!*

They took seats facing Roberts, who said, "Welcome."

"We appreciate your help," Morgan said.

"We are happy to help our American friends, but to be honest, I have an ulterior motive. We can always use goodwill and favors out here. A little additional support from the US goes a long way."

"Congratulations, by the way," Conley said, pointing to the Father's Day card on the desk.

"Thank you, my wife and my first," Roberts said, breaking out into a wide grin.

"Enjoy this time," Morgan said. "Before you know it, they judge you and make fun of your music."

Roberts gave an involuntary laugh and said, "Noted. Now we've put together the records you asked for. I have both a file and a thumb drive for you." He paused and then added, "Can you tell me anything about the... situation you are looking into?"

"I'm afraid we can't," Morgan said.

"Your office will have to call ours for that," Conley said.

"Of course, but can I ask you if there is anything we should be worried about?" Roberts said.

"We really don't know anything. We're just here to pick up the material," Morgan said, putting a firm note in his voice.

"Well, that is our business, I suppose, but I had to ask," Roberts said. "Let me get the items. Would either of you like coffee, or water?"

"Both, if you don't mind," Morgan said.

"And herbal tea, if you have it," Conley added.

"No worries," Roberts said and stepped out.

"Herbal tea?" Morgan said.

"It might buy us another minute or two. Plus, it amuses me to make them root around for it. What tipped you off?" Conley said.

Morgan gestured to the desk. "They didn't clean all of the blood off the stapler. You?"

"Father's Day isn't until September in Australia. So if he's a new dad, his first Father's Day is two months away," Conley said.

"How do you know that?" Morgan asked.

"Long story. What's the plan?" Conley said.

"Working on it. I don't think he knows we know, so we have the element of surprise," Morgan said.

"Great. And we have his letter opener and some paper clips. Piece of cake," Conley replied.

* * * *

Alex woke with a start. Her first thought was that she was late for her shift, or rather, for the two hours of side jobs before her shift. And last night had been hard, even after she'd resolved the situation with Sorina.

She'd put her former roommate to bed and then gone back to finish out her shift, which ran until midnight. It was surprisingly busy, partly because with Sorina gone, the lido deck was down a server. Then there'd been an hour of cleanup. By the time she'd gotten to bed it was nearly two, but that was still better than most nights of training.

Alex checked her alarm clock. It was only eight, which meant she had a little time.

Her next thought was mortification at the fact that she'd forgotten about Schmitt's message that they were being tracked on radar. Someone was watching them and keeping careful track of their position.

They could be pirates, or terrorists, or worse, and Alex was worried about staying on the good side of the headwaiter. She didn't know if that made her a great undercover operative or a complete failure.

Schmitt did tell her the situation wasn't urgent—at least, not yet. So, for the moment, pirates and terrorists were out of her control. However, there was one job she could still do, and it involved lemon-scented industrial cleaner and an ice machine.

Alex showered quickly and came out to find Rebecca up and reading in bed. "Good morning, Alex," Rebecca said. "I missed you last night. I guess I was asleep when you came in. How was your first day?"

"Eventful. I'll have to tell you about it later," she said.

"I'd get breakfast with you, but my first appointment isn't until eleven," Rebecca said, taking a second to yawn and stretch.

"I think I want your job," Alex said.

"It's okay, but you'll meet more people at yours," Rebecca said.

That much was true and would actually mean something if she was on board to meet people.

"Don't worry about it. I have an errand to run before my shift anyway," Alex said.

She got dressed quickly and found her way to Sorina's cabin. She knocked on the door. Silence. Then she knocked again; there was still no reply. "Sorina," she called out.

"Go away," a familiar voice replied.

"It's Alex, let me in," she said.

Silence, then the shuffle of feet from inside. The door opened.

As Alex stepped into the cabin, Sorina padded back into bed and said, "Hello prince—" Remarkably, the woman stopped herself and said, "Good morning, Alex," using Alex's actual name for the first time since they had met.

"I just wanted to see how you were doing," Alex said.

"Terrible. I can't go to work today," Sorina said.

"You can stay in, but Rosa will probably send you home. She talked about it last night," Alex said.

"I don't care," Sorina said.

"Really? You want to go back to Romania?"

"No, it sucks. Plus, I'll make more on this three-month contract than I could in a year there," she said. Her voice started to break when she added, "But I can't see him…"

"It's true that you might see him. Okay, you probably will, but don't think for a second that you are stuck on the ship with him. The fact is that he's stuck on the ship with you," Alex said.

"What do you mean?" Sorina said.

"Look at you. You've been crying half the night, but you still look amazing. Let Ramón see that you don't care. Then let him see you with someone else, even if it's just to torture him. Meanwhile, he'll be with that Ukrainian woman, who is nothing compared to you."

Sorina thought about that for a second and said, "She is a stupid pig."

"You can always quit, but why not have some fun first?" Alex said.

Sorina was uncharacteristically quiet. Then she looked up at Alex and said, "Why do you help me?"

"We're friends. Wouldn't you do the same for me?" Alex asked.

"No, never," Sorina replied.

"Well, I didn't say we were good friends," Alex said. "Now get up and get ready."

Once Sorina was squared away at her own station, Alex reported to Rosa just before ten o'clock.

"Alex," Rosa said coolly.

Alex wondered how difficult she'd made it for herself. She had challenged Rosa last night. She'd also come dangerously close to threatening her supervisor with the crack about Sorina's father being a human rights attorney.

Had Alex just traded one problem with Sorina for an even bigger problem with Rosa? Her father had the reputation at Zeta of acting first and thinking later. It wasn't entirely fair, but it wasn't entirely false either.

Alex decided it was a Morgan curse, one of a growing list.

"Reporting for my side jobs," Alex said.

As if Alex hadn't spoken, Rosa said, "I see that Sorina is at her station. How is she?"

"I think she will be okay," Alex said.

"I heard about her and that Ramón," Rosa said, shaking her head. "Thank you for taking care of things."

"Of course," Alex said.

Then Rosa handed Alex off to one of the other servers, who introduced her to the ice machine. She scrubbed it out with a strong, terrible-smelling lemon cleaner. It took her over an hour and she had time to think about Rosa. The woman obviously didn't hold a grudge and Alex was glad it had worked out.

Alex knew there wasn't much difference between acting without thinking and acting on instinct. She supposed that the only meaningful distinction was whether what you did worked in the end. In this case, it had, and Alex decided she would take the win.

Her next job was mopping the two staircases that connected her deck to the one above, where Sorina's station was located. Remarkably, the mopping was much more pleasant than using strong chemicals on the ice machine.

She finished the job, stowed the mop and bucket in a storage closet under the stairs, cleaned up, and was at her station by twelve.

It wasn't busy, for which Alex was grateful. Most people were at lunch and her customers were a few families who decided to eat by the pool. It gave her a chance to keep an eye on Sorina, who seemed to be keeping it together.

Alex saw someone she recognized sitting in a chaise lounge and looking toward the upper level. Alex had to think for a second to come up with a name. "Hi, Eric," she said.

He turned toward Alex and looked embarrassed, as if he'd been caught staring at Sorina—which, of course, he had.

"Can I get you anything?" Alex said.

"What? No," he said.

"Why don't you go up and say hi to her," Alex said.

"I thought you said she had a boyfriend," he said.

"Not after last night. But it didn't end well, so I'd go easy," Alex said.

"Of course," he said, as if it was unthinkable that he would handle it any other way.

Alex decided she liked this boy. He might be just what Sorina needed. Then she saw the logo on his white polo shirt. It was an embroidered eagle with the word *Airborne* above it.

"You were 101st?" she asked.

"Hmm, oh, yeah. One tour," he said, distracted. Then he added, "I wanted to serve, but this is closer to what I really want to do."

She looked around at the pool, the deck, and the sea beyond and said, "I get that."

He chuckled. "It is nice, but I meant my job. It's as close to Broadway as I can get for now. My show is actually pretty good training," he said.

"I'll have to come see it," Alex replied. "I'll see if I can bring Sorina when we have the same night off. In the meantime, go say hi. Tell her you are an *American* friend of mine. Stress the word *American*."

"I will," he said, getting up. He actually looked nervous. "See you later, Alex." And then he headed for the stairs leading up to Sorina's pool.

"Hi, Alex," a familiar voice said to her. She turned and saw the British guy from yesterday. That was something: She knew exactly two people on the ship, and she had run into both of them in the last five minutes.

"What can I get you, Devan?" she asked. Even as she spoke, she saw Schmitt sitting at the edge of her station.

"Just a lemonade," he replied. "Listen, Alex—" he began.

"Sorry, I have to run. One of my more demanding customers is giving me the look," Alex said. "I'll bring the lemonade right away."

She headed over to Schmitt at a brisk walk. Schmitt was wearing khaki slacks and a gray Renard Tech polo shirt, which Alex recognized as her work outfit.

When Alex arrived, she said, "I didn't think this could wait. We are now no longer just being tracked, we're being followed, or—more accurately—pursued."

"Aggressive pirates?" Alex said.

"Maybe...probably," she replied. "Our radar suggests it's a small ship that has broken off from a group and is coming our way pretty fast."

"What's the captain's move?" Alex said.

"He's had some experience with piracy from merchant shipping. He thinks we can outrun them or just outlast their fuel," she said. Schmitt thought about it and added, "He's probably right, but it will mean turning and putting us deeper in the open sea."

Alex understood. At the moment, they were hugging the Australian coast and heading north to the Australian city of Cairns. That would be their first port stop. From there it was on to Papau New Guinea and Port Moresby. Turning toward the middle of the Coral Sea would give them more room to run.

"At what point does the captain call for help?" Alex asked.

"Not for a while. It looks like there's a storm brewing, so the Australian coast guard and naval ships are busy taking precautionary action. They won't come unless we have an actual emergency. Plus, even the threat of rough seas will favor us and likely make the pirates break off."

"What will the captain tell the passengers?" Alex asked.

"Standard course change because of shipping traffic. With luck we'll lose them and add speed to make up the time, putting us at Cairns on schedule."

There was one possibility that Schmitt hadn't mentioned. "Do you think there's any chance it's Ares?"

Schmitt gave it a second's thought before she said, "No, and for the simple reason that if it were Ares, I don't think we'd see them coming."

# Chapter 19

Jenny Morgan couldn't ignore it any longer. She put down her cards and said, "Dani, I don't have a good feeling about this."

Dani gave Jenny a knowing smile and said, "I never have a good feeling when those two are off alone together."

Though Jenny liked that Dani was getting comfortable enough to make jokes with her—something she did more and more frequently—Jenny couldn't even smile. "No, I mean I have a very bad feeling."

Dani looked at her for a moment and said, "Okay, let's go."

"That's it?" Jenny said. She expected that she'd have to do some explaining—about her family and about the accuracy of her own "feelings" in the past. Apparently, none of that was necessary; Dani was already on her feet.

"Bring your weapon," Dani said.

"It's already in my purse," Jenny replied.

Jenny had bought the gun just over a year ago and had Alex teach her to shoot as a surprise to Dan. She was comfortable with the weapon and was satisfied with her progress at the range. She had fired the pistol hundreds of times and had even pulled it once when she and Dan had been threatened.

She hoped that would be unnecessary today, but the more time that passed, the worse her feeling became. It had started as a flutter in her stomach; now it was a full-on ball of worry.

They headed out the door and made their way quickly to the lobby. "What about transportation?" Jenny asked.

Renting a car would be ideal, but there was no time for anything but a cab.

"I'll handle it," Dani said.

The woman went to talk to the concierge, who listened to her for a few moments before he reached under the counter and handed her a set of keys.

"What just happened?" Jenny asked when Dani returned.

"He's loaning us one of the hotel vans," Dani said as they walked outside.

They quickly found the van, and Dani handed her the keys. "Would you drive? I'll check in," Dani said, pulling out her phone.

"Of course," Jenny replied as they got into the van, which was simply a nondescript oversized van for airport pickups.

As she got into the driver's seat, Dani asked, "Can you drive a manual?"

"Sure," Jenny said. She could drive a standard four-speed before she'd met Dan. Now she was pretty sure she could drive one of the new eight-speeds in a pinch. The van was a standard five and wouldn't be a problem.

"I'll direct you," Dani said as Jenny started the van.

They pulled out and Jenny was pleased when she saw that traffic was moderate at best.

"They are at a local trade office, just a few minutes away," Dani said.

They were driving for less than two minutes when Dani added, "Something has happened." Jenny glanced over to see Dani studying her phone. "I've lost their GPS signals."

"How?" Jenny asked.

"It could be nothing. They might be underground, or in a protected structure," Dani said.

That was possible, Jenny knew, but her gut was telling her there was something more serious—and more dangerous—going on.

"Does Zeta know anything?" Jenny asked, feeling the worry rise up from her stomach into her throat.

"No, they arrived at the office and the GPS signal just stopped. Zeta can't reach them," Dani said.

"What does that mean?" Jenny asked.

"The phones could have been destroyed, or Peter and Dan may have been taken underground," Dani said.

"Is there a non-scary reason why anyone would have done that?" Jenny asked.

Dani's phone beeped; she checked it quickly and said, "The Australian consulate can't reach their office."

"So that's a no," Jenny said as they pulled up to the building.

It was a simple two-story structure, with a laundry on the bottom and what looked like offices on the second floor. All the windows were dark and a large CLOSED sign hung on the front door.

Jenny parked, and she and Dani jumped out to check the building. It was locked up tight and appeared deserted.

"If they are being held, they need help," Dani said. "Keep the car running; we may need to get out of here quickly. I'll go around back, get in, and see if I can get to them."

"Or we could give whoever it is a surprise," Jenny said.

"What do you have in mind?" Dani asked.

Jenny pointed to the bulldozer in the empty lot next door. It was just sitting there, obviously waiting to break ground.

"Can you get it started?" Dani asked.

"Of course," Jenny replied.

"Can you drive it?"

"How hard can it be?" Jenny said. "Just wait around back. I'll make some noise around front, then you can do what you need to do."

"Good luck," Dani said, already moving. "Signal me when it's done."

"If it works, you won't need a signal. You'll know," Jenny said.

* * * *

Not surprisingly, the first system that Jack Watson and Chief Engineer Cabato wanted to learn was the radar. In the main engineering office, the two men leaned over Schmitt's shoulders to watch the monitor that showed the *Grandeur* in the center and a flashing light near the left edge of the screen. Beyond that was the image of the Australian coast.

"It's no longer pacing us," Watson said, his voice steady.

"No, they are increasing their speed. They mean to catch us," Schmitt said.

"That will be harder than they think," Cabato added.

Then another flashing light appeared near the top of the monitor just as a red light flashed on the console in front of her.

"Ms. Schmitt," Watson said. "Is that—"

"Another ship tracking us?" she said. "Yes."

That put one ship roughly at the monitor's nine o'clock position and another at their twelve.

A third flashing light appeared at their six and then one at their three.

"Looks like they forced us out into the open sea intentionally," Watson said.

"To surround us," Schmitt finished for him.

Then, as if in response, four more flashes appeared on the screen, which now showed eight ships roughly in a circle around the *Grandeur*.

"I presume the ships are all closing," Watson said.

"Yes, and much faster than before," she replied.

"Chief, maintain course and speed. Ms. Schmitt, let's go see the captain."

\* \* \* \*

"Anything yet?" Conley asked.

"I was thinking of hiding under the desk, but I don't think we'll both fit," Morgan said.

Conley reached out and took the letter opener. Morgan grabbed the stapler. Then both men pulled at the buckle of their belts and removed the short blade that was hidden there.

Morgan missed his Walther, but what they had was better than nothing.

"How long do you think before they…" Conley started.

"I think he'll try to get us talking for a few minutes so they can learn something before they kill us," Morgan said.

"Before they *try* to kill us," Conley corrected. Morgan's partner was smiling, but it was a grim smile. They had been in tough spots before, but there was no denying that there was a lot going against them here.

They were underground, so the elevator and the stairs next to it were the only ways out. And between the two agents and those exits were at least six trained killers. If they were Ares—and Morgan would bet that they were—they were very well-trained killers.

And that was just the operatives in the basement office with them. There might be more up top, and they were likely Ares as well.

But first things first. Morgan and Conley had nearly impossible odds to beat down here before they would have to worry about the nearly impossible odds above them.

"We'll wait until he's behind the desk and talking," Dan said. "Then wait until I go for him and take cover by the door and grab the first guy to come through. With any luck, they will both have weapons. If we get our hands on them, we'll have a fighting chance."

"That's the whole plan? Even if it works, and even if they do have weapons, we'll still be on their turf and outnumbered two-to-one. Plus, we'll be in here and they'll be out there," Conley said.

"If we're really lucky they will just come after us one at a time," Morgan said.

"Here's to hoping," Conley replied. He kept his blade with the belt buckle hilt firmly in his right hand and the letter opener in his left.

Morgan gripped his own knife tightly. If he had a clear line of sight, he could throw the knife and take out one of the enemies if they got within twelve to fifteen feet. If Conley did the same, the odds against them would still be high, but much better.

And he always had the stapler. Morgan assumed the blood on it had belonged to the real occupant of this office who Morgan presumed Ares had killed to set up this ruse. Whatever happened in the next few minutes, Morgan hoped the stapler would be able to take out at least one of the people who had taken that man's life.

Morgan heard footsteps and casually turned to look over his shoulder and out the door. The man pretending to be Roberts was walking toward them, carrying a folder under his arm and a coffee cup in each hand.

*No water*, Morgan thought. *Typical.*

So Ares would keep up the charade a little longer to get some information. That was something. In that scenario, Morgan and Conley would have the element of surprise.

"Gentlemen," the man said. "I have—"

He was interrupted by what Morgan assumed was an explosion. It must have been on the ground floor, but it was powerful enough to shake the structure down here. Dust fell from above them, and then the lights went out.

Morgan didn't hesitate. He dove out the door, swinging his knife at where he calculated Roberts's throat would be. The knife made contact with something and then Morgan threw himself at the man.

He heard Conley sprint out of the office and slip behind him to the left.

The lights flickered for a few seconds and then went out again. When the red emergency lights came on, Morgan was wrestling with Roberts, who had managed to pull a pistol.

The man was remarkably fast and strong for someone who was already dead but didn't know it. Morgan saw that his swinging knife had made solid contact with Roberts's throat and the man was losing blood fast.

When the two men stopped rolling, they were both on their sides, with Roberts struggling to raise his gun. Morgan pushed at the pistol with his own right hand, which still held the knife. The man yelped and the gun fell to the floor, sliding out of sight.

Then the imposter calling himself Roberts was distracted by the large volume of his own blood running onto his chest. The sight allowed his mind to catch up with his body, which was already slowing and weakening. Morgan shoved the man away, his movements slowing badly.

Keeping behind the desk nearest to Roberts's office, Morgan used both feet to shove Roberts's dying body into the center aisle. The Ares agent rolled a few more feet and then shots rang out, at least two slugs hitting him.

A split-second later, Morgan heard the sound of a knife whooshing through the air and the wet smacking sound of it hitting flesh.

Conley must have taken out a target.

Morgan risked a look down the center aisle. He saw the man who had introduced himself as Givens creeping toward them, holding out a gun. Though he was reluctant to part with it, Morgan let fly with his own knife. He made a direct hit in the center of the man's chest.

"Do not let them reach an exit," one of the Ares men shouted.

In the low red light, Morgan could now see Conley behind the desk across from the one giving him cover. Conley was leaning toward the center aisle, keeping the letter opener in front of him.

As a result, Conley didn't see the agent creeping down the aisle behind him. The man was crouch-walking, and if Morgan had a pistol or even his knife, he would be an easy target, but all Morgan had now was a stapler.

Morgan had spent months training and years perfecting his knife-throwing technique. With a well-balanced knife he was remarkably accurate.

Of course, he'd never trained with a stapler, so he just made his best guess and threw it as hard as he could.

Morgan was aiming for the man's face because it was the biggest target. It hit a little high and to the back, making contact directly with the man's temple.

Without hesitating, Conley rolled backwards and came up facing the Ares man, who was reeling from the blow. Conley thrust upward with the letter opener. It pierced the skin under the man's mouth and Conley kept pushing, forcing it well into the man's skull.

The enemy fell forward, and Conley managed to grab his gun before he hit the floor. Morgan decided to take a second to scan the floor for Roberts's fallen gun, which was against the wall in the corner.

"Anyone behind me?" Morgan whispered.

Conley scanned the area and then shook his head. Morgan scrambled quickly for the weapon, grabbed it, and returned to his position behind the desk.

Things were looking up, he realized. He and Conley were each behind steel desks. They had a wall behind them and if they kept behind their cover, they could each watch the other's backs.

"Throw out your weapons and we won't kill you—at least not right away," a voice said.

"I tell you what—you throw down *your* weapons, give yourselves up, and we'll put in a good word for you with the International Criminal Court," Morgan said.

"You're outnumbered and our people are close by. This will be over soon," the voice said.

"There's something very important you are forgetting," Morgan said.

He could see the question on Conley's face and shrugged.

"Do you think we could come in here without a plan for getting out?" Morgan said.

"I think that is exactly what you did," the voice replied.

"Not true. Our plan is to kill all of you and walk out of here," Morgan said. He looked at his partner. The voice was right about one thing: Time wasn't on their side. Their best chance would be to rush whoever was out there and hope for the best.

By Morgan's count there were only two Ares men remaining. It was almost a fair fight, except for the fact that if Morgan and Conley rushed them, the Ares people would have the defender's advantage. They could stay behind cover and just pick the Zeta agents off as they approached.

And yet that was still their best chance.

He looked at Conley and saw that his partner had come to the same conclusion. They had worked together long enough that they were able to communicate with nods and gestures. Morgan held out his hand with three fingers out.

Then two…

Then one… There was a series of gunshots from the other side of the basement office. It sounded like someone had come from the elevator or the stairs and was firing at whoever was in the middle of the room. Morgan heard two bodies fall.

There were several seconds of silence, and then he heard Dani's voice say, "Peter? Dan?"

"We're here," Conley said.

"The room is clear," Dani said.

Morgan got up from behind the desk as Conley did the same.

"How does it look upstairs?" Conley asked.

"Empty," Dani said. "But we should hurry. Jenny is waiting in the van and they may have other assets in the area."

# Chapter 20

Virtually the entire lido deck serving staff was packed into a lounge that was used almost exclusively for comedy shows. Rosa had greeted them at the door and told them to take seats anywhere.

The room was brightly lit and colorful, with comfortable couches that curved around tables. Even with the harsh house lighting on, the space was much too cheery for what Alex assumed they were about to hear.

Sorina sought Alex out and squeezed in next to her. "What do you think it is, Alex?" the woman asked, clearly nervous.

It was still odd to have Sorina call her by name instead of an insulting nickname, but the nervous woman didn't behave like the same person who Alex had trained with. Since their fight outside the bar in Brisbane, and Sorina's meltdown in the pantry, they were apparently friends, with Alex in the unlikely position of senior partner.

And at the moment, Sorina was looking at Alex for reassurance. "Do you think it's about the storm?"

There was talk about an unusual weather system forming in the south. There was additional speculation that it might turn into a hurricane, or what they called in the southern hemisphere, a tropical cyclone.

Alex knew for a fact that the meeting wasn't about the weather, but she had to tell Sorina something. "I'm not sure, but whatever it is, I'm sure they have things under control."

Remarkably, that seemed to satisfy Sorina, who relaxed her posture, though she leaned in even closer to Alex.

Alex knew she was there to protect the passengers and crew of the ship. For now, it looked like the best she could do was to offer a little reassurance to one member of the crew.

When everyone was seated, Rosa took the stage and introduced a safety officer named Matthews, a young man with a Scottish accent.

"Good morning," he said. "I'm here to talk to you about an emerging situation that you all need to know about. I know there are rumors of a big storm, but we're watching the weather, and I can tell you that is not why we are here. We are being approached by a few unidentified vessels, and we have not been able to establish radio contact."

There were a series of gasps throughout the crowd.

Matthews lifted his hands and said, "I know there is a tendency to assume that a situation like this might indicate piracy, but we have no reason to believe that to be the case at this time. For all we know, these are simply fishing vessels or pleasure craft."

The crowd started murmuring and he said, "You have all been trained for situations like this. As you know, pirate attacks on cruise ships are almost unheard of, especially outside the African coast. And there has never been even an attempt in these waters."

That was, Alex knew, true—at least strictly speaking. All acts of piracy in the Coral Sea were against merchant vessels.

"Even in an extreme situation, your only job will be to help keep the passengers calm and, if necessary, in their cabins. In the event of a serious emergency, you'll be directed to your muster or workstations for further instructions. For now, proceed normally with your day and wait for further instructions."

Then, as an afterthought, he said, "Are there any questions?"

Alex raised her hand and he said, "Yes."

"How many vessels are involved?" Alex said.

He shrugged and said, "We don't have an exact number at this time."

That wasn't true, Alex knew. The ship's normal radar would give them that information. And the new Renard Tech system would give them very detailed data.

Alex could have pushed him on speed and projected rendezvous time with these mysterious ships, but she resisted. He was obviously trying to keep the staff—and by extension, the passengers—calm.

It wouldn't help to trap him with questions he wouldn't want to answer and which would only make the crew even more nervous. He'd already told her what she needed to know. And the fact that they were being spoken to by a safety officer and not one of the security officers told her something else: All the security people were too busy at the moment.

"What do you think, Alex?" Sorina said.

"I think things will be okay," Alex said. "I know for a fact that the captain is the best in the company's fleet. I'm sure he can handle whatever it is. Come on, let's get something to eat and get to the deck."

As they got up, her phone beeped and she read the message from Schmitt. **Lifeboat 42, 9:45.**

Alex would have just enough time to get Sorina to the dining room and grab a quick bite. Almost as soon as they reached the mess, a tall figure approached them. "Sorina," he said.

It was the actor, Eric.

"Hello," Sorina said.

"I just wanted to make sure you're okay," he said, looking directly at Sorina. Then he caught himself and glanced at Alex. "I know you are both new to the ship."

"Eric was in the military," Alex offered.

Sorina shrugged and said, "He mentioned that."

*Good*, Alex thought. That meant that the two of them had spoken a bit on the deck.

Sorina looked up at Eric and said, "What do you think?"

"I think they are not telling us everything, but it will be okay," he said.

Alex liked that he was frank and Sorina seemed to take it well. "Look, I'm going to look for my roommate," Alex said. "Why don't you two have lunch, and then I'll see you on deck."

"Sure," Sorina said, and walked off with Eric.

*That was easy*, thought Alex. Now she just had to grab breakfast and meet with Schmitt. Maybe then she'd be able to do some actual good on this mission—at least something besides matchmaking.

Alex had just sat down when Rebecca called out her name and sat down across from her. "How are you?" she asked.

"Fine," Alex said, as Rebecca studied her.

"I just came to see how you were. Did you have your staff meeting?" Rebecca asked.

"Yes," Alex said. "They said there were some ships approaching, but it was probably nothing."

"Yes, you shouldn't worry. I know this sounds scary, but situations like these usually don't amount to anything," Rebecca said.

Alex was amused and a little touched that her roommate was concerned about her. After all, they barely knew one another.

"Have you seen many of these situations before?" Alex asked.

"Never," Rebecca said and smiled. "It's just that most unusual situations on board never turn into anything. Most of ship life, like most of life, is anticlimax."

Alex realized what was going on here; Rebecca was trying to comfort *her*. Did that mean that Alex was the *Sorina* in this relationship? She had to suppress a smile.

She knew that usually what Rebecca was saying was true—worst-case scenarios almost never came to pass for most people most of the time.

However, that was usually not the case in Alex's line of work.

"I'm from Boston," Alex said. "Until we see the black sails, I'm not going to worry."

That seemed to satisfy Rebecca, and the two chatted normally until Alex got up to meet Schmitt. "I've got to run and see someone," Alex said.

"Do you want company?" Rebecca asked, concern on her face.

"No need. I'm really fine," Alex said.

Schmitt was next to the lifeboat when Alex arrived. They nodded their greetings and Schmitt began. "We're surrounded by eight small vessels and they are closing in," Schmitt said.

"Pirates or worse?" Alex asked.

"I don't know yet," Schmitt said. "They did draw us out into open sea first. That was clever. They are either smarter than normal pirates or they are being directed by someone worse."

"I'm ready for whoever it is," Alex said.

"Good, but remember that for now we are both here only as observers," Schmitt replied.

That was true. And Director Bloch's rules of engagement were very clear. They were not to take any action that would compromise their covers unless there was loss of life, or the imminent threat of loss of life.

"I know what you're feeling, Alex," Schmitt said, as if the woman had been reading her mind. "Sometimes, even when we know we can help, we have to stand by and let people do their jobs. If this is just pirates, they won't be the first the captain has faced. And if it is Ares, or Ares is directing a third party, we can't reveal ourselves unless we have to."

Alex understood the order and the caution behind it, but she didn't agree with it here. People could die because two Zeta agents were waiting for Ares to unveil some master plan.

"I can tell you that I have very strong faith in the captain and the crew," Schmitt said. "They can handle almost anything that comes up out here, and if they need us, we're here. Until then, think of this as a vacation…"

Schmitt stopped herself, looking over Alex's uniform: her white shirt, black slacks, and server apron.

"Okay, maybe not a vacation-vacation, but at least a break from getting shot at," Schmitt said.

"We also serve who stand and wait tables..." Alex said.

Schmitt laughed out loud at that and said, "Exactly. Now I'm due on the bridge."

# Chapter 21

As soon as Bloch stepped into the lab, Shepard handed her a pair of headphones.

"Please put these on, Director," Shepard said. "And make sure they fit snugly."

Then Bloch realized they weren't headphones; they were hearing protection. That both made more sense and was more worrying.

As soon as she placed the headset over her ears, the everyday sounds of the lab disappeared. There was no sound from the air vents, none from the movement of the staff, and none of the hum of the computers and equipment. Nothing but complete, dead silence.

Shepard led her to the center of the room, where there was a simple wooden worktable. On the surface were what looked like a dozen small, white stones. Shepard pointed to them and gestured for her to pick one up. She did and realized they were teeth, or—more accurately—dental caps.

They were no doubt replicas of the caps used by Ares operatives. Bloch was also sure the materials used by Shepard to make these were identical to the ones used by Ares. Now she understood why he had requisitioned an industrial kiln.

Bloch put the cap back down and followed Shepard to a large bank of half-a-dozen machines that she did not recognize. They were all new and from a variety of manufacturers. Whatever Shepard had cooked up, Bloch was sure it would have surprised the makers of each component.

In front of the largest machine was a stainless steel parabolic cone that was a little less than three feet in diameter. The cone was about six feet from the worktable and was pointed directly at it.

On the outside of the cone was a handmade sign that said kill-o-zap.

That was something. She hoped Shepard had made it, and that it meant that he had gotten back a little of his sense of humor.

Shepard checked the readouts on the large machine and made some adjustments on the various dials and switches on its side. He nodded once to her and then hit a red button.

Even through the artificial silence of her headgear, Bloch could hear the sound of something powering up.

Shepard was watching intently and then his eyes went wide as if he'd suddenly remembered something. He grabbed her upper arm and pulled her back a few feet to a point just behind a line of masking tape on the floor.

Then he quickly handed her a pair of plastic goggles, as he hurriedly put on his own. She barely had time to pull hers over her head and in front of her eyes when he pointed at the worktable, telling her to look there.

Nothing happened for a full second, and then the dozen teeth lying on the plywood surface exploded at once.

Bloch was glad for the extra distance from the table as well as the eye protection when she was pelted by small pieces of what she assumed were exploding ceramics.

Shepard held up a finger, indicating for her to wait, and then he headed to the machine and hit a number of switches and buttons. On top of the device, a red light turned green. Shepard took off his ear protectors and then his goggles.

Bloch did the same and said, "That looked very effective."

"It is," he said, looking a little sheepish. "But calibration has been an issue."

"Clearly, but it was an impressive display," Bloch said.

He gestured at the bank of machines and said, "Portability and power consumption are still tricky."

That much was obviously true. However, those were engineering problems—technical problems. The miracle was that Shepard and his team had cracked the science behind it all.

She couldn't imagine how those remaining hurdles could be overcome in time to help her agents currently in and around the Coral Sea, but after what she had just seen, she wasn't ruling anything out.

Bloch could see that Shepard's mind was already on the challenges in front of him. He gave her a tight smile that betrayed his impatience to get back to work. Shepard had shown her the results of Zeta's investment, now he wanted to get back to it.

Bloch understood that her job now was to get out of his hair. "Excellent, Mr. Shepard, keep me posted on further progress."

Her phone beeped and she saw a text from her office. It was just two words: **Code Yellow**.

That meant she had an urgent call from an angry head of state other than the president of the US. Bloch headed for the elevator, shaking white flakes from her hair.

As she got into the elevator, Bloch realized something important: Shepard had looked normal—at least for him. There was very little trace of the haunted, desperate look that he'd worn for the last few days.

Like the test she had just witnessed, it was a small victory but a very real one.

\* \* \* \*

Jenny drove with a look of intense concentration on her face. No one in the van spoke until they had put a few miles between themselves and the trade office. The two couples were too busy searching the road and the space around them for any sign they were being followed.

In the end, Jenny pulled into a large parking lot, choosing a spot that was near the road and gave them a good vantage point to look out for pursuers.

Morgan's phone beeped and lit up. It was Bloch and the call seemed perfectly timed as if Bloch were monitoring their every move—which was something Morgan didn't rule out. He answered his phone without hesitation.

"Morgan," he said.

"I just heard an earful from the Australian prime minister," Bloch said.

"I understand why he would be upset," Morgan replied. "But Zeta wasn't responsible for whatever happened at that trade office."

"Really? Because until I arranged a visit for you and Conley to that office, the staff was still alive."

"I know that is how it must look to the Australians," he said.

"It's not how it looks," Bloch said. "That is how it is. They lost their entire staff after two Zeta agents visited the location and then fled the scene."

"It was Ares. They murdered and replaced everyone," Morgan said.

"I'm sure it was, but right now the Australian authorities want you and Conley in custody," she said.

Morgan thought it was interesting that Bloch didn't mention Dani or Jenny. For whatever reason, she was content to leave them out of it—perhaps because the Australians didn't know they were involved.

That was something.

"Director, you know we are the only agents in the field on this side of the world," Morgan said. It was true. Zeta needed them out here, and more importantly, *Alex* needed them out here to help with whatever was coming.

"We're close," he added. "That's why Ares went through the trouble of setting a trap for us. If nothing else, we exposed the fact that Ares has infiltrated Australian intelligence."

"Everything you are saying is true, but I have to ask you to turn yourselves in to the Australian consulate. I have been assured of your safety. Do not go back to your hotel; proceed directly to the consulate," she said. Then her voice softened. "I'm sure it will only take a few days to sort this mess out. The Australians will need to conduct an investigation, and then I'm confident I can get you cleared for release."

"I can't do that," Morgan said. "What we're doing out here is too important. The mission is too important," he said.

There was something else he didn't say. If Australian intelligence had been compromised, there could well be one or more Ares agents embedded at the consulate. Despite whatever assurances that Bloch had been given, Morgan was not sure the consulate would be safe. And while Morgan and Conley were being detained, Jenny and Dani would be nearby and in danger.

"Are you speaking for your partner as well?" Bloch asked.

"Yes," he replied.

"Then you both give me no choice. I am ordering you to the consulate right away," Bloch said, her tone final.

It was one thing to bend the rules, but it was quite another to disobey a direct order—especially when he and Conley were at the center of a massacre that could cause an international incident.

"Of course," Bloch added. "I appreciate your commitment to the mission, and we both know how important it is. I also know that you have a considerable personal interest in remaining free to operate in that area. However, I have to insist that you put aside your personal feelings and your long-standing tendency to break whatever rules you find inconvenient at any given moment. I absolutely cannot have you ignoring the international relations angle here because you think the mission is more important and will save lives. This is the time for you to be a team player. If you decide to act like a maverick now, lives might be saved, but there will be a lot of bruised feelings and long, angry meetings that high-level people will have to suffer through."

For a moment, Morgan was at a loss for words. This didn't sound like Bloch. It was almost as if she was reading from a script. In addition, she was actually making a good case for ignoring her instructions.

"I know you will do the right thing here," Bloch said.

"I always do," Morgan replied and hung up.

He quickly relayed Bloch's side of the conversation to the rest of the group. They listened and seemed as befuddled as he was.

"She did give us a direct order," Conley said.

"But what Diana Bloch really did was give you permission to go rogue," Jenny added, giving a voice to what they were all thinking.

"What do you make of that?" Conley said.

"Well, it kind of takes the fun out of it," Morgan replied.

"But it leaves us free to go to the Solomon Islands," Dani said.

"Yes, but we don't have anything, not even our passports," Jenny added.

"And the Australians will have personnel at all transportation hubs looking for us," Conley said.

"There is a way, but none of us are going to like it," Morgan said. He and Conley had done it more times than he could count, but it was his least favorite way to travel. And he definitely didn't want to drag Jenny through the process. "Fishing boats," he said to Conley.

"Looks like we have no choice," Conley said.

"No," Dani said. "Too slow and not reliable enough. We need new papers, cash, and weapons. And we need a mode of travel that gets us out of here this afternoon."

"All hard to do if we're fugitives and don't have access to Zeta's resources," Conley said.

"It won't be a problem," Dani said. "I know someone."

# Chapter 22

"What's your analysis, Ms. Schmitt?" Captain Garrett asked.

She felt the captain's and the rest of the bridge crew's eyes on her as she watched the eight ships move closer on the monitor at her terminal. The radar didn't lie; the ships were closing. And they were doing it in a remarkably coordinated manner.

"They mean to board," Schmitt said. "They want to hit us all at once. Possibly from eight different points, but maybe fewer. Since they will all arrive at roughly the same time, it will force you to spread your security personnel and countermeasures thin. If they try boarding from eight points simultaneously, they could overwhelm efforts to protect the ship. But even if some of the ships are decoys, we won't know where the boarding party or parties will be coming from. And it will take time to prepare fire hoses and other defenses," she said.

"Thank you," he said. "I have no doubt you are correct and that is their intention. At least that is what they will likely attempt to do," Garrett said.

"Up ahead, Captain," one of navigators said.

Schmitt turned in the direction the man was pointing and could see something moving in the distance. It was a small ship, likely a skiff, but it was too far away to make out any detail.

Since the bridge crew could now see the craft with the naked eye, it wouldn't take long for the ship (and the others in the eight-vessel fleet) to arrive.

"Mr. Watson, would you please escort Ms. Schmitt to the engine room," Garrett said.

"Yes sir," Watson replied. Then he turned to Schmitt and said, "Ma'am."

"Of course," Schmitt said and headed for the exit.

When they were on the deck, Watson said, "Protocol. If there's a threat of a boarding party, the captain stays on the bridge and I stay in the engineering control room."

"Where in an emergency or in the event that the bridge is compromised you can assume control of the ship," she said.

"Like most of our protocols, it's a precaution and will probably be unnecessary," he said.

"You don't have to do that. If there are eight boarding parties coming from different directions, there's at least a fair chance that one or more will get on board," she said.

Watson stopped for moment and turned to her. "Then I pity the poor fools," he said. "They will wish they had stayed on their ships."

Schmitt liked his confidence, and he would no doubt be right if this group were ordinary pirates. However, they had already shown more coordination and sophistication than any reported, modern pirate attack.

She was suddenly in a rush to get to engineering. Once she was at her terminal, she could start making real contributions. If nothing else, she could give Watson and the captain real-time updates on the other ship's positions.

And there were a few other tricks that she might be able to coax out of the system.

* * * *

*Arrived Choiseul* the message from Jenny Morgan said.

In Bloch's entire career, this was the first time that she had received a mission update from the wife of an agent who had gone rogue. Nevertheless, Bloch was glad to have it and pleased her people had gotten off Papua New Guinean soil so quickly. In fact, she'd have to look into how they managed that when the full might of the Australian intelligence network in that country was looking for them.

And not just the Australians, but all officials of Papua New Guinea as well. That cooperation was a given, of course, due to the close relationship between the two countries.

Bloch had already fielded angry calls from the State Department and bad feelings would only get worse as more time passed, at least for the next few days, while Australian and local authorities investigated the scene of the massacre.

So far, their only progress was in finding the bodies—twenty-two Australians and locals who had been murdered by Ares and left in a storeroom. Of course, at the moment, all the authorities could see were twenty-two of their people dead, and two Americans at the site of the murder.

That was fair enough. And if time wasn't a factor, the smart move would have been to let them take Conley and Morgan into custody.

Zeta's chief advantage in its work was that it operated outside of the normal diplomatic and bureaucratic channels. Those channels had important safeguards, but they also created very real inertia that could be deadly when time was short and lives were on the line.

Many of the same nations that knowingly or unknowingly benefited from Zeta's successes were the first to curse it when things went wrong. That was the nature of the secrecy necessary for Zeta's mission. And while Zeta was independent, to perform its function it still depended on cooperation from allies in various world governmental and security organizations.

When Bloch had suggested that her people run, it wasn't just Morgan and Conley who had gone rogue—it was Zeta as well.

Now Bloch had to hope that the investigation would be completed before the attack they were waiting for happened. Once that started, Zeta and her people in the Coral Sea would likely need support. And that support wouldn't come if Zeta's agents were wanted for committing a massacre.

Bloch had allowed them to run because time was short. However, now she was depending on Ares and whatever they had planned to wait so she could patch up the relationships on which the lives of her three agents and Jenny Morgan might depend.

*My lord*, she thought. Morgan had bent the rules into unrecognizable shapes and gone off on his own more times than she cared to remember. If this was what it felt like, he could keep it.

Yet Bloch was certain that she had made the right choice.

And like the times Morgan had gone off the reservation, the ultimate test wouldn't be whether or not her decision was justified at the time, but whether or not it produced good results.

To that end, she truly hoped Ares would wait a few days. It would be good to be able to count on the Australian navy. And she would like her agents on the scene to have the benefits of a practical and working prototype of the weapon that Shepard and his team had created. At the moment, unless Morgan, Conley, and Guo had a crane to move the device and a good-sized municipal generator to run it, the weapon wouldn't do them any good in its present form.

The phone on her desk buzzed. She hit a button and said, "What is it, Rand?"

"Director, we've received a message from Alicia Schmitt. She confirms that eight vessels are closing on the *Grandeur*."

As Bloch hung up the phone, she came to two very clear conclusions. One, the bad guys never cooperated when you needed them to. And two, she had been spending far too much time with the Morgans.

* * * *

Leaving the forward crew dining room, Alex felt the deck beneath her shudder and then she both heard and felt the sound of a large motor reverberating somewhere underneath her. It took her a few seconds to place the sound; it was the ship's stabilizers being retracted.

The stabilizers were pairs of retractable wings—which looked remarkably like airplane wings—under the waterline on each side of the hull. When deployed, they helped keep the ship remarkably steady, so that even in moderately rough seas, the passengers didn't feel any roll or movement.

Usually the stabilizers were deployed within minutes of the ship leaving port and kept out until the ship was approaching its next port.

At the moment, the sea was relatively choppy, so Alex could only think of one reason for the captain to retract them now: He was going to try to use speed to escape the ships closing in on them.

Alex heard a loud clang that told her that the wings were back inside the ship, and then she felt the deck shift under her feet as the ship swayed. There were gasps and grunts from the people in the hallway.

"This is Captain Garrett. I am instructing all passengers to return to their cabins, effective immediately. There are unidentified vessels approaching, and we have not been able to establish communications. In the unlikely event that the ships intend to act aggressively, I have retracted the ship's stabilizers so you may feel some chop. Because of that and because of the risk posed by the approaching vessels, I need everyone stay in their cabins. For passengers with balconies, you are instructed to lock the exterior doors. And for all passengers in outside cabins, please avoid windows and portholes.

"In the event of very rough seas or high-speed maneuvers, the safest place for you to be is sitting on the floor of your cabin. If the ship undergoes a serious emergency or we are boarded, you will hear the general emergency signal. There will be seven short blasts on the ship's horn, followed by a single long blast. In that event, report to your muster stations and await instructions. Thank you for your patience. We hope to have this matter resolved quickly.

"For the crew, I am ordering safety protocols. Off-duty crew should return to their cabins. On-duty personnel should meet at their work areas for further instructions. Garrett out."

That last order was significant. Most emergency scenarios required all crew to report to their more centralized muster stations. From there, they would engage in whatever activities the emergency required—up to and including evacuation via lifeboats. However, piracy was so rare that the normal rules didn't apply.

Even so, if this were a simple pirate attack, Alex was sure the captain and crew could handle it. If, however, Ares was involved, the crew could throw out whatever rule book they were working from.

Alex walked up a crew staircase and came out at the edge of an indoor lounge that led directly to the lido deck. She saw that the lounge and the passenger corridor beyond were full of passengers heading for their cabins.

The big surprise there was how orderly the passengers moved, even though the deck was now regularly rocking under their feet from the rough seas. There was a loud murmur of voices, but no running or signs of panic. The only overt emotional response came from passengers complaining about the inconvenience. One particularly loud woman walked past Alex, telling her husband that the line had better compensate them for the time lost in their cruise for this unnecessary "drill."

That made Alex smile. Annoyed was better than scared.

Alex had just reached the server station behind the Four Corners of the World bar when a voice called out, "Alex."

It was Sorina, who pushed through the assembling servers and grabbed Alex's hand. "What do you think? What is happening? Is it pirates?"

Alex was pleased to see that Sorina looked nervous—as did most of the people around them—but not scared.

"I think it's just like the captain said," Alex replied. "I think it will be fine. Even if it is pirates, the captain has experience dealing with them from his merchant sailing days. And no pirates have ever boarded a cruise ship carrying passengers."

That much was true. There was a single incident over ten years ago when pirates managed to get on board a ship, only to find a skeleton crew and no passengers. Disappointed, the pirates quickly left the ship.

The *Grandeur* rocked, and Alex swayed on her feet. Then she heard the clang of glassware nearby.

"Everyone," Rosa called out. "Lockdown procedures right now. We've been instructed to secure all equipment and glassware, offer assistance to passengers who need it, and then get to our cabins. Security and safety officers will take it from there."

The glassware was important. If the seas got much rougher they would have shattered plates and glasses everywhere in minutes. There were also chairs and tables that would go flying around the deck if they weren't secured.

As they started to work, Sorina stuck close to Alex. That might be a problem. Alex wanted to hang back after cleanup. If possible, she would be the last one on the lido deck. She'd stay as long as she could in the event she was needed.

Schmitt would be on the bridge or in the engine room. It wouldn't hurt to have one of them on the deck for as long as possible.

Alex's phone beeped. She pulled it out and saw a message from Schmitt: **Estimate no more than forty minutes until contact.**

Alex felt the deck shift under her feet as the ship made a sharper turn than she would have thought possible.

Alex worked faster.

# Chapter 23

"Can I help?" the tall man said as he approached.

For the second time, Alex mistook Eric for a guest. He walked up to where Alex and Sorina were stowing margarita glasses. She checked her watch; they could actually use the help.

"They don't need you at your theater?" Alex said.

"No, the tech crew doesn't like the performers touching anything if we're not performing," he said. Then he shrugged and added, "It's a whole thing."

"We could use the help. We're running out of time and we need to get everyone to their cabins," Alex said.

"What can I do?" he said.

"Sorina, can you show him what needs to be done back here?" Alex said.

The large Romanian woman looked up at Eric with a shy smile and said, "Of course."

Alex had to struggle to keep from smiling herself.

While she didn't have an easy fix for the pirates and the fact was that she might not even get a chance to help, she thought she might have already solved Sorina's man troubles.

"Thanks," Alex said to Eric as she sprinted outside and onto the deck. Alex nearly fell as the ship rocked under her feet. She saw that the sea was getting rougher and without the stabilizers she could really feel the change.

Alex jumped in to help two short-order cooks from the bar who were locking down a stack of deck chairs. That done, the trio moved on to another stack. Within fifteen minutes, the entire outdoor portion of the lido deck was secured—in addition to the smaller decks around the two pools above them.

Rosa was everywhere, directing the action. She then started sending people who had been working outdoors back to their cabins. Alex avoided her and headed back inside to check on Sorina and Eric. While she was just outside the door, Rebecca stepped out to meet her.

"Rebecca?" Alex asked.

"I came to check on you," Rebecca replied. She looked around and said, "We finished locking down the spa and I wanted to see if you needed help finishing up out here."

"Thanks..." Alex said. She was impressed by how well the crew worked together—which was a minor miracle, given that they were all from different parts of the world. And Alex once again appreciated her roommate's concern, but she couldn't do her real job if she couldn't shake her concerned friend.

"We're almost done out here," Alex said. "If you head to the room, I'll just check in with my boss and be right behind you."

"You sure?" Rebecca said.

"Yes, right behind you. I'll meet you in the room," Alex said.

Just then, the deck tilted under their feet and Alex had to struggle to keep upright. The feeling continued for far too long and Alex realized that the ship was executing a turn that was extreme for a ship that size—and it was doing it without the stabilizers to steady it.

"Okay, but come right down," Rebecca said when the ship seemed to right itself.

"Will do," Alex replied as she stepped inside. Alex found Sorina and Eric stowing the last of the dishes. Alex jumped in and they were done in a few minutes.

Rosa appeared behind them. "Okay, it's time to get downstairs," she said.

"What about you?" Alex said.

"I will be in my cabin before any of you," Rosa said with a grin. Then she walked toward the employee stairwell.

"Let's go, Alex," Sorina said.

"Sure," Alex replied. The three of them headed toward the stairs that Rosa had used. "This is you," Alex said to Sorina. "I'll use the port stairs," she added, grateful that her room was in a different part of the ship than Sorina's.

"Good luck, Alex," Sorina said as she and Eric slipped behind the door.

One of the safety officers raced past Alex and said, "Get to your cabin."

Alex said she would, but she doubled back to the entrance to the outdoor deck. Then, for the first time since she had been onboard, Alex looked out across an empty lido deck. The sight was unnerving in a place that was defined by crowds and movement in which there were always people around, even when Alex was closing up at midnight.

She was torn. On the one hand, she wanted to remain where she was, or find a hidden corner on the deck to wait out whatever was coming. On the other, she knew that Rebecca would be concerned. She might even come looking for Alex, call security, or send up some sort of alarm.

Alex wanted to remain in a position to help if she was needed, but she hadn't heard from Schmitt. And if security had to spend time rounding her up or escorting her back to her cabin, they would have fewer resources to fight the pirates.

Her orders and mission required her to do nothing for the moment, which was something that her entire nature rebelled against. Her body was tensing, her mind becoming hyperalert, and it took an act of will not to race across the deck to try to get a visual on any of the pirate teams.

Before Alex could move, she saw two dark figures emerge from the lounge across from her. As her eyes focused, she realized that the figures weren't just dark; they were dressed in all-black tactical gear, including helmets.

And they were carrying rifles.

As both men raced forward to the bow of the ship, Alex saw that they carried IWI Dan .338s, which were very effective Israeli sniper rifles. They were bolt-action and good for long-distance work.

Alex realized the pirates must be getting close.

* * * *

"Five hundred yards," Schmitt said to Watson over the comm on her terminal, which was now communicating directly with the bridge console.

Schmitt shifted her glance from one monitor to the other. One was a radar screen, and one was an eight-feed split-screen showing an outward view from eight of the system's sensor/camera arrays that circled the ship

That feed only gave them glimpses of the skiffs, but those views were coming more and more often as the fast-moving ships moved closer. The skiffs were managing to keep a relatively uniform distance from the *Grandeur*, even though the cruise ship had to be making in excess of thirty knots.

That required a number of things that she didn't associate with pirates: fast ships, skilled pilots, and remarkable coordination.

On the plus side, now that they were so close to the *Grandeur*, Schmitt had more options.

"Mr. Watson, I've identified how they are communicating," she said. "They are using ordinary VHF walkie-talkies, with all parties on the same frequency," she said.

"How can we use that?" Watson said.

"I think I can jam them," Schmitt said.

"Get it ready," Watson said, then he hit the comm button on the panel and conferred with the captain. Less than thirty seconds later, he said, "Do it."

"A few more seconds," she said.

The system wasn't designed with traditional jamming hardware, but she was able to use its RF tower to broadcast a very strong signal on the pirates' frequency. It should overwhelm their relatively low-powered walkie-talkies.

"Got it," she said and turned on the transmitter.

There was nothing obvious happening. The ships were still tracking the *Grandeur* visually so their formation didn't automatically fall apart. However, half a minute later, she saw that they had changed frequencies on their walkie-talkies. Schmitt made the same change to continue the jamming. The pirates and then Schmitt repeated the process again. And again.

In the end, the pirates gave up.

"Hang on," Watson said.

Schmitt didn't ask any questions. She simply held tight to the grab bar on the side of the console. The ship turned so sharply that gravity pulled her body starboard for perhaps a full minute.

From her aircraft carrier days, she was very sensitive to the tilt on a turn. Any more than a 4 percent, and ship ran the risk of having planes and other expensive equipment slide off the flight deck and into the ocean.

However, the *Grandeur* had no flight deck and thus had considerably more leeway in its turns. The only limiting factor was the risk of capsizing, which was greater with the stabilizers retracted, but the captain still had plenty of room for maneuvering.

Schmitt guessed that the turn was as much as twelve degrees. The much smaller skiffs would have no trouble following. However, that could quickly turn into a problem for them.

On the video feed in front of her, Schmitt watched as two of the skiffs that had been trailing the *Grandeur*'s rear, suddenly found themselves sailing into the ship's large wake, which was even larger with the vessel's increased speed.

That was when the pilots of both skiffs made the same fatal choice. Had they turned into the wake they could have hit the large wave directly. Instead, they opted to try to turn away from it. Here, their high speed worked against them and they couldn't come close to making the turn.

Schmitt watched as the first skiff hit the wave at a forty-five degree angle at about thirty knots—which was approximately thirty-five miles per hour. What followed was similar to what would have happened if the boat had hit a ramp at a sharp angle. It flew into the air while it flipped over.

Several figures dropped or were thrown out of the ship, which rotated a second time and landed in the water upside down. The second skiff saw that happen and turned harder, so it hit the wake broadside but with less forward momentum.

It didn't fly into the air quite as spectacularly since it hit the wave sideways and at a lower speed.

It was only in the air for a moment while it turned over and landed upside down.

Schmitt turned to Watson and said, "That was amazing."

"Yes," he replied. "That was the captain."

It was something. The captain had taken out two of their eight pursuers with a simple maneuver—and that was before the crew rolled out any of their actual security equipment and procedures.

Schmitt was beginning to think that she and Alex might be here only as observers.

* * * *

Alex waited a few tense seconds for a reply from Schmitt.

The snipers are on our side, Schmitt's message said. After just a few more seconds, there was another text. Crew seems to have situation under control.

If Schmitt thought the crew could handle the threat, Alex knew she could relax.

In fact, it looked like it was time to return to her cabin. She and Rebecca could wait out the attack there, and she could catch up with Schmitt later to get the full report.

Alex had barely turned toward the door to get back inside when a voice behind her said, "Alex."

She turned to see Devan Martin approaching her from the other side of the lido deck. She realized he must have come up from below.

"Mr. Martin, the captain has asked all passengers to stay in their cabins and wait for further instructions," she said.

He smiled a surprisingly disarming smile and said, "I believe the same instructions apply to the crew, at least the ones not on the security or safety teams. It looks like we're both breaking the rules."

"I'm doing my job," Alex said.

"I'm sure that's true, and that's exactly what I wanted to talk to you about," Devan replied.

"I'm afraid I have to get back to it," she said. Then she made her voice firm. "I can escort you to your room or have someone from safety do it."

His smile was still there and his posture relaxed, but there was something wrong here. Alex didn't like where this was going.

"I tell you what, Alex," Devan said. "Let's sit in the lounge and talk for a few minutes. It looks like you have no customers waiting and I definitely have nowhere to be."

Alex noticed that he had stopped several feet away from her. He wasn't close enough to be menacing, but he was a few steps further out than he would be for a normal conversation.

"I'm sorry, Mr. Martin, but I have to insist," Alex said.

"Call me Devan, Alex," he replied. And then while he maintained eye contact and kept his smile in place, he very quickly reached behind his back and pulled out a gun, aiming it straight at her stomach.

Alex accessed the situation. She had to assume that he knew what he was doing with the gun, and that if she rushed him he would have time to fire. Similarly, she was too far from the door to make it to cover before he shot her.

"Now I have to insist," he said. "We both know that you are not really here to serve fries. Let's sit in the lounge and get to know one another."

Scanning the deck, Alex saw no one. And her ears told her that there was no one behind her.

"I'm more comfortable out here. That way, when security comes along we can all have a conversation," she said.

"Get inside!" he replied. "I'd prefer to keep this friendly, but there's a limit."

Alex considered refusing and making a very loud fuss, but the odds were that any security officers that came by would be unarmed. If they tried to intervene they would likely get shot for their trouble.

"Okay," Alex said. Then she turned and headed for the door that would take her inside.

She heard Devan's footsteps behind her, and she sensed he was a professional. That meant she would likely not have any more tactical options indoors. Unfortunately, at the moment, there was nothing she could do but follow his instructions and wait for an opportunity.

# Chapter 24

"Have you seen the footage, Mr. Brown?" Bloch asked.

"What footage?" the British man on her computer screen replied.

"The security footage from the trade office," Bloch said. "The footage that you and the Australians couldn't access until my people created a back door for you through the Ares encryption. The footage that shows Ares agents overpowering the Australian personnel, murdering them, and then staffing the office with their own people. The same footage that shows what my people did when they were lured into the same office."

Fortunately, when Ares took the office, they kept the security system running, though they added a robust level of encryption to the material. Ares clearly expected to keep up their ruse a bit longer. And they definitely didn't expect that three badly outnumbered Zeta agents and an interior designer from suburban Boston would take them all out in a matter of minutes. Brown didn't reply for nearly thirty seconds.

"It looks like we've both seen the footage, Director Bloch," Brown said. Then he sighed. "It doesn't really change anything. If you decrypted the footage, how do I know that your team didn't fake it?"

"Because as good as my computer people are, you know they didn't," she said. "If for no other reason than there wasn't time."

"Tell that to my bosses, and their partners in Australia," he said.

"No, thank you," she replied. "There's a reason I'm talking to you. We both work for a living and if we let politics rule, we'd never get anything done."

"It's not just politics, Diana. The Australians lost a lot of people," he said.

"Yes, Peter, and because of my people, every single person responsible for that massacre is dead," she said.

"Yes, but because of *your* people, there's no one left alive to question," he replied.

"Fair enough, but in a perfect world, the Australians wouldn't have sent two of my agents into a trap. So why don't we figure out how to put that all aside and work together?"

This was delicate, even within the framework of international intelligence interagency cooperation. The Australians had ruled Papua New Guinea until 1975, which made sense since it was just off their own coast. But the UK had ruled the Solomon Islands—which were just off the coast of Papua New Guinea—until 1978.

Meanwhile, Australia was and remained a member of the British Commonwealth, which meant the Queen was still on their currency. Thus, the two countries were more-or-less family. As such, their relationship was close but volatile.

Theoretically, the UK was the senior partner—or older sibling—in this relationship, but that often meant it had to tread more lightly than it wished to. Of course, like any family relationship, there could be tidal shifts on a nearly daily basis.

Bloch wasn't helping matters by going over the Australians' heads to get the help Zeta needed from a contact in British intelligence.

"What are you proposing?" he said, resignation in his voice.

"I'm proposing that you and I trust one another," Bloch said. "It will take days or weeks for the diplomats and politicians to unruffle each other's feathers. I propose that we can't wait for that. My intel points to a major incident in the area that we may have only days to stop, or if we're lucky, a week. I want us to share information and resources while we wait for the politics to catch up. I further propose that you do whatever you can to get the heat off my people so they can do their job."

Bloch had to fight the urge to add *as well as your job*, but it wouldn't help to antagonize the man. And she remembered very well what it was like to be constrained by a bureaucracy driven by politics. That experience was why she was at Zeta and not still in Naval Intelligence or in one of the civilian intelligence services.

"I agree. I presume you got your people out of Port Moresby," Brown said.

"They got themselves out," Bloch replied. "Officially, they've gone rogue. Unofficially, they are about to investigate a potential Ares facility in the Solomon Islands. If they find something I'd like to know I can count on your support."

"Diana, you know you can always count on my support," Brown said.

That much was true. She didn't want to trade on their personal connection, but she had no choice. The fact was that over the years they had both gone out on a limb for one another so many times that they were past counting who owed who.

Though, as a practical matter, Brown had definitely done Bloch the most recent favor when he recommended Lily Randall to her.

"And I can turn down the heat," Brown added. "No one will be falling over themselves in the manhunt for your people. In fact, I suspect that we are about to receive solid intel that they are on the Australian mainland."

That made Bloch smile. It was better than a report that put the Zeta agents far away. This would keep the Australian intelligence agents busy on their own soil. In fact, it would likely mean that some of the ones searching for her people in Papua New Guinea might be recalled to search at home.

"Thank you, Peter," Bloch said.

"I just hope that whatever your people are doing is worth it," Brown said.

"No, you don't," she said. And Bloch didn't either. If Morgan and the others found something, things would likely get much worse before they got better.

"No, I don't, but it was good to talk to you, Diana," Brown said and then her screen went blank.

The irony was rich here. If nothing came of this situation, then she and now Peter Brown would have no end of hassles from some very upset people in a number of governments. Still, she found herself hoping those were the worst consequences they—and the people who lived in that part of the world—would face.

Of course, Bloch rarely got what she wanted.

\* \* \* \*

"That's far enough," Devan said.

Alex stopped and turned around. Devan was still pointing his gun at her. "This is a good place for us to talk."

It was one of the private little corners of the lounge, near the exterior wall. Here, no one racing through to or from the lido deck would see them.

"This isn't the first time you've had a gun pointed at you," he said. It wasn't a question.

"As I told you, I'm from Boston," she replied.

"That was the final giveaway. They can train you to wait tables and act like one of the staff—even though you are the only American server on the ship. But it's harder to train you to forget your other training. You remain cool. You calculate the distance between you and I, and you estimate my reaction times. You also note the nearest exits and the nearest cover. Those things are automatic and are necessary for survival, which always takes precedence over maintaining your cover."

"That's an interesting theory. However, you're ignoring the obvious: That I have no idea what you are talking about and I just don't find you intimidating, even with a gun."

"That's unfortunate. This would go much faster if you took your situation seriously," he said.

"It's hard to take you as seriously as you would like me to when you can't keep up your embarrassing posh accent. I think you are the one who's getting nervous," she said.

That seemed to amuse him. "You think my accent is fake?"

"I know it is. You're drawing out your t's and just plain gargling your k's. Personally, I have nothing against people from Liverpool, but the question is: Why are you embarrassed to be a Scouser?"

Alex could tell she had hit a cord with that one. His eyes flared and he actually sputtered.

She had once asked her father if he'd ever been staring down the barrel of a gun with no good options. Dan Morgan said he had. In fact, he'd been in that position a number of times. And his strategy had always been the same: Antagonize his enemy.

*"To keep them off-balance? To give yourself time to think of something?"* she'd asked.

*"No,"* he'd replied.

*"To get him angry enough to make a mistake?"*

*"Nothing like that,"* he'd said.

*"They why do it?"* she'd asked in exasperation.

*"I like pissing them off."*

And that had been Dan Morgan's final word on the subject.

Alex realized that she liked it too. Another Morgan curse, she supposed.

Devan recovered his composure and said, "I thought you only could spot London and Cockney?"

"Well, I know who the Beatles are," she said.

"An American your age. How is that?" he asked.

"Two reasons: I have parents, and I'm not a savage," Alex said. For the next one she had to reach to recall the details of a phone call that her friend Lily Randall had made to her brother in which they argued about soccer.

"Tell me, is it hard to pretend to root for Manchester now?" she asked.

"You have no idea what you are talking about," he said.

"No, I imagine it isn't for someone like you who was probably just a glory supporter for Liverpool."

That one really hit the mark and she could see genuine anger in his eyes.

"There it is," she said "You can learn a new accent—badly—and learn how to point a gun, but the hardest thing to do is train away your automatic reactions. That's the same reason they don't train show dogs to sit. They can't afford to have a dog at the Westminster Dog Show plopping down every time a smart-ass in the crowd shouts the word. I guess it works on *robber's dogs* with guns too," she said.

Alex knew robber's dog was an insult to people from Liverpool and hoped she was using it correctly.

Before he could react any further, a familiar voice called out. "Alex!" Rebecca said.

Alex looked over and saw Rebecca approaching. The woman was looking at Alex with concern and Alex realized that Rebecca couldn't yet see Devan, who was obscured from her angle behind a large column. However, if Rebecca took another few steps, Devan would be in Rebecca's line of sight, and then her friend would be in trouble.

"Rebecca, stop. Get out of here. There's a creep with a gun," Alex said.

Nevertheless, Rebecca not only kept walking but sped up.

"No!" Alex called out. Then, just as Rebecca was able to see Devan holding a gun on her, Alex shouted, "Run!"

Rebecca froze and simply stared at Devan and Alex for a moment. "Oh, Alex," she said.

Alex kept her eyes on the gun. If Devan shifted it off her for even a second, Alex would be able to try something. But the man kept the gun steady and pointed directly at her midsection, even as his eyes darted to Rebecca.

"Hello, Devan," Rebecca said, her voice cool.

"Hello, Rebecca," he replied. "I was just having a talk with our friend Alex here," he said.

"Any progress?" she asked.

"No, but we just started. Of course, it will go faster if you help."

Alex cursed herself for not seeing through Rebecca. She had barely known Devan, but Alex had lived with the Taiwanese woman. They had spoken, joked, eaten together, and slept in the same room.

Then Alex realized that Rebecca had likely been right about one thing: July was unlucky.

* * * *

"Jenny, it's just recon, there's nothing for you to worry about," Morgan said. His wife didn't look convinced.

"Dan," she said in a tone that told him that this conversation was going to get much worse if he didn't nip it in the bud.

"Peter and I can move faster if it's just us. You wouldn't want me at a client design meeting," he said.

"I wouldn't want you at a meeting because most of your meetings end with someone bleeding...or worse," she said. "Are you afraid that I'll add too much color, or bring a clichéd rococo touch to your *recon mission*?"

Morgan took a deep breath and said, "Okay."

"Okay? Just okay?" she said.

Morgan knew better than to argue further, not because he didn't enjoy a good argument, but because he didn't enjoy fighting a battle he knew he would lose.

To her credit, Jenny didn't gloat and said, "You and Peter can get the car. Dani and I will meet you downstairs."

When Morgan and Conley were in the hallway, Conley said, "We'll look more like tourists if we all stay together."

"And if things go... If things go the way they usually go for us," Morgan said.

"We both know that's a lot less likely to happen if Jenny is there," Conley said.

Morgan grunted. "That's a good thing now. Bloch is working on getting us local support. And she says Shepard is working on a weapon that we can use against Ares."

"Unless Shepard can email us the weapon, I don't think it will do too much good," Conley said.

"Either way, it won't hurt to take a day to collect information. If this is Ares's base, we need to know what we're up against before we charge in."

Morgan knew his partner was right, but he couldn't shake the feeling that they were close to something. And that meant Alex was close to that same thing.

"Dan, if this is the place, is there a better one to make a stand?" Conley said.

Once again, Conley had a point. They were in Honiara, the capital of the Solomon Islands. In the six-month Battle of Guadalcanal, Allied forces in 1942–1943 had turned the tide of the fight in the Pacific. When it started in August of 1942, America was on the defensive. By the time they were done in February of 1943, they had begun the offensive that would press the Japanese forces back to their mainland.

There was no better place, Morgan decided.

Since the hotel was in the capital of the Solomons, it was modern and very friendly to Westerners. Their car was waiting for them and Morgan took the key from the valet.

It was warmer than Port Moresby, but less humid, so it was more comfortable—and the air smelled clean. It was overcast—which Morgan knew was normal for this time of year—but it didn't look like rain.

Their Ford SUV was another good sign. Morgan knew they needed a vehicle that could go off-road since less than 20 percent of the island's roads could be considered "fair" by American standards. And they needed a vehicle that could travel over the coral, gravel, or dirt that made up a large number of the unpaved roads.

And given where they were going today, they would likely try out every type of road the island offered.

Jenny and Dani joined them and the four were off. Since the islands had been administered for years by Great Britain, English was the official language and virtually all islanders spoke it reasonably well. On the downside of their membership in the British Commonwealth, they drove on the left side of the road and Morgan had to concentrate for a few minutes to reset his driving habits.

The capital was on the northern coast of the island and their destination was close to the island's center. Though the trip wasn't far, as the crow flies, there were no direct roads. However, they were able to take one of the island's few highways for most of the way.

The trip was an hour and a half, and for the last twenty minutes Morgan was grateful for the SUV. The coral-covered roads were surprisingly smooth, but some of the dirt-only paths would have been impassable if they didn't have the four-wheel drive.

Using a combination of maps and GPS, they found an almost completely overgrown mining road that ringed the compound they were looking for. Morgan took the road to a rear entrance and stopped at a gate the held a large sign that read Gold Ridge Mine, No Trespassing!

"Looks like no one has been here for years," Conley said.

"Officially, it's been abandoned for a long time," Morgan replied.

"Who abandons a gold mine?" Jenny asked.

"There was some violence in the area that shut the mine down. Then a flash flood. And there were persistent rumors about giants," Morgan added.

"Giants?" Jenny asked.

"Local legends. There were also reports of very large footprints, which were probably the locals having fun with the mining company," Morgan said.

The four of them exited the car and approached the gate. Jenny pointed to green stickers that had been added to all four corners of the sign. It was the universal symbol for biohazard—three open circles arranged into a rough triangle with another circle in their center. The signs read either caution biohazard or quarantine biohazard.

"I'll talk to them," Dani said, pointing to one older and one younger man slicing bark off of a felled tree with machetes.

"Maybe that's why it was abandoned," Jenny said, pointing to the stickers.

"No," Morgan said. "That's how we know someone is hiding something here."

"How does that work?" Jenny asked.

"People camp out all year around Area Fifty-one, and nobody in authority cares because there's nothing to see there," Morgan said.

"The real action is in Utah at the Dugway Proving Ground," Conley added. "But for years the official story has been that it's a testing facility for biological and chemical weapons."

"I'm guessing that no one camps out there to get a peek?" Jenny said. "Okay, but that can't be true one hundred percent of the time. How do we know this is a cover story and not a real hazard?"

"Because we know that some of the items we tracked in Jakarta to Port Moresby ended up in this area, and this is the only industrial facility—closed or open—around here."

Dani returned and said, "They say the place is dead. There was activity there up until about two weeks ago, and then it stopped. They recommend we stay out. They don't believe the sign, but a number of young men from the area have disappeared in the last six months."

That made sense, Morgan thought. Abandoned places were like magnets to the young just about everywhere. It this was an Ares facility, disappearances would keep anyone from telling about anything they saw there, and would stand as a warning to any others who might also get curious.

It would be a ruthless and effective method of insuring privacy, which meant it definitely fit Ares's brutal and murderous MO.

"Jenny, for this part, Peter and I need to go in quietly. If you and Dani can wait in the—"

"No," Jenny said firmly. "And not because I don't want to spoil your fun or get in your way, but because it's a terrible plan."

Now it was Morgan's turn to put a firm note into his voice. "This is what we do. I need you to trust me."

"If I'm not mistaken and Dani's new friends are right, whoever runs this place specializes in making young men with more curiosity than brains disappear. If they have decent electronic security, they already know we're here, and they will see you coming a mile away."

"So what do you propose?" Morgan asked.

"We open the gate, drive down into the compound, and knock on the door. We'll tell them we need to use their ladies' room," Jenny said.

"Let me get this straight: Your plan is to just walk into the command center for a dangerous group of international terrorists and ask to use the facilities?"

"Yes. They've been picking off locals. We are undercover as tourists, American tourists, the kind that buffalo their way through the jungle in their big, American-made SUV and start making demands. If this was your evil lair, would you want the authorities combing the countryside, looking for the four of us?"

Jenny looked at him expectantly, waiting for him to challenge her, and knowing she was right.

Morgan didn't have to look at his partner to know that Conley was smiling. In fact, his peripheral vision told him that Dani was as well.

He simply grunted and headed back to the SUV. "Let's get moving. We need to wrap this up. The sky is getting dark and it's supposed to rain this afternoon."

# Chapter 25

There was an instant when Alex saw that while the gun was pointed at her midsection, Devan's attention was on Rebecca. It wasn't much of an opening, but it might be the only chance she got.

She leaned back on her right foot, slightly bending that knee as she prepared to spring forward. Alex waited for an instant when Devan's eyes were fully on Rebecca and then she would—

"Don't try it, Alex," Rebecca said.

Of course. Alex had been so focused on Devan that she didn't realize that Rebecca had been watching her like a hawk.

"I've seen him work," Rebecca said. "No matter how good you are, you wouldn't be fast enough."

"I would really rather not shoot you," Devan said.

"That would be messy," Alex said. "Easier, I suppose, just to toss me over the side."

That was true. Disposing of a body was absurdly easy at sea. Most people who went overboard were lost even when were spotted right away. In this confusion, even if someone saw her in the water alive, there was little chance of rescue while all security and safety officers were fighting pirates.

"There's plenty of time for that. For now, why don't we just sit down and talk," Devan said.

Before anyone could move, Alex heard automatic gunfire from the bow. Instinctively, she leaned forward and prepared to dash to the front of the ship to help.

"Don't do it," Rebecca said as Alex's roommate drew a gun and pointed it at her.

It took all of her will for Alex to keep herself from lunging at the woman. "And I thought you were the nice roommate," she said.

"The problem is that you chose the wrong side, Alex," Rebecca replied. "Now I'm going to insist you sit down so you don't run off and make Devan and me shoot you."

Alex sat on a small love seat facing Rebecca and Devan. They took seats opposite her with coffee table between them.

It was a smart move on their part. Alex had many fewer options when she was sitting. She'd have to get up before she attacked them or tried to run, and that would give them plenty of time to shoot her.

Alex heard a gunshot up ahead at the bow. *Sniper fire*, she thought. *Good, security is fighting back.* She hoped they were giving Devan and Rebecca's pirate friends hell.

Alex smiled, leaned back, and said, "Yes, let's talk. The fact is that I have a number of questions for you both."

She heard running footsteps and saw the black-clad snipers racing across the lido deck. Alex considered calling out to them, but realized she would only be putting the men in danger.

Two Ares agents—one dressed as crew and one dressed as a passenger— would have little trouble shooting them before the security men even knew Rebecca and Devan were a threat.

Besides, they had a pirate attack to fend off. For now, Ares was her problem. If nothing else, she would keep them talking until the pirates were dealt with. Then Alex could force them to use their weapons on her when security was close enough to see or hear the commotion.

Alex would likely not survive, but these two would be exposed and that would give the ship a chance.

"Now where were we?" Alex said.

\* \* \* \*

The gate wasn't locked, which was one of a dozen things Morgan didn't like about this operation. Actually, there were more than a dozen, but that was where Morgan stopped counting.

"Maybe the disappearances and biohazard signs kept people out," Conley said.

That was certainly possible. The problem was that it just didn't feel right to Morgan. As they got closer to the compound, that feeling was one more thing Morgan could add to his list.

"You hear that?" Morgan asked.

"It's too damn quiet," Conley said.

Aside from the sound of the car and the normal rustle of the jungle, there were no sounds—no voices, no hum of a generator; nothing mechanical at all, in fact.

The place was either on silent running while the people there planned an ambush, or it was staffed entirely by ghosts. There was a short drive on a well-maintained mine road, and then the jungle opened into a clearing that was at least a quarter mile square.

There was heavy equipment, a pond, fuel tanks, at least one generator building, one large garage, two long structures, and a number of smaller outbuildings. It looked like what it was: a large, modern, working mine. The only thing that was missing was people or movement of any kind.

And while there was a large generator—along with fans, compressors, and other equipment to run a large physical plant—nothing was running and no lights were on anywhere.

The mining road ringed the compound and Morgan drove up to the building nearest to them and parked. He and Conley stepped outside and headed over. As they approached the door, Morgan was already pulling out his small lockpick kit. They walked up to the door and Conley said, "Hold on, Dan."

Conley pushed at the door and it simply swung inward. "Hello," he called.

There was no answer and the two men stepped inside. Morgan automatically tried the light switch but there was no power and the partners pulled out their flashlights, though there were enough windows that they could see reasonably well.

As Morgan had suspected, this was an administrative building, filled with offices and cubicles. It looked like it had been recently occupied, but there were no signs that anyone was there, or had been recently. There was nothing personal in any of the work spaces, and even the office fridges were empty.

The only other oddity was the complete lack of computers—or rather, CPUs and data storage. There were monitors on most of the desks and they looked fairly new. They were all just not hooked up to anything.

That part made sense. If Ares had been here and left, they wouldn't want to leave any devices that held real information that could be used to track them.

Morgan and Conley went back to the car and drove a few hundred yards and repeated the process in the next building, which stored office supplies. After that, Dani and Jenny came with them.

The extra flashlights helped, and all four of the party took pictures of the empty buildings. Perhaps Shepard and O'Neal's team back at Zeta could make some sense of what they were seeing.

There was a mess hall, a gymnasium, and a building that looked like it had been designed for storage but had been retrofitted to be a shooting range—though there were no signs of weapons or ammo.

One of the long buildings was full of industrial equipment: pipes, fittings, stacks of steel I beams, tools, and pallets of miscellaneous equipment and raw materials.

The other long building contained a large, open space. On one end was the entrance to the mine with tunnels that led underground. The rest of the building was clearly a factory.

It was a full industrial machine shop, with tooling to make large metal parts to stamp out casings, or bend pipes and beams. There was also a large vacuum-forming machine and injection-molding devices.

There was equipment for cutting sheet metal, and an electronic assembly area, with bins of circuit boards, wires, and power supplies.

The two couples spent quite a bit of time photographing it all. When they were finished, Jenny asked, "What could they have been making here?"

Morgan had been thinking about that and said, "Just about anything."

"Whatever they were doing, it looks like they finished and moved on," Conley added.

Morgan didn't like the sound of that. It pointed up the fact that, once again, they were at one step behind Ares. And if Ares had been building anything destructive, that meant they were ready to deploy it.

The place felt cold and he understood why the locals had avoided it. It actually felt worse than cold, it felt dead—so much so that even the lure of valuable equipment was not enough for anyone to even come close.

"Let's get out of here," Morgan said.

* * * *

"When did you both know that you wanted to be henchmen?" Alex asked. Rebecca and Devan didn't react, except to give each other quick glances. "Is it a calling, or something you just fall into?"

Devan raised his gun and said, "Alex, we'll ask the questions."

Alex waved off his comment and continued. "I think you should really think about finding a better organization. The current standards aren't very high. I took out five of your friends after they snuck up on me."

"You're referring to the recent incident in Boston?" Rebecca asked.

"Have there been many more incidents like that lately? Like I said, you really should think about trading up on your workplace."

"Let's talk about you," Devan said. "My hat is off to your team. Your bio holds up very well—an article about some neighborhood cleanup project when you were a kid, high school transcripts, followed by vocational school records and a work history. It goes all the way back and includes a remarkable social media presence. For someone who doesn't exist, Alex McGrath has quite a detailed history. And the material fits you, but I thought your social media team hit the Dungeons and Dragons boards a bit hard. That culture is too specific and raises too many questions."

The Dungeons & Dragons material must have been Shepard. She would have to talk to him about it. Devan was right about that much. She wouldn't be able to answer anything past the most basic questions about "her" D&D campaigns.

Of course, to have that problem in the future, she'd have to survive the next half hour and that was looking less and less likely.

There was shouting on deck somewhere behind them. Alex thought it was a security team, which was confirmed when she heard the term *water cannons*. She knew they were usually a very effective tool for discouraging pirates trying to board a ship.

"Your team did their job, but what blew your cover was the cruise line's database. Your application was received and you were hired the same day, even though staffing was completed for this cruise. They actually moved someone to another ship to make a place for you on board. There were three levels of manual overrides necessary to make that happen. All this because I guess they really needed a motorcycle mechanic on the serving staff."

"I'm a *very good* motorcycle mechanic," Alex said.

"Apparently," Devan agreed. "I assume 'taking out' people who sneak up on you is a hobby?"

"I'm also a concerned citizen who doesn't like international terrorists and lowlifes. It's a Boston thing," Alex said.

Neither Devan nor Rebecca responded to that.

"Did you know that we call you *Ares*? I've come up with another name for you, but I don't think you'd like it," Alex said.

Now Devan looked uncomfortable and shot Rebecca a long glance.

There was clearly something going on with them, but Alex was focused on the sounds of shouting nearby. More calls for hoses and pressure. From the sound of the voices, whatever security was trying to do was a struggle.

"Alex, where did you get that ring?" Devan asked.

That came as a surprise to Alex. The ring was on her right hand. On its face was what looked like a crest but was really two antique keys that formed an X.

"My friend Pierre gave it to me," Alex said.

Devan looked genuinely surprised and said, "We both know that's not true."

"Okay, my friend Lily did; she's a friend of Pierre's," Alex said.

"Who is Pierre?" Rebecca asked.

"The founder of *Les Clefs d'Or*, an elite group of hotel concierges that also operates as an informal white hat intelligence service for a very, very select group," Devan said.

Alex didn't like the idea that *Les Clefs d'or* might have been compromised by Ares. The elite concierges were very visible. They worked in top hotels and wore gold- embroidered keys on their lapels. If Ares knew about them, those keys might as well have been targets.

"Let's talk about your friend Lily…" Devan began and then a realization flashed over his face. "Wait, Lily Randall?"

"The girlfriend of that billionaire, Scott Renard?" Rebecca asked.

Alex was too shocked to conceal her own surprise…and then dread. If Ares knew that Lily Randall was in intelligence…

"Alex, you need to tell us who you work for, and you need to do it right now," Devan said.

"My employer is the Great Adventure Cruise Line," Alex said flatly. She'd already said too much and she felt a cold dread when she thought she might have compromised Lily.

"Oh my God, you're Zeta," Devan said.

"I don't know what you're talking about," Alex replied.

"Zeta, are they even real?" Rebecca asked.

"It fits. The rumor is that Zeta was the group that came up with the name Ares," Devan said. For a moment, it looked like he was genuinely wrestling with something. In the end, he said, "I'm MI6. I've never met Lily Randall, but she was still serving during my first year. There were rumors she'd joined Zeta. Alex, if you're—"

Before he could finish, two security men wearing dark blue uniforms raced by. They weren't carrying sniper rifles, but they were carrying large, bulky pistols of some kind that she did not recognize.

Alex watched as the new security men dashed across the lido deck to far starboard and started engaging with someone over the side. Instantly, there was automatic weapons fire, and then Alex watched as one of the security men fell back. She realized with horror that he'd been shot.

That was it. Alex started to get up. "Don't do it," Devan said.

Alex froze. There just wasn't time for this.

"We still don't know who you are," Rebecca said.

"I'm here to protect this ship, and it needs protecting *right now*. I don't know who either of you are, except that you're both pointing guns at me, which isn't a great start. Now I'm going to tell you what's about to happen so you won't be surprised. I'm going to head over there and help make sure that whoever is shooting at security doesn't board this ship. If you're really MI6 you can help me. If you're Ares, I guess you'll just shoot me in the back."

Now Alex didn't hesitate. She leapt out of her chair and raced for the lounge's exit.

# Chapter 26

Alicia Schmitt watched on her monitor as the snipers took position in the front of the ship. The forward camera attached to the sensor array she'd installed showed them taking shot after shot from a position just to the right of the stern. This continued for at least two minutes. She switched to one of the lower cameras and could see the motor on the skiff was in flames. Two of the six men on board seemed incapacitated and the other four were trying to put out the flames.

Whatever happened, they were clearly out of the fight. The snipers set up a position on the left side of the deck and waited for a shot on another one of the skiffs.

The captain's initial maneuvers had swamped two of the boats. Now the snipers had taken out a third. That still left five. It helped that they couldn't coordinate with each other, but they were armed with AK-47s and still a threat.

Her monitor told her that while the snipers were struggling with the remaining forward skiff, the pirates on that skiff had clearly seen what had happened to the other boat and were keeping their distance.

As soon as the snipers fired the first shot, the pirates darted back to the starboard side and moved closer—taking advantage of the fact that the snipers weren't set up there.

And since Schmitt wasn't in direct contact with the snipers, she couldn't tell them. And even if she could, the pirates could continue racing back and forth just out of range, which would keep the snipers occupied indefinitely.

Unless…

Schmitt hit her direct line to the bridge and said, "Watson, this is Schmitt. There's a skiff five degrees to port and getting closer. If you could change course and put on a burst of seven to ten knots I don't think they could get away in time."

"Acknowledged," he said. It took less than five seconds for the order for speed to come down to the chief and then she felt she ship turn.

Her radar told her the skiff was less than one hundred yards out when the *Grandeur* executed its maneuver. At this point, the skiff must have seen the danger. The problem was that it was still heading toward the ship, and even with a relatively sharp turn away it still had quite a bit of forward momentum.

It took valuable seconds for the skiff to arrest that momentum and to actually start heading out of the *Grandeur*'s path. Unfortunately for them, during those seconds, the massive ship was closing the distance between the two vessels.

At this point, the forward cameras were useless, since their line of sight prevented them from seeing the ocean that close to the hull. However, Schmitt's radar told her that the skiff was less than sixty yards from the front of the *Grandeur*. Her system's collision warning system told her that there was an imminent danger of a collision.

The skiff actually managed to get maybe twenty-five yards to starboard, which meant that it came only ten yards short of clearing the front of the hull.

The skiff's radar blip disappeared into the center of her screen as her collision alarm sounded. Schmitt didn't need a camera to show her that the skiff had been obliterated—though it had no doubt barely scratched the *Grandeur*'s paint.

"Thank you, Ms. Schmitt," Watson's voice said through the comm.

"Well done, Mr. Watson," she replied. "That's four down by my count."

"Yes, and we've only just started. We have more surprises for the others," he said.

\* \* \* \*

Alex ran onto the lido deck and was pleased that she didn't hear any gunshots behind her or feel the crushing blow of a bullet hitting her in the back. She didn't know what to make of her encounter with Devan and Rebecca. However, she now had a mission and that helped drown out those questions.

If Devan and Rebecca turned out to be allies, that would help Alex complete her assignment. However, Alex would be satisfied if they just stayed out of her way.

"Behind you," Alex called out as she approached the two security men near the railing. "I can help."

One of the men was down, holding his shoulder while he lay on the deck. The other was holding his strange pistol but seemed torn between doing his job and tending to his partner.

"I have him," Alex said as she skidded to a stop next to the men. She grabbed a towel from a nearby pile. She knelt by the injured man and applied pressure to the wound. She couldn't be sure because of the uniform, but it looked like the bullet had hit his tricep. And because he didn't scream in pain when she applied pressure, she knew the bone hadn't been hit.

"You're okay. It's superficial, looks like through and through. We'll get you down to the medical center and you'll be fine," Alex said, though for the moment she had no idea how she would do that.

The security man next to them fired his pistol and Alex heard a hiss that told her it was probably a flare. The problem was that his single shot was met with automatic weapons fire—*a lot* of automatic weapons fire.

They definitely had AKs, Alex thought. And they had brought plenty of ammunition.

"What can we do?" someone said behind her. The accent told her it was Devan.

Alex glanced back and saw Devan and Rebecca standing there. She noted they had put their guns away. Whatever their missions were, they weren't ready to reveal themselves to the crew.

"Devan, go behind the bar and get a serving cart. We need to get him to sick bay. Rebecca, collect as many towels as you can and pile them right there," Alex said, gesturing to the railing in front of her. "Just don't get too close to the edge."

Devan returned quickly with the cart and Alex helped him get the man into a sitting position on it. She read the name tag on the man's uniform. "Michaels, listen to me. You're going to be fine, and Devan is going to get you to the medical center. But I need you to hold the towel against the wound."

He nodded. "I can do it," he said. He looked pale and he was clearly going into shock, but the bleeding wasn't bad, and he was only minutes away from real help. "Devan. Take him to deck five. Use the center guest elevator and follow the signs."

Rebecca had already created a stack of folded white towels a couple of feet from the railing. Moving quickly, she went back to get more.

Alex picked up the strange pistol from the ground. Remarkably, Michaels had been able to hold on to it even after he'd been hit in the shoulder, which kept it from falling into the ocean. It was oversized in every way, but the most striking feature was the round ammunition cylinder that was just forward of the grip. That feature made it look like a cross between a cartoon pistol and a tommy gun.

A quick examination of the very wide barrel told her what it was.

"It's a flare gun," she said. "What do I need to know?" she asked the security man next to her. Looking quickly at his name tag she added, "Mr. Benitez. I'm Alex."

"Just point and shoot and hold it steady after you fire. It doesn't have a traditional recoil—it's more sustained. And at this range it will shoot pretty true," he said.

Rebecca piled up more towels in front of the railing, while Alex grabbed another serving cart. The two women started piling the towels on top of it. To Benitez she said, "Best guess on their position?"

"Directly below us," he said.

"Rebecca, take the cart to the edge of the pool. When I say, get a running start and ram the cart into the railing," Alex said.

As Rebecca took her place, there was a loud clang near the railing in front of them, and Alex saw two metal hooks appear on the railing. The skiff had hooked a ladder to them.

They were about to be boarded.

Alex took a position a few yards away from the top of the ladder on one side and Benitez did the same on the other.

"Rebecca, now!" Alex shouted as the sound of automatic gunfire filled the air.

The pirates were shooting straight up to make sure that no one tried to stop them. To her credit, Rebecca didn't hesitate; she pointed the cart toward the railing and started running. Her distance gave her several good strides to get up to speed, and then she let go when she was a few feet away from the railing.

The cart hit the railing hard, and the pile of towels flew into the air in an impressive display. Predictably, the pirates started shooting at this new threat.

Alex and security officer Benitez didn't hesitate—they leaned over the railing and aimed their flare pistols at the skiff, which was at a point directly between them. They fired almost simultaneously and caught the skiff in their crossfire. Benitez had been right about the recoil; it lasted almost a full second. Then the cylinder spun to chamber the next round. Alex adjusted her aim, targeting the center of the skiff. Her second flare was off before the first one hit the rear of the small ship, where it flashed rather spectacularly.

Five of the pirates were still shooting at the towels, which fluttered toward the boat in a confusing mass of white. As Alex took her third shot, she saw two of the pirates notice her and Benitez.

Alex fired and shouted, "Cover."

Pulling her head back, she held the gun for another fraction of a second so she wouldn't throw off her last shot. Alex pulled her weapon back and rolled away just as she heard new gunfire coming in her direction.

It stopped suddenly. Alex could hear shouts and she could see a series of flashes as the flares ignited something on board the skiff. There was silence for a few seconds and then a short burst of fire from a single AK-47.

One of the pirates had made it to the ladder, Alex realized.

They wouldn't need weapons to handle him. "Rebecca, give me a hand," Alex called out.

She grabbed the serving cart and rolled it back over to the railing, lining it up with the hooks of the ladder. There was another short burst of fire, but Alex could tell the pirate's heart wasn't in it. With his friends gone, he was no doubt trying to conserve ammo in the event he found himself on the ship alone.

Of course, Alex was going to make sure that didn't happen.

"Ready?" she asked, and Rebecca nodded. Together, they lifted the serving cart and let it rest on the railing. There was a burst from the AK but all the pirate could do was shoot straight up.

"Now!" Alex called out, and she and Rebecca pushed the cart over the railing, taking care not to lean over and give the pirate a target. There was a dull thud, followed by a double splash as the pirate and the cart hit the water.

Looking down, Alex could see the wooden skiff burning brightly. She realized that those flares were designed to do more than act as emergency signals. Alex suspected they walked a fine line between safety equipment and incendiary ordnance.

Combined with their semiautomatic firing mechanism, she realized they made very effective weapons.

Alex could hear commotion and saw two security officers struggling with a fire hose across the deck. There was gunfire and she could see ladder hooks on the railing.

Benitez was struggling with the hooks of the ladder in front of them and said, "Help me get rid of this."

He was right. If they left it on the side of the ship, the crew of another skiff could use it to climb on board while they were occupied somewhere else.

"No," Alex said. "I have an idea. We can use it."

# Chapter 27

*She can't help herself,* Schmitt thought as she watched Alex join the flare gun team after one of the men went down. Technically, Alex had stayed within their mission parameters. The shooting of the security man constituted an imminent threat of loss of life.

But even so, Alex hadn't appeared to reveal herself as an agent. She even managed to enlist the help of one of the guests and a member of the crew—who Schmitt thought might be Alex's roommate. Together, they eliminated a skiff.

Maneuvers and the ship's snipers had taken out the two forward and two rear skiffs. And the hose team had taken out two of the starboard skiffs. And Alex had helped eliminate another. It was an excellent effort, but that still left one heavily armed skiff, and its crew had managed to get one of their ladders on the side of the ship while heavy AK fire kept the hose team from getting a line of fire.

So far, this had likely been the most sophisticated, most aggressive, and most coordinated pirate attack in modern shipping history. And the *Grandeur*'s crew had performed admirably, eliminating seven of the eight threats.

However, the remaining pirates remained a real problem. Six committed men with AK-47s—and God knew what else—could do a lot of damage on board. Once they were free to roam the ship, it might not be possible to stop them from taking over.

Schmitt hadn't known about the snipers on board, or the remarkable flare pistols. The water cannons were a tried-and-true method of deterring pirates, but they were obviously less effective against such heavily armed and aggressive foes. And of course the ship itself—with the right person at the helm—had turned out to be another surprise and had executed defensive maneuvers with military precision.

Despite all of those efforts, the fight might be over unless Alex, a masseuse, and a security team with a water hose came up with something in the next few minutes.

* * * *

It took longer than Alex would have liked to pull up the ladder. It was a rope ladder—though a more advanced one than Alex would have expected from a group of island-based pirates. The steps were manufactured, well-machined steel—relatively lightweight and strong. The rope was some sort of composite nylon.

The rope ladder had advantages over the traditional rigid steel or iron siege weapons used in every other pirate attack she had studied. A rope ladder was lighter and easier to manage but required something to launch it into the air. That meant some sort of gas-powered device and a targeting mechanism.

That was sophisticated tech and from what Alex had seen, the pirates were able to get it into position on the first try. Alex decided that she definitely didn't want these people running loose on the ship.

"Where are we?" Devan said from behind her. When Alex turned, he added, "Looks like Benitez will be okay."

"We need to help them," Alex said, pointing to two men handling the water cannon. It was firmly mounted to the deck, but the men were paralyzed by the gunfire. Like the flare gun team, there was simply no way for them to effectively use their hose without leaning over the side of the ship and making themselves targets for the pirates' AK-47s.

In a world where there was virtually no danger of pirate attacks on cruise ships, the defensive options available were more than adequate. However, if this was the start of a new trend, ship's security would need new options—chief among those was the ability to use their existing weapons behind cover.

However, Alex suspected this wasn't a new trend, but an Ares operation. Given their level of sophistication and armament, there was an excellent chance that these pirates were funded and supplied by Ares operatives—if they weren't Ares people themselves.

That raised all kinds of questions that Alex didn't want to think about—in fact, couldn't think about it until she had dealt with the killers with machine guns that were trying to board the vessel.

"Rebecca, get the other end of this. Devan, grab two café tables, we'll need one on each end."

Neither of the two asked any questions. Rebecca simply picked up her end of the ladder and Devan raced across the deck to grab the tables.

As Alex picked up her end of the ladder, Benitez appeared next to her and said, "What can I do?"

"Do you have any flares left in your weapon?" Alex said. She knew that the one she had used was out.

"Just one," Benitez replied.

"That will do. Stand by. You'll know when to use it," she said.

The water cannon team was shooting water out toward the ocean, but it wouldn't affect anyone on the ladder. The security men saw Alex and her unlikely team coming and one of them said, "What have you got?"

"A way to clear the ladder if you can pull the cannon down," she said.

The men didn't hesitate. They quickly closed the valve on the spout of the cannon and pulled metal base out of the mounting hole in the floor.

"Devan, twist your side of the ladder around the legs. Rebecca, give me a hand," she said.

The café tables were simple squares, designed for two people. They each had a propeller-style base with four "blades" that were heavy enough to keep the tables steady in moderately rough seas.

The nylon composite rope that made up the sides of the ladder was flexible enough that it was easy to secure two of the ladder's metal "steps" over the opposite blades from the table's base.

"Benitez, find a spot a few yards over and fire when this goes over," she said. She hoped he could do it. He'd be taking the most risk, since he could have to expose himself to gunfire to take his one shot.

"Okay, now!" Alex said to Devan, who had taken position about twenty feet away from her. She and Rebecca heaved their table on to the side of the railing, as Devan did the same on his end. All three of them took pains to keep from leaning over and giving the pirates a target.

As they pushed at the tables, Alex heard automatic weapons fire—not from beneath them but from practically right next to them. When she and Rebecca gave the table a last push, Alex saw why: One of the pirates was at nearly the top of the ladder. She could see his head and the barrel of his AK, which he fired straight into the air—presumably to scare the ship's defenders.

It might have been effective, but the defense of the ship was out of their hands and was now in the hands of simple physics—or more specifically, gravity.

The ladder, which had been strung between two heavy tables about twenty feet apart, started its journey to the ocean, sweeping through anyone who was climbing the ladder.

Alex heard a series of thuds, followed by sounds that were more yelps than screams and then a series of splashes as the two tables and anyone in their path hit the water.

Just as the first splash sounded, she saw Benitez throw himself forward, fire his one round, and them pull himself back. There was no answering fire from the skiff. There were, however, two short screams and more splashing sounds.

Alex didn't have to look to know that Benitez's aim had been true. She let herself slump to the deck and sat for a moment to catch her breath.

It was over, which was just as well, since Alex was out of tricks. She smiled at Rebecca and then at Devan.

Devan, however, wasn't smiling. He looked concerned and called out, "Alex!"

She looked toward the ladder, where a man's head was just peeking up from below the deck. He looked like someone from the local islands; he also seemed very, very angry.

And he was looking directly at her.

His head popped up quickly, and then his torso was visible through the railing. Then, as if in slow motion, he reached up with one hand, which Alex could see was not holding an AK-47 but a pistol.

He was swinging it up and preparing to shoot. And given that there was less than ten feet between them he could hardly miss.

But before he could take final aim, an invisible hand threw him off the ladder and several feet backward.

It took Alex a full second to realize that it wasn't an invisible hand, but a concentrated blast of water that had hit him directly in the chest.

Turning her head, she saw the water cannon team lying on the deck and holding the nozzle between them as it shot its powerful blast of water inches above the deck and through the empty space in the railing.

She smiled at the men, who nodded and turned off the spray.

Alex got to her feet and took a cautious look over the side. There was no one on the ladder and no one in the water that she could see. The skiff was burning and looked empty, thought it was hard to see detail because it was already falling back as the *Grandeur* moved forward.

At that moment, Alex realized that she was right in the middle of her serving section, station four. She decided that Rebecca had been wrong there. The number four wasn't unlucky here—unless you happened to be a pirate.

"Come on, Alex," Rebecca said, standing above her and holding out a hand. "It's starting to rain. Let's get you inside."

Alex took her roommate's hand and let the woman pull her to her feet.

* * * *

"Director, I would have been happy to come up," Shepard said when she appeared at his workstation.

She waved off the concern. "At the moment, your time is more valuable than mine."

"I took the intel you relayed from Morgan and we're still examining the photos," Shepard said. "Whatever they were manufacturing there, it was very advanced. And since there were no high-tech manufacturers licensed to operate at that location—or anywhere on the island, for that matter—I think it's safe to assume that it was dangerous. And based on our other intelligence, Ares is a safe bet."

"Good work," Bloch said. "Any chance of finding other locations on the islands?"

That was a tall order. There were over 900 islands in the Solomons, and most of them were uninhabited. She'd been on the phone full-time with the CIA and Renard Tech to re-task satellites, but bad weather over the area was making satellite imaging difficult.

"We've had some luck there as well, Director," Shepard said. "The shipping manifests from Jakarta and Port Moresby helped us narrow it down. We tried to coordinate those with missing person reports like Morgan suggested, but the islanders have spotty reporting. And local law enforcement isn't computerized on all the islands. However, when we cross-checked with information provided by your contact at MI6 we got some hits."

"How many hits?" she asked.

"Several, but there's only one with a port deep enough to be useful to Ares as a base. Plus, MI6 has seen signs of a helipad. If Ares is in the area and I'm certain they are, they're on Savo Island. It's only twelve square miles, but I think any base would be near the port."

Shepard looked pleased and he had every right to be. There was a real chance that for once they would have the jump on Ares and be able to take the fight to them for a change.

"More than I could have hoped for," Bloch asked. "Thank you both." Bloch turned to O'Neal, who was looking at Shepard and actually grinning.

"Of course," she continued. "You know that I have to pass this information along to Morgan."

With a looming threat, they had to act. However, that would mean putting three agents and a civilian at risk. Once she told Morgan and the others the location, they would go charging in. It would be hard to imagine an assault like that happening without some losses on Zeta's side.

"Shepard, I want to thank you for your work on the new weapon as well. I know you did your best," she said.

He had blamed himself for the death of a single civilian. She wondered what would happen if one or more of his friends died in the coming fight.

Part of that would be on her. She had given him an impossible task with the artificial deadline for the new weapon. She'd done it to motivate him, to get him out of his particular dark place, but she'd also done it selfishly. She needed him and his and O'Neal's department at the top of their game to get this far.

"It has been difficult. I know I can do better on miniaturization and power," he offered.

"No one could have done more," she said. "It will help us in the future. For now, Morgan and the team will make do with the resources at hand."

Shepard looked at her as if he didn't understand what she was saying.

"Lincoln, Morgan made it very clear that unless you can email him the weapon…"

"I know. He told me the same thing," Shepard said. "I was putting together the email when you got here. Give me five minutes and I'll send it out to him."

# Chapter 28

The captain's voice boomed over the public address system. "I want to thank all of our passengers for your patience during the recent attempt by a number of parties to unlawfully board this vessel. I know it was a frightening time for everyone, but I am pleased to report that all members of our crew—especially our security and safety officers—performed exceptionally. I can confirm that the Australian and Solomon Islands coast guards have been informed and will be investigating the incident to insure that it is not repeated.

"In the meantime, we will resume full activities and services tomorrow. Tonight, all food service will resume by five o'clock, except for service on the lido deck due to the rain. Most entertainment options will be available tonight, but please check with individual venues to confirm scheduling. All crew should report to their duty stations for instructions.

"All security and safety crew will report to the Capital Theater for a brief reception at nine a.m. tomorrow.

"Once again, I am very proud of the *Grandeur*, her crew, and her passengers, and I want to commend you all for your performance. Garrett out."

Alex waited by the waitress station until Rosa arrived. Others were already gathering around, but Rosa ignored them and sought out Alex, pulling her to the side.

"Alex, I just heard from First Officer Watson—who I have never spoken to before. He says you helped repel the pirates," she said, looking up at Alex with something like awe.

"I happened to be here," she said. "My roommate and me, and one of the guests, tossed some tables over the side and applied first aid to Security Officer Michaels."

"The first officer sees it differently, and don't talk him out of it. You have made all of us look good. We're reassigning some lido servers tonight, but he's instructed me to give you tonight and tomorrow off. Good work, Alex."

Then Rosa was off, talking to the staff one at a time. Alex wasn't sure what she was going to do with a full day off during the week. Since training, she'd been used to constant long hours for six days at a time, followed by a day that was spent either sleeping or numb.

Alex would meet with Schmitt tomorrow, but otherwise she supposed she would have to try to relax.

Alex saw Sorina approaching with Eric in tow. The woman didn't stop until she had Alex in a tight hug.

"Alex, is it true you helped fight the pirates?" Sorina asked.

"A few of us helped a little," she said with a shrug. "We didn't do much."

"Rosa doesn't think so," Sorina said. "And she gave me tonight off—I think because we're friends." She pointed to Eric and said, "Because we're off tonight, Eric has invited us to his play."

The man next to her looked embarrassed and said, "It's a revue. If you're not too shaken up."

Alex could feel Sorina's eyes on her. Though she would like nothing better than to crawl into her bunk, Alex knew that she could do one more good deed today. And this time no one would be shooting at her.

"Definitely, it sounds like fun," Alex said.

"Nine o'clock," he said. "I'll have tickets waiting for you."

"Eric, can you have dinner with Alex and me before?"

"Sure, if it's early. I have to be at the theater by eight," Eric said.

"Okay, Alex?" Sorina said.

She and Sorina weren't going to have dinner together, but once again she could feel the Romanian woman's eyes on her. Sorina wasn't ready to go alone with Eric. "Sure, six, okay, Eric?" Alex said.

He nodded enthusiastically.

As the two left, Alex decided that she would draw the line after the show tonight. If those two were going to kiss, they would have to do it on their own.

* * * *

When it was over, Chief Cabato quietly thanked Schmitt for her help, left the office, and went to talk to the men working in the actual engine room. About fifteen minutes later, he returned and smiled for the first time since the pirate attack began.

He opened a cabinet and pulled out a bottle of ordinary-looking red wine. Then he took out four glasses and poured, giving one to each of his two lieutenants, one to her, and raising his own.

"To the *Grandeur*—her captain, her crew, and her new friend and protector, Alicia Schmitt." They all raised their glasses and drank.

Then he quietly conferred with one of his men who disappeared and returned, carrying two epaulets from an engineering officer's uniform. The epaulets had two stripes each, with a purple band between them, which was the designation for a second engineer officer.

"Ms. Schmitt," Cabato said. "Please take these as a small token of our thanks."

Schmitt took the embroidered pieces and said, "Thank you, but no thanks are necessary."

"On this we disagree. Tell me, Ms. Schmitt, do you use purple on your aircraft carriers?"

"Yes, for flight deck crew, the ones who fuel and de-fuel the planes. It's one of the most dangerous jobs on the ship," she said.

"On cruise ships, it's the color of the engineering crew. We wear it because it was the color of the engineers of the *Titanic*. We wear it to remember their bravery," he said.

That was an understatement. Those engineers fought desperately to save their ship, keeping the boilers running, the bilge pumps working, and the power on until the very end. All crew departments on that ship suffered heavy losses, but for the *Titanic*'s engineers, their losses were the heaviest at 100 percent—since not a single certified engineer was among the survivors. Even the engineers who were off-duty raced to help and then went down with the ship.

For a moment, Schmitt was actually speechless and then Cabato added, "I'd like to make you an honorary member of our crew and our department."

He and his two lieutenants raised their glasses and said, "Welcome."

Schmitt smiled and muttered her thanks, for a moment not trusting her voice.

And then Jack Watson entered the room. He had a broad smile on his face and said, "Well done, Chief. To all of you, and to you, Ms. Schmitt. Chief, if you don't mind, can I borrow your consultant?"

The chief nodded his agreement, and Watson turned to Schmitt and said, "Could I have a word?"

When they were in the corridor, he said, "Alicia, I can't thank you enough for your help."

"You know it was mostly the system that did the work," she said.

"A system that you helped design," Watson replied. Then he glanced down at her right hand, which held the epaulets the chief had given her.

"Did the chief give you those?" he asked.

"Yes," she said.

His eyes went wide and he said, "Wow."

"Is that not allowed?" she asked.

"No, it's just surprising," he said. "The captain would like to meet with you later to thank you personally, but I didn't want to wait to thank you myself."

"You've done that twice now. You're welcome," she said.

Schmitt couldn't tell if he wanted to say something else, or he was just embarrassed. She decided it was neither of those things.

"You're very welcome," she said, then she leaned in to kiss him.

It was a full minute before they separated. She took his hand and said, "Come on, my cabin's closer."

\* \* \* \*

Alex had barely taken ten steps when she was approached by Devan and Rebecca. "Alex, can we have a word?" Devan said.

"Can it wait?" Alex replied.

"I think there are a number of things we need to talk about," Rebecca said.

That was true. Alex needed to have an open discussion with these two. However, she was undercover and working to thwart a devious and powerful enemy. Could she really be sure she could trust these two, simply because they helped fight off some pirates? An open discussion might not be a good idea.

"We really need to talk," Devan repeated.

"Can we just agree to disagree on that?" Alex replied.

"Let's stipulate that none of us want to do it," Devan said. "But we have a common enemy, and we may need each other."

They stepped into the rear of the lounge off the lido deck. It was only when they sat down that Alex realized they were in the same seats that they had sat in an hour ago. The difference was that this time Alex didn't have any guns pointed at her.

"What is it?" Rebecca asked.

"I was just remembering the last time we sat down like this; right here, in fact," she said.

"If you'd like to move..." Rebecca said.

"No, it reminds me to be careful," Alex said.

"Given what we do, Alex, do you really take it personally when someone points a gun at you?" Devan asked.

"No," she said. "But I like making you both uncomfortable."

Devan smiled at that. "Fair enough. Since we were the first ones to draw weapons, I'll go first. I'm MI6 and I'm here because there was a pirate alert."

That made sense. The UK had clear interests in the Solomon Islands. Turning to Rebecca, Alex said, "Are you also MI6?"

"No, I'm NSB," Rebecca replied. "I'm here on my own. In fact, I was surprised to see Devan on board."

That also made sense. The National Security Bureau was Taiwan's intelligence agency. Rebecca's presence was logical, given Taiwan's relationship with Mainland China and China's proximity to the Solomon Islands. Then there was China's recent and unsuccessful attempt to purchase one of the islands, which had made a lot of people uncomfortable.

"Now it's your turn, Alex. Are you really Zeta?"

"I'll answer that question when Rebecca tells us both why she's really here," Alex said. NSB explained who Rebecca worked for, but the woman hadn't said anything about her mission.

Now it was Rebecca's turn to look uncomfortable.

"Rebecca?" Devan said.

"My orders are to prevent trouble," Rebecca said.

"What kind of trouble?" Alex asked. "If it's piracy, mission accomplished. If it's something else—and we three are going to be working together—we need to know."

That was one of the problems with espionage work. To do your job, you had to keep secrets. And sometimes, to do your job you had to trust other people. Those two requirements often came into conflict.

"Rebecca?" Devan repeated.

"We didn't formerly discuss our missions," she said to Devan.

"I think now would be a good time," Alex added.

Rebecca took a deep breath and said, "China stole the prototype of a solid-state laser from an American company. It's a self-contained pod that's designed to be added to fighter aircraft—and more powerful than anything currently in service. The theft was the easy part. Transporting it from the US has been tricky, but we traced it to a delivery of spare parts and equipment to this ship. I'm here to make sure it arrives in port where NSB and American agents will be waiting to intercept it."

"It looks like we all have only part of the picture," Devan said.

"Alex, it's your turn," Rebecca said.

"It's true, I'm Zeta," she said.

"You do have the air of a…contractor," Devan said.

"Funny, I thought you gave off a strong corporate MI6 vibe," Alex said.

"It makes sense that you're Zeta," he said. "You're from Boston, and there were reports of a failed Ares operation in Boston. I presume that's the incident you referred to earlier."

"Yes, they tried to take me by surprise," she said.

"That would have been just before you started your training with the cruise line," Rebecca said.

Devan looked impressed. "Did you really take out five Ares operatives?"

"Yes," Alex said simply. She wouldn't gain anything by being modest, and there was no value in keeping that information from her new partners.

"I guess there goes the myth about the invulnerability of Ares operatives," Rebecca said.

"I can confirm that it's only a myth," Alex said. "But I can also confirm they are very dangerous and very committed. And I can tell you that our information indicates a major attack in this area in the next few days, something regional in scope."

"Bigger than what we just faced?" Devan asked.

"Yes," she said. "Our system didn't pinpoint this ship, but it did pinpoint these waters."

"So which is it?" Rebecca. "A hijacking of high-tech cargo? A pirate attack for ransom? Or some global threat?"

"Why not all three?" Alex asked. She'd seen enough Ares operations to know that they almost always included misdirection, or multipronged attacks, or both.

"What if the pirates were here to steal the cargo and…I don't know, sink the ship," Alex said.

"Sinking a cruise ship with six thousand people on board would be very bad," Rebecca said. "And not just for those of us on the ship. It would shut down passenger and probably merchant shipping for an extended period. It would damage the Australian economy and ravage the economy of the Solomon Islands. That would create an opportunity for China to move in."

"Or create an opportunity for someone who wanted regional chaos," Devan said.

"Now that sounds like an Ares operation," Alex said.

"But does that mean we already stopped it?" Devan asked.

"I honestly don't know," Alex said. "In the past, Ares mounted multistage operations and often used local groups as proxies. This could just be the beginning or this could be it. That's certainly possible, given that Ares is spread thin due to the sheer number of operations they have been running worldwide. Or those operations could be the keep the world intelligence community from noticing this one."

"In other words, we don't know anything," Devan said.

"True, but instead of just one of us groping in the dark, there's three," Alex said. She considered telling her new associates that Zeta had another agent on board, but she decided that this was all the trust she could handle for one day.

"We should have dinner tonight and compare notes," Devan said. He said it casually, as if to both Alex and Rebecca, but he was looking intently at Alex.

She recognized the look and knew that she didn't have the time or attention for it. She had one night and one day off. Then it was back to twelve- to fourteen-hour days—on top of her responsibilities trying to prevent a major disaster that would affect the entire region, at least.

"I'm sorry, I have plans," Alex said. "But let's keep our eyes out and keep each other's numbers handy."

# Chapter 29

Morgan hung up the phone to see three pairs of eyes looking at him.

"Well?" Conley asked.

"Shepard found the base," Morgan replied.

"Is he sure?" Conley said.

"Yes, he coordinated the shipping records we found with missing person reports in the area," Morgan said. "There's too much cloud cover to confirm with satellite images right now, but he's pretty sure."

"Is it far? Can we fly or do we need a boat?" Jenny asked.

"It's an island about nine miles from the northern tip of Guadalcanal, just across Ironbottom Sound," Morgan said.

Realization dawned on Conley's face. "Oh," he said.

"What's wrong with that?" Jenny asked.

Morgan shrugged and said, "It's not a good place."

"Why, what's there?" Jenny asked.

"You must be joking, Peter," Dani said.

Jenny was now frustrated and not trying to hide it. "What is there?"

"It's not what's there," Dani said. "It's what happened there during the war."

"We know what happened. After six months of hard fighting, the Americans won the Battle of Guadalcanal," Jenny said.

"Before that battle there was the Battle of Savo Island," Morgan said. "The Japanese fleet had the element of surprise and dealt our forces the worst defeat in the history of the US Navy during actual battle. The reason they named it Ironbottom Sound is because of the number of ships that still lie on the bottom," Morgan said.

"That's it?" Jenny said.

"Jenny, it was the worst—" Morgan began.

Jenny looked at Morgan and then at Conley. "You have got to be kidding me. I don't want to spoil your History Channel moment, but that was a long time ago. So we lost one there and won one here. None of that changes anything we have to do."

"Of course," Morgan said. "I just don't like the history."

"So we'll change it," Jenny said. "How do we get there?"

"No air field, we'll need a boat," Morgan said.

"Then we'd better hurry," Jenny replied. "If we want someone to take us over we should do it quickly. The weather isn't getting any better."

"We can't just yet," Conley said. "Shep's been working on a weapon we can put together to use against Ares. There's some medical equipment we can get locally. Dani, he thought you could make some modifications; he's sending the details. Dan and I can get the actual equipment."

"While you're doing that, Dani and I will work on transport," Jenny said. "You take the truck. We'll work with the front desk and take cabs if we need to."

Morgan liked this. They had an objective and the beginnings of a plan. And if Shepard's weapon worked they might even have a chance.

* * * *

Alex walked up to the nurse at the desk and said, "I'm Alex McGrath, I'm here to see—"

"He's waiting for you. I'll take you right in," the pleasant Filipino nurse said to her with a wide smile.

The woman got up and led Alex through a door and into a short hallway. So far, the sick bay was clean and bright and looked like a modern walk-in clinic.

A middle-aged black man in a lab coat appeared out of an office and said, "Ms. McGrath, I presume."

Alex shook his hand and said, "How is the patient, Doctor?"

She saw that the name tag on his coat said Dr. Benga, Senegal.

"Well," he said. "Mr. Michaels told me that his condition is partly thanks to you," Benga said, with a pleasant French accent.

"I really didn't do much. I was one of the people who applied pressure, and then I asked someone to get him here," Alex said.

"He says you diagnosed his wound. I can confirm that it was through-and-through. Tell me, Ms. McGrath, have you seen a lot of gunshot wounds?"

Alex gave him an awkward smile and said, "Mostly on television."

He nodded and said, "Of course."

"He's okay on board. No need to move him ashore?" she asked.

"He's fine. His wound was cleaned and stitched. We'll watch him for another day to see if there's any infection. Usually we would fly him out, but there's too much wind for the medical helicopter," he said.

That was true. The rain had brought strong winds and rough seas. As if to punctuate his point, the deck shifted slightly under their feet.

"The nurse will see you in," Dr. Benga said and then turned to go back into his office.

The nurse led Alex into one of the exam rooms, where Michaels was sitting up and looking into his laptop—his left arm in a sling. In bed, he looked younger than he did on deck in his tactical gear. Alex guessed that he was maybe twenty-five, good-looking, with sandy brown hair.

He looked up and smiled. "She's here," he said into his computer.

Then he looked up at Alex and said, "Hi." He looked embarrassed and added, "There's someone who wants to say hello to you."

Michaels turned the computer around and on the screen was the image of a blond woman of about Michaels's age. Alex imagined that she would be pretty if she wasn't sobbing.

The woman wiped her eyes, seemed to pull herself together, and said, "Hi Alex, I'm Jess." She stopped to push back a sob and said, "Timothy told me what you did for him, and I wanted to thank you myself. We're getting married in—"

Then Jess lost her fight to hold back the sobs. Alex gave her a minute and during a pause said, "You're welcome, but we all just pitched in. I'm glad that everything worked out."

"—in September," Jess said. Then her image froze.

Michaels turned the laptop back around and punched at the keyboard with one hand.

"I'll have to call her back. Sorry for the ambush, but she wanted to talk to you and the signal has been spotty. I guess the weather. Look, I wanted to thank you too. I was in the National Guard in Virginia for four years. Never called up and never deployed. I'm on the ship less than three months—not even finished my first contract—and then this," he said, glancing down at the sling.

"The doctor said you'll be fine," she said.

"I will, thanks to you and your friends. How did you know what to do? No offense, but you're a server. Yet you seemed pretty in control."

"I am from Boston," she said. Then she realized that sound flippant. "I guess I just watched too much TV with my dad when I was growing up."

That much was true and seemed to satisfy Michaels.

"Thank you. I don't have much pull on the ship, but if you need to get into the comedy club, the bartender there owes me a favor and I can get tickets most nights," he said.

"I will probably take you up on that," she said. "Now I'm going to let you go. See if you can get Jess back on the line. I think it will help her if she sees you some more. I'll check on you tomorrow."

* * * *

Morgan knew things were going well when the hardest part of an operation was driving back. The equipment was safely in the rear of the Ford. Once again, Morgan was grateful for the SUV. There were real roads all the way to the hospital, but they were rough and the rain was heavy.

"Dani says to pull around back and up to the garage," Conley said. "We have it as a work space at least through tomorrow."

That made sense. The island seemed to be shutting down because of the weather. The roads were clear—or even more clear than usual on an island that had little in the way of streetlights or nightlife. And with the high winds keeping planes from taking off or landing, there was little danger of new guests checking into the hotel.

Morgan pulled under the overhang in front of the office entrance to the garage, which had two double doors. It was so far in the back; he hadn't seen the building before. Since the hotel vans and the few guest vehicles he'd seen were parked in an outdoor lot, he assumed it was used primarily for maintenance.

"How did you boys do?" Jenny asked as they got out of the car.

"Well, we got everything on Shepard's list," Morgan said. He opened the back of the SUV, then he and Conley unloaded the equipment while they rolled it through the office door.

"How is this going to shatter their teeth?" Jenny asked.

He pointed to a rectangular box about the size of a waist-high file cabinet. Next to it was a five foot semicircle on a wheeled base. At the top of the circle was a cylinder about the size of a gallon paint cant.

"This is an extracorporeal lithotripter," Morgan said.

Jenny didn't say a word. She just looked at him.

"It breaks up kidney stones with sound blasts," he said. Then he pointed to a second, suitcase-sized piece of equipment. "And that's a sonogram machine."

"They both use sound," Dani said.

"At the right frequency and with enough power, Shepard thinks they'll work," Conley said. "Dani, we're hoping you could make some modifications. Shepard's working on software patches, but some physical tinkering will be required."

Dani examined the equipment and nodded approvingly. "Besides adjusting the frequencies, he'll want to draw out the blasts on the lithotripter. And I assume we'll be tuning the machines to each other to create some constructive interference and take advantage of superposition to get a much more powerful series of waves."

"Right, you can talk to Shep for the details," Morgan said. He turned to Jenny. "How'd we do on transport?"

"Good. It's right in the back," Jenny said, pointing to the interior door that led to the repair floor.

Morgan's heart sank. "I appreciate that you're trying to help, but anything small enough to fit into this space won't be big enough to carry the equipment, let alone the weapons we'll need. We'll have to hire someone to take us."

"I did the best I could, Dan; why don't you take a look and see if you can make do," Jenny said.

Morgan appreciated that she was trying to help, but this was his world. It would cost them some time, but he and Conley would have to find transport tomorrow. Jenny knew something about the water, but this wasn't sailing around Nantucket. This was a mission and had specific tactical requirements.

He pushed through the door, took two steps, and stopped cold. After a few seconds, he realized that he'd forgotten to breathe.

Morgan felt Conley push past him and then stop cold himself.

"Is it?" his friend said.

"It is," Morgan replied. Then Jenny was next to him and he said, "How?"

"You know you can't throw a rock on this island without hitting a plane, or a tank, or a truck from the war."

That was true, Morgan had seen it himself. However, most of those relics were rusted hulks.

"We saw it outside one of the bigger private museums," Jenny continued.

Those museums were run by locals and usually included rusted knives, guns, and helmets. This was something else.

"Does it run?" Morgan asked.

"Yes, but roughly. You'll want to take a look at the engine," she said.

The DUKWs were floating, six-wheel amphibious trucks that could transport equipment and troops over both land and sea. Powered by a General Motors straight-six 369.5 cubic inch engine, they were real workhorses in both theaters during the war. Their watertight hulls made them float and they could literally drive from the beach and into the water, where a propeller in the back took over propulsion.

Morgan had first seen one as kid in Boston where the World War II relics had been painted bright colors and repurposed as "DUKW tour" vehicles. The last time he saw one was when Alex was maybe twelve, and they had taken one of the land-and-water tours around Boston. Morgan usually avoided tourist attractions, but he loved the DUKW vehicles.

This one was a faded and rusted version of the Army green, but it looked like it was in reasonably good condition.

"The man had it on display, but he was also using it as a truck," Jenny said.

That made sense. Planes and tanks had very little use to the islanders, but these would have come in very handy. Nevertheless, Morgan was still impressed that the DUKW was still not just running but making itself useful.

"Do you think she can make it?" he said, circling the vehicle. It was open in the back, which was large enough to fit a midsized car.

"She runs and the propeller works," Jenny said. "But you'll want to see what you can do with the engine. I have concerns about the rudder system, and it will definitely not make nine miles both ways unless we redo the seals. Plus you'll have to get the bilge pump working. Otherwise, if she starts taking water she'll go down in ten minutes."

Morgan took a moment to scan around the garage. It was reasonably well-kept but he wouldn't know if he had what he needed until he got started. Since the islands were controlled for so long by the British, most of the tools would be metric, but like Jenny said, he'd have to make do.

Dani had wheeled the medical equipment into the repair bays and Conley immediately started sizing up the job with her.

Jenny was inspecting the propeller and manually working the rudder in the back with a frown on her face. Morgan walked around front, climbed up onto the vehicle, and found the latch that would open the beast's hood and reveal the engine.

# Chapter 30

The rocking of the ship woke Alex up. That was unusual. Everyone with experience on board told her that yesterday's rough seas would pass by morning. Checking her phone, there was a crew-wide message from the captain that said all on-deck activities were cancelled for the day. Also, there was a weather advisory for the storm. It seemed that rough seas, high winds, and rains would persist throughout the day. There was also the possibility that the storm would turn into a tropical cyclone—which is what Alex knew they called hurricanes south of the equator. The crew was monitoring the situation, and in the unlikely event of a cyclone, they would turn around and make port in Brisbane.

Alex also had a message from Sorina thanking her for coming to Eric's show. Her former roommate gushed about how talented Eric was and then she mentioned that she and Eric would be having breakfast. Notably, Sorina didn't invite Alex, which Alex took as a good sign.

There were also messages from Rebecca and Devan, who wanted to meet with her as soon as possible. That was something she could act on. It was time. If they were going to be allies on this cruise, it was time to start figuring out how that would work. She would also have to set up a meeting to brief Schmitt on Rebecca and Devan's existence. Since she was off all day, it shouldn't be hard to meet with Alicia in person.

But first things first. She made arrangements with Rebecca and Devan and started to get ready.

\* \* \* \*

Morgan woke with a start and saw that Jenny was already up and dressed. "Why didn't you wake me?"

"I wanted you to get a full three hours, and I looked out the window," Jenny said.

Morgan took a look himself. He saw heavy rain falling nearly sideways due to the strong wind. He checked his phone and saw a message from Bloch at Zeta. There was a pirate attack on Alex's ship, but the pirates had been repelled.

"You saw the message from Diana?" Jenny asked.

"Yes," Morgan replied. "Bloch says that Alex was involved peripherally and her cover wasn't compromised." That was something.

"Do you think that's it? Do you think that's the end of the trouble?"

"No," Morgan said. He wouldn't lie to his wife now. And even if he did, she would see right through it. "If Ares was behind the pirate attack, it won't be that easy. And they won't give up if their plan involves the ship. Even if it doesn't, there's a base on Savo Island. And Alex will be on the ship for the next three months. Ares can simply wait for another opportunity. As long as they are there, they're a threat."

"Not with the tropical storm coming. There's even talk that it might turn into a hurricane. They'll be stuck in their base through the bad weather," Jenny said.

"They'll also be at their most vulnerable," Morgan replied.

There was a symmetry there. The Battle of Savo Island was such a disaster for the American Navy because Japan's Vice Admiral Mikawa's seven-ship task force took the American naval forces completely by surprise. If Morgan and Peter could do the same with Ares, maybe they could get the same result as Mikawa.

"There's only one problem," Jenny said. "The same weather will ground us."

"Maybe," Morgan said.

"No, Dan, not maybe. These things are designed to be stable and to land on beaches, but it's still a floating truck. If it gets rough out there, it will turn over and sink like one."

Morgan knew she was right. Jenny had been sailing since she was a girl, and she definitely knew boats. Given the stakes for Alex, if Jenny said it wouldn't work, it just wouldn't.

"Then we wait for our moment. In the meantime we'll finish the work on the DUKW and on Shepard's weapon," Morgan said.

If the storm broke soon and Morgan and Conley were ready to go, maybe they could still catch Ares when they weren't ready. Though by the look of things outside, the storm wouldn't be breaking any time soon.

His father had rarely talked about his experience in this part of the world during the Second World War, but the elder Morgan had said it was always raining and he was wet, or muddy, or both for weeks at a time.

Looking at the constant, heavy rain, Morgan believed it.

Yet the rain would give Morgan time to open up the DUKW's gearbox and properly grease the propeller transfer. He'd also recheck the steering and the lines from the steering system to the rudder. It was a lot of work, but it looked like they would have time.

Morgan and Jenny met with Peter and Dani, ate quickly, and were back at the garage in half an hour. Shepard's weapon was coming along well. Dani had loaded the new software while Peter had mounted the spherical emitter directly to the side of the squat unit itself. That was very good. It reduced the weight by eliminating the heavy half-circle base that was designed to position the emitter over a patient who was lying on a table.

On the other side of the waist-high device, they had mounted the sonogram unit. The wand of the sonogram machine was now facing the same direction as the emitter and was surrounded by the metal cone from a portable work light, making it look like a radar dish. The end result was something that looked like a cross between the scariest medical device ever and a dangerous weapon—which, Morgan supposed, it was.

There was a bolt of lightning and the lights in the garage flickered.

"We'll need power for this thing," Conley said. "Even if Ares lets us plug in, there's always the chance that the power will go out."

Morgan had considered that. Even if he could come up with a transducer, the DUKW's twelve-volt power supply wouldn't be strong enough. He pointed to a portable generator sitting in the corner. It was 8500 watts and would do the trick…if he could get it working.

That was another thing for his to-do list.

Just then, Morgan, Conley, and Dani's phones all chimed. Morgan saw there was a message from Shepard.

To Jenny he said, "Shep says they pulled some recent satellite images. There's definitely a base of some kind there, operating out of an old Japanese bunker. The local government clearly either doesn't know about it, or is looking the other way. They've been receiving a lot of cargo out of an old World War Two port and sending stuff out. They also have a helipad on-site. They're not connected to the local grid, but they're generating lots of their own power."

"How?" Jenny asked.

"Looks like geothermal," Morgan said. He read the next line and a wide smile broke out across his face. He looked up and saw the Conley had seen it too.

"You're kidding me?" Conley said through his own smile.

"What is it? What could possible be amusing about this?" Jenny asked, exasperated.

"The facility is at the base of an active volcano," Morgan said.

"So?" Jenny asked. "As long as it doesn't erupt, what's the difference?"

"Well, the point is that we're planning an assault on the terrorist group's secret lair, which is powered by an active volcano," Morgan said.

Jenny's face went from confused to annoyed remarkably quickly. "So this is a game to you both?"

"Not a game, but it's—" Morgan started.

"Forget it," Jenny replied. Turning to Dani, she said, "Can you believe—" Then Jenny noticed that Dani was smiling as well.

"What, you like this too?"

Dani shook her head. "No. Well, yes. But I just like volcanoes."

"Our first date in the Philippines—" Conley began.

"Really, I don't need to know. Why don't we all just get back to work," Jenny said as she headed to the DUKW.

\* \* \* \*

Devan and Rebecca were already at breakfast when Alex arrived. They chose one of the guest-only cafés far from the lido deck. Technically, Alex and Rebecca were breaking the rules, but Devan was a guest so Alex would risk a reprimand later.

"My people don't think the threat has passed," Alex said.

"Mine aren't sure," Rebecca said. "But the pirate attack could have been an operation to grab the laser prototype. Of course, we won't know for sure until we make port."

"Which port?" Alex said. "I know that if the storm gets worse, they're considering turning around."

"Possibly," Devan offered. "But depending on the severity of the storm, the open sea might be safer than port."

"So we can all agree that we don't know anything," Alex said. "Except that July hasn't been unlucky for us."

"It's only the middle of the month," Rebecca said.

"MI6 doesn't have anything specific either. I've been instructed, alternately, to remain vigilant and to be careful."

"I don't know about you both," Alex said. "But that describes what I need to be every single day of my job."

While they ate and chatted, Alex came to a decision. If the three of them were going to work together, she needed to be honest with her new partners.

"We have another agent on board," Alex said. "She's got naval experience and she's signed on as consultant to oversee the installation of and training for a new navigation system. She's working with the senior crew as well as the engineering and IT staff. She was already able to help them eliminate some of the pirate teams. She also has access to communications, navigational, and security equipment."

"Can she get me into the cargo hold to inspect the laser?" Rebecca asked.

"Not without blowing her cover, but if it becomes necessary, probably," Alex said. "For now, she'll know if anything unusual happens."

"So we have nothing to do but wait and enjoy the ship," Devan said.

"Maybe you do, but we have to get back to work tomorrow," Alex said.

From Alex's point of view, that wasn't a bad thing. She would try to relax a little today, but she knew she'd spend most of her free time wandering the ship, looking for anything out of the ordinary.

After that, work would be a welcome distraction.

The ship lurched under them again.

Then Alex realized that something was off in the café. For several seconds, it went dead quiet. Then there was a buzz of conversation, and the beginnings of an actual commotion outside in the corridors.

Alex's phone beeped, telling her there was a message from Schmitt.

**There's been an attack. Automatic weapons fired on board. Wait for info,** it said.

"What is it, Alex?" Rebecca asked.

"I don't know yet," Alex said. "But whatever we've been waiting for, it's started."

# Chapter 31

"Thank you for breakfast, Jack," Schmitt said.

"You're welcome, but I can't take all of the credit. As a contract employee, your meals are provided by the cruise line," Watson replied.

She gave him one of her rare—and dazzling—smiles. "Then thank you for the company."

"That was my pleasure, Ms. Schmitt," Watson said. "The captain has a short reception this morning, and then he will be busy with his incident report for most of the day. However, he wanted me to invite you to his table for dinner so he can thank you properly for your assistance yesterday."

"Of course," Schmitt said.

Watson headed to the bridge. He was also quite busy today. Besides assisting the captain with his report, Watson had all of his regular duties, plus he had to inspect the lido deck so it could be cleared for passenger use when the weather finally broke.

The storm had calmed a bit, but he didn't like the long-term forecast and they would be watching the storm carefully to see if there was any chance of it becoming a cyclone.

Once again, Schmitt and her new system would be very helpful there. Though his schedule was tight, he decided it might be worth asking her to lunch so they could discuss it.

"Good morning, Captain," Watson said when he entered the bridge. Garrett was early today, which made sense, given all they had to do.

"Good morning, Jack," Garrett replied.

Watson called each of the department heads to take their morning reports. At nine exactly he said to the captain, "It's time, sir. Mr. Giotto reports that his staff has assembled," Watson said.

The entire team was waiting for their reception with the captain to begin. It was a thank-you from Garrett to the team, and there was no doubt they deserved it. It would be an informal buffet-style meal with the captain—who many in the department had met once, if at all.

Before Watson could reply, a call came through from the Australian coast guard to the captain. Watson informed Giotto there would be a brief wait, and fifteen minutes later the captain was off the line.

As soon as he hung up, the comm panel at the captain's station beeped and Garrett hit the speaker button. "I'll be right down, Mr. Giotto. Tell the—"

The immediate reply was a scream, which was then followed by Giotto's voice. "Captain—" There was shouting in the background. "There's been a breach—"

What followed next was the unmistakable sound of automatic gunfire, followed by more shouts, and then more screams. The voices died down after less than half a minute, but the gunfire continued for long seconds afterward.

*All of them are in there*, Watson thought.

Had more pirates somehow boarded the ship? Had one or more slipped on during yesterday's confrontation? And had they just executed every security and safety officer on board?

Watson was afraid that he already knew the answer to that question.

If someone was really taking the ship. He knew where their next stop would be. He had to stop himself from calling Giotto or one of his security officers. For a moment he didn't know what to do next, then the captain's voice cut through the haze that had descended on his brain.

"Call down to Cabato, tell him to lock down," Garrett said.

As Watson made the call, he realized something awful. Whoever had attacked the security team had known they would be there. In fact, if he hadn't been delayed by the local coast guard, the captain would have been there as well.

That thought, however, made him feel better. If they still had Garrett, they still had a chance. Whatever was happening, the captain had probably seen it—or something worse—before.

The comm line to the engine room wasn't responding, so he tried his only remaining option. He went to the new navigation panel, hit the direct line to the engine room panel, and said, "Schmitt. Get Cabato over to you. There's been an attack. There was automatic gunfire and there are armed intruders on board."

Before any reply could come, the doors on both sides of the bridge flung open and two men with guns raced in from each side. The four gunmen were dressed in all-black tunics and pants.

They also all carried rifles. Watson didn't know much about guns, but they looked dangerous, and he'd heard machine-gun fire in the security lounge. He had no doubt they could wipe out the bridge crew just as effectively as they had the ship's three-dozen security and safety personnel.

One of the men stepped toward the center, where the captain was standing and said, "Hands up. The first person to hit a Mayday will die."

The captain's hands went up, and all of the bridge officers followed suit.

"Captain," the man in black said when he was directly in front of Garrett. Like the others, he was a fit man in his early to mid-thirties.

"Yes, I'm Captain Garrett. Who are you and what do you want?"

"You can call me Mr. Sticks," the man said. "As for what I want, that is not something you need to concern yourself with. Your reputation precedes you, Captain, and I want you to know that this is not personal."

There was a blur of motion as in a single movement, Mr. Sticks drew a pistol, pointed it directly at Garrett's forehead, and fired.

Even as his mind screamed to Watson that what he was seeing was not possible, the captain fell to the deck.

* * * *

*Oh my God, Jack*, Schmitt thought as she listened to what was happening on the bridge.

Cabato shouted something in Italian and then came closer to the speaker. "The captain..." he said.

"And I think they hit the security reception," Schmitt said.

There were groans and exclamations from the lieutenants, who leaned in closer to the speaker on the console. Watson had left the line open. Whatever happened next, they would hear it.

Schmitt composed and sent a short text message to Alex to tell her partner what little they knew.

The next voice from the bridge was one that Schmitt didn't recognize. "Mr. Watson, I regretted having to do that, but it was important that you understand that we are very serious. I know that you can run the ship and get me what I want. If you are thinking about resisting, your captain's death will serve as an example of what will happen to you and anyone on this crew who doesn't follow my instructions to the letter. Do you understand?"

"Yes, I understand," Watson's voice said.

"Good, that will save time and save lives, starting with your own," the man who called himself Sticks said. "First, I want you to get me a direct line to the engine room."

A moment later, the comm panel at Chief Cabato's station beeped.

The chief looked at it wide-eyed and then got up.

"No, Chief, you can't," she said.

He looked at her and said, "You heard what he said."

"I did, and I heard what he did to the captain. They don't know about the comm panel on the new system, so they expect to talk to you on the regular comms. You can't do that. You can't give them anything they want, and you can't even talk to them. Look, I don't know if we can save the ship, but I know that our only chance is to disrupt their plans. So far, they've killed almost forty members of the crew, including the captain. And Watson has a gun to his head, which means he's compromised—and that means you are in command right now. As soon as you start talking to Sticks, you put him in charge. Now, I can help you, but I can't give the orders that you can."

In an instant, Cabato's face went from that of a baffled man who had just had his entire world shattered, to an officer who was ready to act. "What can we do?"

"Don't answer the comm. Better yet, shut down the circuit. In fact, can you shut down all inter-ship comms and phones?"

His eyes went wide, and he said, "Yes, but—"

"Then do it. It will be like what we did to the pirates. If they can't communicate with each other, they can't coordinate. And if they can't threaten us, they won't have any reason to act on their threats," she said.

Then Watson's voice came through the public address system. "To all passengers and crew, this is First Officer Watson. The *Grandeur* has been taken by a group led by a Mr. Sticks. He has killed the captain, but he assures me that no one else will be harmed as long as all crew do precisely as instructed. Please cooperate with any and all members of this group, and this will be over soon."

"We need to shut it all down," Schmitt said.

Cabato nodded and barked out orders to one of his men in the control room, who quickly went to work.

"Then can you shut down power to the ship-to-shore and satellite transmitter?" she asked.

"Yes," he said, barking out another series of orders.

Watson's voice resumed. "Passengers are free to move about the ship as long as they don't interfere with the new command team. All crew should resume normal duties," Watson said.

That was bad. Most people would stay in their cabins, but some would venture out. And if the crew remained at their posts, that would give Sticks and his men an endless supply of hostages to threaten at will.

"Chief," Schmitt said.

"That's public address and inter-ship comms. Also Wi-Fi. They're out," he said.

That was a start.

"Now we've cut ship-to-shore and satellite," he said.

That was also good. It meant that Sticks wouldn't be able to negotiate with any outside government or contact confederates nearby. He would be cut off.

She'd have to scan all frequencies to see if they were using walkie-talkies. If they were, she could use the same jamming tactic she'd used on the pirates. Sticks and his team might also have satellite phones, but she might be able to jam that signal on board ship as well. However, she'd prefer not to because once she did that, she eliminated any chance she had of calling out to Zeta.

That gave her an idea. The team at Zeta might be able to temporarily disrupt the satellite phone signal in this area, and perhaps even shut off whatever phones Sticks and his team were using.

Of course, Sticks would still be roaming the ship with who-knew-how-many heavily armed men, but she had to focus on one problem at a time.

"And Chief, there are two more things we need to do right away. One, you need to lock us in. And two, you need to shut down the helm on the bridge."

"The doors are locked now. There is only one way in," he said.

"I've seen the doors. They're steel and reasonably strong. I'm guessing it will take them twenty minutes to break through when they figure out what we've done," she said.

"We can close the watertight doors outside of the engineering area manually. Once that's done, it would take a welding team and a few hours to get through," he said.

"Once we shut off their controls, they will have nothing but time. And they will be very committed," she said.

"Maybe, but all of the welding equipment on the ship will be on this side of the doors," Cabato said.

That was something, Schmitt realized. And it would give them time to come up with a real plan.

"And they'll want to use the ship's security cameras to keep an eye on things," she said. The fact was that the law now required virtually all public spaces to be covered by security cameras.

"Cut all feeds to the security offices," she said.

Cabato nodded grimly at the reminder that every security and safety officer on board the ship was dead. If those feeds were kept running, the only ones to see the images would be the people who had murdered them.

Twenty minutes later, it was done. All communications were shut down within the ship—with one notable exception. The Renard Tech system had its own signal that would allow Schmitt to contact Alex through her Zeta phone. Depending on where Alex was on the ship, voice communication might not be possible. However, there would be enough signal almost everywhere for texts. The system would also maintain a line between the bridge and the engine room—if Schmitt could figure out how to use it without getting Watson killed.

"What now?" Cabato asked.

"Now we figure out how to fight back and retake the ship," she said to the chief and the four assembled lieutenants. "There's another Renard Tech–affiliated person up there. She has some training and can help. And I understand she has some allies as well. We'll offer support from here, but I want you to think of this ship as a weapon. You people know it better than anyone. Think of every accident and malfunction you've ever seen, heard of, or trained to avoid. I can watch the security feeds from here. Once we identify where these people are and how they move, we can figure out how to defeat them."

Cabato and his men had taken a blow. Their leader and their friends had been killed and they were facing long odds. But when she looked at their faces she didn't see any of that, she simply saw purpose.

They returned to their stations and got to work.

Schmitt didn't doubt her move to cut off communication with Sticks and his men. It was never a good idea to negotiate with people of that kind. And communication gave them leverage. The hijackers on 9/11 had gained entry to the cockpits of passenger jets by holding knives to the throats of the flight crew.

Here, Schmitt had cut off their ability to even threaten violence. What would Sticks and his people do now, when they had already killed Captain Garrett to insure compliance? Nevertheless, Schmitt was sure she'd done the right thing.

However, she was just as sure that she'd signed Jack Watson's death warrant.

# Chapter 32

"They killed the captain and every security officer on board," Rebecca said in disbelief as they headed to Alex's cabin. Rebecca seemed to be an experienced agent, but the brutality and suddenness of what Ares had done had shocked her. Alex knew how the woman felt. However, this was not the first time she'd come face-to-face with Ares's handiwork.

"That means we have to assume they have control of all ship's weapons," Devan said.

"Yes, so we only have what we brought or what we can put together," Alex said. There were still possibilities there. After all, they had taken out committed, heavily armed pirate teams with towels, a desert cart, and café tables. Who knew what they could come up with when they had a full ten minutes to think about it?

They reached Alex and Rebecca's cabin and stepped inside.

"Our chief advantage is that we know the ship and they don't. My partner says they are mostly patrolling the guest areas," Alex said. That made sense: those areas were well-marked with plenty of maps telling the guests where they were and signs telling them how to get to important locations. The crew areas, on the other hand, were notoriously hard to navigate with no helpful signs.

That had been one of Alex's chief complaints on both her training ship and the *Grandeur*. But like everyone else who joined the crew, she'd had to memorize the layout of the ship.

According to Schmitt, it looked like the Ares gunmen had been on board since the beginning of the cruise, posing as passengers. Thus, it was safe to assume they understood the ship as passengers did.

"They can always commandeer crew to get them around, but their default will probably be to stick to the guest areas—if for no other reason than those spaces are nicer," Alex said.

Ares might be cold, brutal killers who would stop at nothing to achieve their objectives, but human nature was human nature.

"We still don't know what they want," Devan said.

"I'd say the laser is a safe bet," Alex replied. "At least it's somewhere to start. And my rule with Ares is that just imagine the worst thing they could possibly do, and you'll be on the right track. Now, I need to get my weapon."

"I searched your things," Rebecca said. "There's nothing here."

"You went through my stuff? Really?" Alex said.

Rebecca gave a sheepish shrug and replied, "I thought you were with them."

"You searched by looking for places I could have stashed something," Alex said, retrieving her Swiss Army knife from her bedside. She opened it and jammed the blade into the tiny gap between the small bathroom's mirror and the wall. "However, my people placed this while I was still in training."

The mirror came free of the wall, and from the now-open space, Alex retrieved her weapon, holster, and spare clips. She took pleasure in the look of surprise on Rebecca and Devan's faces. "In our business, there are some advantages to working in the private sector."

Alex put on her shoulder holster and added a clip to her Smith & Wesson 9mm.

"What is our plan?" Rebecca asked.

"I say we go out and kill the bad guys before they kill us and everyone else on board," Alex said.

"I love the enthusiasm, but where are we on details?" Devan said.

"I can't do all the work here," Alex replied.

"We could stake out the laser," Rebecca said.

Alex thought about that for a second and said, "That's actually a good idea. Of course, we'll have to find it first."

Her phone beeped and Alex saw a message from Schmitt. She read it out loud: *"Looks like twenty armed Ares men. They're moving in four-man fire teams. They all seem to have small arms and AKs. If they have grenades or anything heavier, it's not showing on the security cameras. And they've definitely emptied the weapons lockers."*

"That's a shame; we could have used one of those semiautomatic flare guns," Devan said. "Even regular flares would be something at this point."

"No chance. We know they've taken all weapons and most likely any safety equipment that could be used as weapons," Rebecca said.

That was true, Alex thought, since Ares had definitely emptied the security lockers. On the other hand, she realized, not all of the flares on board were in lockers.

"Lifeboats…" Alex said.

"What?" Devan asked.

"Each lifeboat has four parachute flares and six hand flares," Alex said, remembering the safety information drilled into her during her training. "And that's not all. There are two hatchets and a jackknife in each boat. Even the compact fire extinguishers would be useful."

"How do we know that the Ares men haven't thought of that?" Devan asked.

"They might have, but we almost didn't. And remember, they were expecting to have access to security cameras and instant communications. Now they have to physically patrol the ship, and their fire teams are cut off from their command structure and each other. Even if they've thought of it, they don't have time to strip fifty lifeboats of anything useful, not if they are going to maintain control of the ship and achieve their objectives."

Alex reached into her closet and grabbed the only piece of civilian clothing she had that would also properly hide her weapon—her tan, collarless riding jacket. It was light enough that it wouldn't look suspicious indoors, and it also had interior breast pockets that would carry her spare clips.

There were a few seconds of familiar noise coming from the corridor. Alex had just identified the sound as Sorina's voice when her cabin door pushed open and Sorina stepped inside. Speechless for a moment, the woman looked at Devan, Rebecca, and Alex, who was wearing her holster over her polo shirt and holding her gun.

"Alex," Sorina final said. "We came to make sure—" And then the Romanian's eyes fixed on Alex's weapon. "What is—" she began.

Eric entered behind Sorina, and the cabin went from a little tight to downright crowded. "Close the door, Eric," Alex said as she holstered her weapon.

He looked at her warily and closed the door behind him.

Sorina was still processing what she was seeing and said, "Why are you wearing that?"

"Are you with the terrorists?" Eric asked, his voice firm.

"No, in fact, I'm going to go out and try to stop them," Alex replied. Sorina looked at her as if she had just announced she was joining the circus. "Look," Alex continued. "I'm a security consultant for US intelligence. They put me here because there were reports that an attack like this might happen."

Because they were short on time, Alex came to a quick decision. "Sorina and Eric, this is Devan and Rebecca. Devan is with British intelligence, and Rebecca is with the Taiwanese intelligence service. We were all put on board the way you would put air marshals on a plane."

"That's why you were able to help with the pirates," Eric said.

"Yes," Alex replied.

"Can you stop them?" Sorina asked.

"I don't know. Besides the captain, they have also killed the entire security and safety staff. We're on our own, but they are not expecting any resistance, so we'll see. There's another agent on my team in the engine room who was able to shut down their communications."

"Our cell phones are out too," Eric said.

Alex nodded. "That was the only way."

"I want to help," Eric said. "You know that I did two tours in the Middle East."

"Yes, I want to help as well," Sorina said.

"Really, the best thing you can do is go back to one of your cabins and keep your heads down," Alex said.

Before Eric could reply, Rebecca interjected, "There is something they can do: the lifeboats."

Alex hadn't thought of that. She presumed Eric could handle himself and Sorina had gotten lifeboat training, as did the whole crew. At that moment, Alex realized she just didn't want them involved. She didn't want to have to worry about Sorina, but that was selfish on her part. Alex wasn't going to deny the woman the chance to contribute, especially now that she had something to fight for.

"Okay," Alex said and then laid out the plan. "The focus is on the flares. Grab as many as you can, and bring a pack or something to carry them in."

"What are you going to use them for?" Eric asked.

"I have no idea, we'll improvise," Alex said.

"What about the knives and hatchets?" Sorina asked. "We can't carry them all, but we can stow them in the life-preserver lockers at the lifeboat stations."

That was a good idea, Alex realized. The lockers were just outside the lifeboats and were easily accessible. It would be nice to have ready weapons if they found themselves in a fight on deck.

"Start in the back of the ship at number forty-two and work your way forward. We can always follow your trail and catch up to you. We won't be able to communicate, so let's agree to muster in the lounge behind the Four Corners bar in one hour," Alex said. Then she leaned in to Sorina and whispered, "Thank you for doing this, but be careful. The seas are rough. Just climbing in and out of the lifeboats will be dangerous."

Sorina smiled and cupped her cheek. "You worry too much, princess. I'll see you soon."

A moment later Sorina and Eric had disappeared into the corridor.

"Where do we go first?" Devan asked.

Alex checked her phone quickly and read the last message from Schmitt. "One of the fire teams is on deck five, nosing around the cargo areas," Alex said.

"That means they're looking for something," Rebecca said.

"Probably your laser," Devan added.

"And they will never be more vulnerable. They won't expect anyone to fight back. I say we give them a surprise," Alex said, heading into the corridor with her new friends behind her.

\* \* \* \*

Cabato conferred with one of his men and then came over to Schmitt.

"They got the Wi-Fi system up, probably with crew from IT helping them," Cabato said. Before Schmitt could speak, he raised his hand and said, "Don't worry, we cut the power. Even if they can run a line from somewhere else, it will take time, and we'll cut that circuit too."

Cabato and his engine room team had done an excellent job of disrupting the Ares forces so far, but it required constant effort from all of them. Ares had retrieved backup walkie-talkies from the security offices and had actually set up basic communication between the teams, until Schmitt had been able to identify the frequency and generate a jamming signal. Ares then changed the frequency and Schmitt had followed suit. In the end, Cabato had assigned a man whose job it was now to play whack-a-mole with the frequency changes.

"It's okay," Cabato said. "If they are running around playing with their walkie-talkies, they aren't doing anything...worse."

That was true. However, Ares did have access to people from every department on the ship and could force them at gunpoint to do just about anything. Eventually, they would likely figure out that they could stop the jamming by sabotaging the ship's transmission towers.

For the moment, Schmitt was out of tricks for disrupting their plans. She hoped Alex came up with something soon.

Schmitt saw a light flashing on her board and realized it was a weather alert. That surprised her, since she'd cut the ship off from the outside world, she'd stopped receiving real-time satellite weather updates.

This alert must have come from the system itself, which couldn't see nearly as far as the satellite weather services.

Calling up the weather readings, Schmitt saw what she had missed.

"What is it?" Cabato asked.

"It's a tropical cyclone," Schmitt said. "It's coming from the north, and it's getting closer."

"Protocol would be to head back to Brisbane and lock the ship down in port," Cabato said.

"We have no way of knowing what the attackers would do," Schmitt said.

"True, but they know the protocols. They certainly knew the protocol for a reception after a major security incident and took advantage of it to murder an entire department," Cabato said. He thought for a moment and asked, "Do you think there is any chance they will let us make port in Brisbane?"

"No," Schmitt said. "I don't think we'd make it. There's a reason they struck while we were at sea."

"Then I say we turn into the storm," Cabato said. "We know we can do our jobs in a cyclone. If nothing else, they will make less trouble if we keep knocking them to the deck."

Schmitt couldn't argue with the chief's logic. So far, their strategy had been to disrupt Ares's plans and a storm like this was about as big a disruption as they could get.

Cabato gave the order and turned the ship on a course straight into the swirling mass of clouds that made up the storm.

That done, Cabato huddled with his entire team, looking over one of their consoles. Schmitt decided that she didn't like their body language one bit.

Schmitt got up from her station and walked over. "What is it, Chief?" she asked.

"They have started launching lifeboats," Cabato said.

"Why would they do that, are they abandoning—" She didn't finish the question. There was only one reason she could think of for Ares to launch the lifeboats: When they had whatever they came for, they intended to sink the *Grandeur.*

And they wanted no survivors.

Compared to that, heading full speed into a hurricane looked much more appealing.

# Chapter 33

"It's a hurricane, Dan, or whatever they call them here," Jenny said. "You know there's just nothing you can do." As soon as she said it, his wife caught herself and added, "At least right now. Not until it clears."

*There's nothing you can do*, Morgan thought. He always hated hearing that, and he hated it most of all when it was true.

"They're calling it Cyclone Maeve," Conley added.

There was something familiar about that name. Something his daughter had told him recently. Then he remembered. Maeves was the name of a female motorcycle gang. Apparently, they were pretty tough.

The leading edge of the cyclone had just hit the island and based on the heavy winds, he knew it was going to get much worse before it got better.

Morgan knew the storm would also hit Alex's ship directly if it kept to its original course, but how likely was that now? According to the last report from Bloch, Ares gunmen had murdered dozens of people on board and taken the ship. After that, Schmitt had shut down communications, so Zeta had no idea what was happening.

They did know that Alex and Schmitt were there on their own, facing a superior, heavily armed force. And Ares had a base on Savo Island that could provide support or extraction as soon as the weather cleared.

In fact, Ares had a helipad on-site and could get to the *Grandeur* in ten minutes or less. Whereas the DUKW could do maybe six-and-a-half miles an hour in calm seas. It would take Morgan and Conley at least an hour and a half to get to Savo. In that time, an Ares helicopter could get to the ship and back three or four times if they wanted to.

And there would be nothing that Morgan could do...

*Damn*, he thought.

And the DUKW was ready. It wasn't right off the assembly line, but Morgan had no doubt it was operating better than it had in decades. The DUKW would almost definitely make it to Savo, but it would probably be too slow to make a difference.

"Alex can handle herself, Dan," Conley said. "And she's not alone. Schmitt is there."

*But I'm not*, Morgan thought.

"Dan, do you want to head back to the hotel?" Jenny asked.

"No," he said. "I want to wait it out here."

When the weather broke, he wanted to get onto the DUKW and be on his way. It would only save a few minutes, and given the situation, that would probably not make any difference.

But Morgan was determined to do what he could.

\* \* \* \*

They're on deck 6. They just left cargo hold 4 and seem to be headed for cargo hold 5, the message from Schmitt read.

*Finally*, Alex thought. For once they might be ahead of Ares. If they hurried, they could get to the hold first. Alex and her team ran. The crew corridors were almost empty. The people they did see had the same look—more numb than scared. That made sense. This had been going on for a while, and people could only keep up the extreme fear response for so long.

The storm been helpful there. While Ares had instructed crew to maintain their routines, the increasingly rough weather had made that impossible.

The crew-only stairwell dropped Alex's group right next to the cargo hold's large double doors. "Devan, you stay inside the stairwell in case any of them get past us. Rebecca, come with me."

Inside, the cargo hold was two decks tall and full of pallets of what looked like computer equipment. Alex knew there was talk of a major upcoming IT upgrade, and she assumed this equipment was going to be used for that.

The two women picked spots about twenty feet from the door and about that far apart from one another. They each had good cover and would catch the fire team in a solid cross fire. They had a few seconds, so Alex racked back the slide on her weapon to chamber a round and then put in a fresh clip, giving her a full load plus one bullet.

As soon as that was done, Alex heard voices outside. Then one of the double doors opened and a single black-clad figure slipped inside.

Like all Ares operatives Alex had seen, he was fit and in his early thirties. He was also black. She had now seen white Europeans, Latin Americans, and black operatives. Whatever else you could say about Ares, they had managed to recruit a diverse group of murderers.

Alex definitely approved of his attire, which was some sort of formfitting long-sleeved tunic that was not covered with any sort of body armor. That was an unfortunate choice for them, but made sense when they didn't expect any armed resistance. Working without armor was more comfortable and gave them more freedom of movement.

One at a time, the others slipped into the hold. All four men now scanned the room with their weapons cocked and pointed forward. They may not have been expecting resistance, but they weren't stupid.

However, they were still in the open and made good targets.

Alex said, "Now!" and opened fire, putting two rounds into the chest of one of the men on her side while she heard Rebecca's pistol fire. Alex just had time to shift to the second target when she saw the man's AK-47 swing in her direction and open fire with a spray of automatic fire as she heard one of the men on Rebecca's side do the same.

Alex barely had time to pull her head down and weapon back. From Alex's quick glimpse of the AKs she thought they carried standard, thirty-round clips. When she'd counted off about that number, she popped her head and weapon out from cover and fired at the only target she saw: a single gunman who was standing in front of the door. He was in the middle of replacing his clip when she hit him directly in the chest. Now there were three bodies on the deck of the hold.

Then she heard two shots from in the corridor. She hoped those shots were Devan's, and the entire Ares team was dead.

Carefully, Alex stepped away from her cover as Rebecca did the same. "You okay?" Alex called out.

"Yes, you?" Rebecca replied.

"Yeah, but I can't say the same for these three," Alex said.

All of them were motionless and had dropped their weapons, but Alex and Rebecca approached them cautiously. The two women checked their pulses and confirmed that they were all dead.

There were two quick raps on the door and Devan's voice said, "Alex? Rebecca?"

"We're coming out," Alex said and pulled open the door.

Devan was outside, looking down on the man on the floor. The Ares operative had a wound in his chest, but he was still breathing, though each breath was labored.

Leaning down, Devan gave the man a shake, "Hey, we want to talk to you."

"No!" Alex said, pulling at Devan's arm, but it was too late. The Ares man opened his eyes and took in the three people standing over him.

"Don't do it!" Alex shouted at the man, but she could see him working his jaw.

His eyes met Alex's, and he grinned briefly before his body was wracked with convulsions. In half a minute he was still and Alex didn't have to check to know that he was dead.

"What was that?" Devan asked.

"Cyanide tooth," Alex replied. "They don't allow themselves to be taken alive."

"I didn't think he had long, but a few answers would have been nice," Devan said.

"We have sixteen more chances," Alex replied.

Alex insisted on dragging the bodies into a nearby supply closet so that any other fire teams who came looking for the men near the cargo hold would be left wondering.

The four weapons and four sidearms were a different problem. Alex didn't want to leave them, but it wasn't safe to carry the AKs openly—not with four more fire teams roaming the ship.

Their compromise was to bring them up two floors to a guest floor and stuff them all in a housekeeping cart. Then they headed up to the lido deck level and wheeled the cart through the lounge to the lifeboat 42 station.

It was quiet outside and the first thing Alex did was check the safety locker. There was a hand-scrawled S near the latch. It was written in red lipstick.

*Sorina*, Alex thought. That was clever. Tagging the lockers she and Eric filled with supplies from the lifeboats would help them identify the lockers with weapons later.

Sure enough, inside the locker were a few flares, one hatchet, and two compact fire extinguishers. Alex took the flares and extinguishers while she put the guns from the cart inside.

"What now?" Rebecca asked.

"I say we take the bridge," Alex said. "I presume that's where their leader is."

"I thought it was cut off?" Devan said.

"It is, but their original plan was to operate from there, and they haven't adapted their new circumstances," Alex said.

"What do you mean?" Rebecca said.

"They lost surveillance and communications," Alex said. "But they are still moving in four-man fire teams—despite the fact that two-man teams would give them better coverage of the ship. Because they have stuck with their original plan, they just lost twenty percent of their forces at once. That's the problem with rigid, evil organizations: They don't value individual initiative and, thus, are slow to adapt."

"They will still be on their guard, especially if their leadership is there," Rebecca said.

"That won't help them," Alex replied as they headed forward toward the bridge.

* * * *

The ship rocked heavily and Schmitt had to clutch her station's grab bar to keep in her seat. Remarkably, during the same period, Chief Cabato simply walked over to her station, somehow automatically adjusting to the ship's movement as he stepped.

In her entire time on an aircraft carrier, Schmitt had never seen seas like this. Of course, in her entire time on an aircraft carrier, they had never intentionally steered directly into a hurricane.

"Chief, Alex and her two companions have taken out one of the fire teams," she said as the chief settled in next to her.

"Good. If we're lucky the storm will wash more of them off the ship," he replied.

"About that..." she said. Then she called up security camera footage outside one of the cargo holds where one of the fire teams was scanning the corridor.

The hallway was empty. That was one advantage of steering into the storm. The constant bucking of the ship kept almost everyone in their cabins. And the Ares teams were too preoccupied to roust passengers and crew to keep them in the line of fire.

"If they follow procedure they will search the hold. Is there some way we can keep them in there?"

"The hold is protected by a watertight door," the chief said. "We can trip it from here, but all of the doors can be opened manually from both sides. It will take them a few minutes, but they will be able to get out."

"That qualifies as disrupting their plans," Schmitt said, thinking out loud. "Maybe we can close a series of doors to tie them up."

\* \* \* \*

The chief studied the monitor, but Schmitt decided that she didn't think much of her own plan. Her console could show her the feed from hundreds of security cameras. However, her monitor could only show a few feeds at a time. The camera system was meant to be monitored by at least two people who were watching a wall full of monitors. And, even then, that would be inadequate to watch all corners of the ship during an armed assault.

Even if Schmitt could tie up one fire team indefinitely, the process would also tie her up and reduce her ability to offer Alex and her group support anywhere else in the ship.

"There's something else we can do," Cabato said, studying the screen. "There's a pipe that runs through the hold to the saltwater filtration system. We can increase the pressure and blow a valve."

"Can you flood them once they are inside?"

He shook his head. "Not really; the pumps will kick in before the water gets to one inch. But we can overload the electrical circuits, create a short, and..."

"Electrocute them," Schmitt said.

"I've seen it happen before, by accident," he said.

"Then let's do it. Do you need much time?" she asked.

He was already on his feet and heading over to his people. "No."

Schmitt watched as the Ares team entered the hold. "They're in," she said.

Because they had no communication, the fire team hadn't learned from the other team's experience with Alex. They didn't know enough to be wary.

They entered one at a time and started searching once they were all inside. Schmitt presumed they were looking for the prototype laser.

"Ready," the chief called out.

"Close the door," Schmitt said to one of his people

Almost immediately she saw a heavy door start to slide across the entrance. The men inside noted it but didn't panic. Schmitt assumed that was because they knew how to use the manual releases.

"Building pressure now. Tell me when the door is closed," Cabato said.

It took half a minute for the door to close completely, and then Schmitt said, "Now!"

She didn't see a blast of water, but within a few seconds she could see a growing puddle on the floor. By the time it covered the entire surface, one of the Ares men had headed for the door and was looking for the manual release.

Schmitt could tell the water was rising and got up to join Cabato in front of one of the control panels. He was keeping his hand over a red switch.

Gently, Schmitt took his hand in hers and said, "I can do it, Chief."

He seemed surprised but he also seemed to understand. He was a civilian engineer. This wasn't the military, and no matter what the Ares men had done, taking their lives would weigh on someone like the chief.

"It's my job," she said.

For a moment, the chief simply looked sad. "The captain was my friend, and they killed so many others."

Chief Cabato hit the switch.

Schmitt wasn't at her station so she couldn't see what happened. When she got back to her monitor, she saw the four men lying on the ground, motionless.

"They're down, Chief. Give me a minute to make sure they're dead," Schmitt said.

"They're dead, Ms. Schmitt," Cabato said, his tone making it clear that he was certain.

# Chapter 34

"Dan, I don't like that look in your eye," Jenny said.

Morgan stared out the window of the garage. The wind and rain were dropping off quickly.

"It's clearing up," he said simply.

"No, it isn't. The eye of the storm is about to pass over us," she said. "It will do that very quickly. Then we'll be back to fifty- to sixty-mile-an-hour winds. Do you know what kind of waves that causes on the open sea, and what that would do to your amphibious vehicle?"

"But I've done the math. We'll be traveling with the storm...at least partly. And the eye is easily twenty-five miles wide. It's only nine miles to Savo, so we should get there with time to spare."

"Sure, that's possible," Jenny said. "But the storm is moving at twenty-five to thirty miles an hour, which means it's very fast, which means it's also unpredictable in terms of speed and direction. Plus, it's partly traveling over land now, so that means a shift in the path is even more likely."

"I've factored all that in. It's still possible," Morgan said.

"Possible, sure. But how likely?" Jenny replied.

Morgan didn't want to answer that because he didn't want to lie to his wife...especially now.

"I'll agree on one condition: I drive," she said.

"What?" he said, unable to keep the surprise out of his voice. "If we get there we'll be making a direct assault on a heavily fortified position."

"*If* you get there," she said. "Which is a lot more likely if I'm at the helm of that thing. I respect that whatever happens on Savo will be your world, but this is mine."

That was the moment that Conley stepped forward and said, "Do you remember the last time you had to work in the water?"

"That's not fair—I slipped once," Morgan said.

A light went on in Jenny's eyes. "Was that the time you hurt your back?"

Sometimes he really hated that his wife had such good insight. He didn't have to answer her; she read the truth on his face.

"You said you just had a fall," Jenny said.

"I did, but first I slipped in a helicopter," he replied.

"And *fell* into the water," Conley added.

Reading his wife's face, he said, "It wasn't that high up. Look, it was ten years ago. Can we focus on what's in front of us?"

"So it's agreed?" Jenny asked.

Morgan didn't reply. He didn't have to.

The DUKW was ready. They'd taken the extra few hours to fashion a canopy over the top. They didn't have the original army-issued canvas, but the tarp they were able to scrounge was undoubtedly waterproof. They had also rigged a waterproof cover for Shepard's weapon and the generator was running smoothly. Everything was loaded and ready, and their amphibious assault vehicle had a full tank and some extra gas in cans stowed with the equipment.

Before they boarded, Jenny and Dani disappeared into the back of the garage and came back carrying rifles. No, not just rifles...

Jenny presented Morgan with a vintage M1 Garand. It was the standard US military rifle in World War II and Korea, and it saw action as late as Vietnam.

"How?" he asked.

"The same man who rented us the DUKW. I don't know what else he does when he's not giving tours," Jenny said.

Morgan didn't know what to say. The M1 was the primary weapon for US forces in the war. In fact, his own father had carried one when he had served in the Pacific theater during World War II. Though his father made passing mention of the Philippines, Morgan realized that he didn't even know if his father had been at Guadalcanal. The elder Morgan would never talk about the war in any detail. In fact, that was just one of a list of things that father and son didn't talk about.

Next, Jenny presented him with a canvas bag full of ammo: 30-06 Springfield ammo loaded into eight-round block clips.

He heard Conley gasp as Dani presented him with a Winchester 1912 pump action shotgun, a weapon that had also seen quite a bit of action during the war.

Then Jenny was rushing them around the rear of the vehicle, where they climbed up and inside. They crowded behind Jenny as she started the DUKW, hit a button to open the garage door, and drove outside.

The rain had stopped, and it was eerily calm. There were branches and leaves everywhere—and more than once they had to drive around a felled tree—but they were at the beach in minutes. The water was calm and Jenny didn't hesitate, she simply drove from the sand into the water. As soon as they were floating, she engaged the propeller, and they were off.

The engine sounded good and Morgan was satisfied that it would get them to the island. Jenny studied the sea, and checked a storm tracker on her phone, making adjustments to course and speed a few times before she seemed satisfied.

It was only then that Morgan looked ahead. Though the sky above was clear, they were surrounded by a giant circle of dark clouds. They formed the eye wall, which seemed impossibly high, and except for occasional flashes of lightning, seemed almost peaceful.

That illusion of calm was a lie, Morgan knew. Because that wall was actually the beginning of the most destructive area of the hurricane, since the fastest and most powerful winds were closest to the eye.

If the wall passed over them when they were still on the water, their trip would be over very quickly.

No one spoke and Jenny's face was a mask of concentration as she kept her eyes forward. In the distance Morgan could just make out Savo Island, which looked impossibly far away.

Morgan checked his watch. They were less than ten minutes into their journey. Just an hour and a half more to go.

* * * *

One fire team eliminated in cargo hold 6, the message from Schmitt read. Alex was glad to hear that, though she had no idea how Schmitt had managed that from the engine room.

Ares is launching the lifeboats empty, the next message read.

That didn't sound good, Alex thought. She couldn't think of a single reason for doing that which didn't involve the murder of everyone on board.

Her next thought made her catch her breath. *Oh my God—Sorina.*

She and Eric were grabbing resources from the boats. If it hadn't happened already, they would eventually run into the Ares men launching the lifeboats.

She wanted to race back down to the lido deck and warn them off, but she, Rebecca, and Devan were too close to the bridge to turn back. All she could do was hope that Eric and Sorina had gotten to safety.

Alex had only been to the bridge once, during her initial tour of the ship. However, she remembered the layout. It was close to the front of the *Grandeur* and near the top of the vessel. Tall windows ran the width of the bridge and gave an impressive view of the sea.

Though wide, the room wasn't deep—maybe a dozen feet. It also had three entry points. On the far left and far right it had doors that made it accessible from the outside. In the center there was a door that led to a stairwell going to the deck below.

They reached the point on I-95 just below the bridge and started climbing the stairs up. The trip was harder than Alex expected, as the rocking of the ship tossed them from side to side on the narrow crew staircase. The bridge was seven decks up, but they left Devan one deck below so he could cover the interior entrance. Then Rebecca and Alex reached the point where they needed to separate so they could each cover one of the exterior doors.

"Be careful out there," Alex said. "Apparently there's some wind."

"You too," Rebecca said and then she broke left as Alex broke right.

Alex came to the door that led to the outdoor observation deck that connected to the bridge. All she could see through the glass of the door was rain and a darkening sky.

Alex didn't hesitate: She pushed through the door and into what was only moderate rain, but stronger winds than she had ever felt before. Schmitt had told her the winds were up to sixty miles per hour, but that number had been an abstraction. This was real, and strong enough to sweep her over the railing, after which it would be seven decks down to the deck below.

Keeping low, with one hand on the railing to her left, Alex moved forward. When she reached the bridge door, she stopped and pulled what she needed from inside her jacket.

There was a small overhang above her that would have given her protection from the rain if it wasn't coming at her sideways. Alex ignored it and pulled out one of the fire extinguishers that Sorina and Eric had left for her in the first lifeboat safety locker.

She also pulled out the zip tie she'd claimed from the same locker. She made a loop around the trigger to the device but didn't pull it tight.

Next, she checked her watch. Both she and Rebecca had set five-minute timers on their watches. There was less than a minute to go and Alex counted off the seconds.

When it got to five, she put a hand on the door. When it got to zero, she hit the trigger and pulled the zip tie around it to keep it depressed. As the white chemical powder started to fly out of the extinguisher, she pulled open the door and then tossed it inside, trying to give it a spin as the threw.

She heard voices and worked quickly to pull out and ignite the flare. Then she opened the door again and threw that inside as well.

Rolling away from the door, Alex lay on the deck on her stomach and pulled her weapon, aiming it forward.

If Rebecca had done the same on her side there should be a fair amount of chaos on the bridge. Their improvised devices weren't smoke grenades, but they were pretty close—and Alex thought the flares would be a nice touch. The combination of the fog created by the powder in the extinguishers and the bright light of the flares would be interesting.

Alex kept her focus on the door and it only took seconds for someone to come bursting out. She recognized the white shirt of a crew uniform and held her fire at the last possible instant.

The bridge crewman had actually been tossed out onto the deck and he went sprawling toward the railing. The fact that he fell down two steps later saved him from going over the side. Instead, he skidded on the deck and crashed into the barrier.

Seconds after that a black-clad figure burst out, firing an AK-47 on full automatic in Alex's direction. Several bullets would have hit Alex center mass if she had been standing, but given her position on the ground, they simply flew over her head.

Alex's three shots, however, didn't miss, and hit him directly in the chest. The man went down quickly. She heard gunfire from Rebecca's side and hoped the woman hadn't shot a crewmember forced out by Ares.

She would have called out to the other woman but she'd never be heard over the wind and rain. So Alex waited. It wasn't long before the door pushed open slightly and a voice from inside said, "This is First Officer Watson. I'm coming out."

Alex kept her gun trained forward until she saw the white uniform and recognized the man. "Are there any inside?" she asked, lowering her gun and getting up from the deck.

"No," he said. Then he stepped over to his crewmate, who was leaning against the railing. Watson helped him up and pulled him back toward the bridge. Then Watson looked at Alex carefully and said, "What's happening?"

"I work with Alicia Schmitt. She's locked in the engine room and we're trying to clear the ship. There were five four-man teams. With this bunch there's only one left," Alex said.

"Not quite. There were only three with us. One of them left to force crew to launch the lifeboats," Watson said.

"Alicia has access to the security cameras. She can try to find him," Alex said.

"What can we do?" Watson asked.

She pointed at the downed man and said, "Collect their weapons and stay near the bridge. I'll tell Alicia what's happened and she'll contact you."

Then recognition flashed across Watson's face and he said, "Wait, I know you. You're a server on lido. You were there during the pirate attack."

"Yes, sir. Alicia told me I have you to thank for my day off," Alex said.

"After this you can take the week," he said.

"Thank you, sir," Alex said as she turned and ran back toward the door that would take her back to the ship's interior. Pushing through the door, she found Rebecca and Devan waiting for her.

"I talked to Watson; he'll hold the bridge. Rebecca, did they throw a crewman at you?" Alex said.

Rebecca nodded her head and said, "Cowards. Don't worry, I didn't shoot him."

"I want to get downstairs to see if we can find Sorina and Eric. One of the thugs from the bridge is launching the lifeboats."

The trio made their way down to the lido deck. They started from lifeboat 42 and worked their way down. Seven lifeboat lockers had Sorina's lipstick S on them. The eighth one was unmarked.

There was no blood and no other signs of violence, so Alex held out hope that Sorina and Eric were safe somewhere. At the moment, there was nothing she could do for them, and there was still one more fire team and a single gunman roaming the ship.

Alex holstered her gun and grabbed her phone.

"Don't move," a voice said in front of her. "All of you."

Looking up, Alex saw a black-clad figure pointing an AK-47 at her midsection. Alex's peripheral vision told her that Devan and Rebecca were still holding their weapons. That was something.

"I want you all to drop your weapons," the man said. "Then you are going to tell me how many of you are on board and where they are."

Alex did a quick calculation in her head, factoring in the rate of fire of the AK on fully automatic and the probable reaction times of her new friends. Though Alex would be the first to be hit, she thought there was at least a fair chance that either Rebecca or Devan would get at least one shot off at the man who was about to kill her.

At that moment, the ship rocked violently and for a second Alex thought the storm might save her. However, the Ares operative stayed on his feet and kept his weapon aimed at her.

For a moment, Alex wondered where the security men with the fire hose were when she needed them. Then she remembered that like everyone in that department, they had been murdered.

"Don't listen," Alex said. "Shoot him."

# Chapter 35

While the beach was getting closer, the sea was getting rougher. Jenny had not said a word in a full half hour. And for the last fifteen minutes, she had stopped checking behind them.

He didn't blame her; it wasn't pretty.

When they had gotten onto the open sea, the cloud wall had been a safe distance behind them, but it had drawn closer as they traveled toward Savo.

The first big change had come when it was less than a mile away and their small vehicle was no longer in the sunlight, because the wall was now blocking the setting sun completely.

Now the wall looked darker and much more ominous as it loomed over them. It was at that point that Morgan first wondered if their DUKW was going to end up another World War II relic littering Ironbottom Sound.

To his surprise, darkness wasn't followed by punishing winds and crushing waves. Instead, the water remained calm.

But the eye wall seemed to chase them, and as it did, it became darker and less clearly defined. Like clouds on an airplane, it only looked more or less solid when you saw it at a distance.

In some ways, that made it more unnerving. When the cloud wall was a clearly defined thing he could see, he had a sense of how much time they had before it reached them. Now it felt like things could change at any second.

Up ahead, he realized that the distance to the island was now a few hundred yards, almost close enough to swim. Of course, in the event that they were thrown into the water, Morgan wasn't sure that washing on a beach controlled by Ares was much better than going down with the ship.

For the first time, a serious wave gave them a solid shove. When the DUKW settled, Jenny said, "It's okay. As we get closer to the beach the waves will be behind us, pushing us forward. The real danger was when we were on the open sea and could get capsized by a wave hitting us broadside."

And then another wave hit them on the side. By now, Morgan could feel the wind picking up. He had no doubt that they were now only minutes away from real trouble.

But they were also only minutes away from shore.

When the first serious wave gave them a shove from behind, Morgan realized that his wife had been right. He looked around them and saw that the waves were all pushing toward the beach.

On the downside, those waves were much bigger than he was comfortable with. Morgan put a hand on his wife's shoulder while he held on to his seat with the other. They were now maybe a hundred yards from the beach, then fifty.

And the waves behind them were getting even bigger. He also didn't like the way they were breaking on the shore. Jenny adjusted speed and the vehicle's angle several times, then she looked behind them. Morgan could see her actually choose her wave. Jenny made a final course and speed correction and aimed them toward shore.

When they were less than twenty feet from the sand, Morgan could feel a wave lift them up in the back. For a moment he was afraid that it would flip them over, but instead the DUKW merely rose as the wave passed ahead of them and broke a few seconds before the vehicle's front tires hit the beach.

Morgan engaged the all-wheel drive and the DUKW lurched forward. Seconds later, all six tires were on the sand and their boat had become a truck again. Looking at his wife's calm, focused expression he realized that if they weren't already married, he would propose right there.

As soon as they had reached the top of the beach Jenny turned to him and was about to speak when she saw the way he was looking at her and said, "What? It was basically bodysurfing. Which way now?"

Morgan pointed to their right and said, "Follow that road and keep the lights off for as long as you can."

* * * *

Schmitt was relieved to hear that Jack and the bridge crew were still okay. She told the chief but she couldn't spare another moment on Jack for now. There was still one fire team and one extra operative remaining on board.

If it looked like they failed on their primary objective, which Schmitt assumed was the acquisition of the laser, she had to assume their next move would be to try to sink the ship.

She toggled from one security camera feed to another. Her system was powerful, and could tie into the *Grandeur*'s hundreds of cameras, but all those feeds were still filtering to her single monitor.

The feeling that time was racing forward was punctuated by the occasional shift in the deck as the ship was battered by the large waves, which her system told her were as high as thirty feet.

It would take more than that to endanger the ship—or capsize her—but Schmitt knew the storm must have been battering the passengers and crew pretty good.

She eventually found the fire team in one of the corridors on deck six. Each of them was wheeling large cylinders that had to be six feet long each and at least two feet wide.

"Chief, take a look," she said.

Cabato came over and studied the feed. "What do they have?" he asked.

"I think they're bombs," she said. "Can we box them in?"

The chief started barking orders at his men. But before they could find and engage the right watertight doors, the men disappeared through the door to cargo hold 1.

Thirty seconds later, thanks to the chief, the watertight door outside the cargo hold started closing. She watched the men inside. They seemed to be completely unconcerned.

Switching the feed to the camera in the hold, she watched the men closely. They left the bombs in the middle of the entryway and walked off to pick up some five-gallon containers.

The chief watched over her shoulder and said, "What are they doing?"

"I think they are arming their bombs," she said.

Schmitt suddenly understood how they had snuck the weapons on board. The bomb cases were easy; they could have been disguised among a number of spare parts or equipment. The cases wouldn't set off any sensors or bomb-sniffing dogs because they were simply metal canisters.

And the explosive material didn't have to be hidden among the normal food and supplies because it *was* the normal food and supplies.

She enlarged the image to see that the large containers were vegetable glycerin, but already knew that. It was a common food additive that was used in baked goods, among other things. In diluted form it was "fog juice," the liquid that went into the fog machines in the stage shows.

Once you had the glycerin, all you had to do was add some acid that would have been stored in large volume for use in the pool filtration systems, and you had nitroglycerin. It was twenty-five times more powerful and explosive than TNT. When detonated, it started a self-sustaining reaction that created a shock wave that propagated at thirty times the speed of sound.

But even that was only part of the problem. When detonated, the liquid expanded into a gas that was 1,200 times its original volume. If that explosion was contained in, say, a reinforced bomb casing, the resulting destructive force would be devastating, given the volume that these large cases would hold.

"Chief, we have to hold them in there," she said.

"We can try to keep the door closed, but the manual lever supersedes the electronic system," Cabato said.

"I'll see if we can get some," Schmitt said and sent a message to Alex.

\* \* \* \*

Looking down the barrel of the Ares man's AK-47, Alex's only thought was that she hoped either Rebecca or Devan was fast enough to get him after he cut her down. If they were lucky, they would both survive and that would double the chances of stopping the last fire team.

"Last chance. Talk and live a little longer," he said.

"Sure," Alex said. "Why don't you—"

Alex waited for the crack of the first bullet and the tearing hammerblow of an AK round hitting her stomach at this range.

The man made an ugly smile and she saw his shoulder tensing, which telegraphed that he was about to fire...

And then in one motion his eyes went wide, his body tensed, and his head jerked back as if he was being electrocuted. Then his body jerked again and an expression of surprise flashed over his face before he fell forward to the deck, dropping his weapon.

Shocked herself, Alex's eyes followed him to the ground as she wondered what had just happened. Had he accidentally bitten down on his poison tooth? Could she really be that lucky?

"Alex," a familiar voice called out—a voice with a Romanian lilt to it. Alex looked up to see Sorina holding a knife in a classic throwing position. The woman's eyes were focused on the man on the ground and when Alex looked at him again, she saw there were two similar knives sticking out of his back.

Next to her was Eric, who looked ready to fight, with a hatchet in each hand. "Sorina—how?" she asked.

"Sorry I waited so long, but I had to be close enough to be sure," she said. Eric stepped over to the fallen man and then Sorina approached her, taking her by the shoulders and looking her over. "Are you okay, princess?"

"Yes, I'm fine. Um... thank you. Where did you learn to do that? Romanian military?" she asked.

"No," Sorina said and laughed. "My mother taught me."

Then Sorina smiled at the clear confusion on Alex's face and said, "We're Romani," as if that explained everything.

Was knife-throwing a Gypsy thing? Or was Sorina teasing her? There was no time now to find out.

"We should get out of the open," she said.

Then she felt a buzzing on her phone and picked it up and read the message quickly.

"We have to get downstairs. I know where the last fire team is. They're cornered in a cargo hold," she said.

The five of them raced across the deck and back indoors to the main crew stairwell. If they moved quickly, they could end this soon.

# Chapter 36

The base wasn't hard to find. They simply drove toward the mountain ahead of them, which Morgan also knew was an active volcano. Intellectually, he understood that *active* didn't mean *immediately dangerous*, but the idea still unnerved him. He'd be happy when the job was done and they could get out of here.

The storm, on the other hand, was a much more immediate concern. The winds were insane and he was grateful for the DUKW's two-and-a-half-ton weight and six-wheel drive.

The vehicle could make it through anything the storm could throw at them. Morgan's only real worry was that a large tree might block the roads or paths they needed to use. However, so far, they'd been lucky.

The light held out as well as he could expect and they hadn't needed to use the DUKW's headlights. The final stretch to the bunker was a brand-new, well-paved road, which was unusual for a road leading to a structure built by the Japanese in 1943 and abandoned since then.

There were no lights on the road and he knew that was Ares showing light discipline. There was no point in advertising your secret, evil lair. And so far their stealth strategy had been successful. No one in the international intelligence community had known it was here, even though Zeta and everyone else had been looking for Ares bases for months now.

And the only reason Zeta had found it was that he and Conley had tracked leads from Jakarta to Guadalcanal, and Zeta had put together the final pieces with additional intelligence from a number of other sources.

Morgan had Jenny stop when they came to a fork that led to the large front entrance and the smaller rear entrance. Most of the structure was underground and actually built into the mountain, but if they could cover these two exits they could neutralize the base.

"Is that a…" Jenny said.

"If you mean is that a Russian Mi-24 gunship attack helicopter, then yes," Morgan said.

"Looks like the twenty-four B variant," Conley added.

"You're right, look at the tail rotor," Morgan said.

"Are you boys done showing off?" Jenny asked.

"Not even close," Morgan said and then asked her to drive around back.

From a distance, Morgan used his M1 to take out the camera/sensor over the door. He hoped Ares would assume it was the result of storm damage but, to be sure, he waited a full two minutes for anyone to come to investigate.

No one did, and he had Jenny pull the vehicle as close as possible to the rear door so they could unload the equipment. They pulled down Shepard's odd-looking weapon and placed it on the pavement. Morgan was glad they had covered it with a waterproof tarp. He had no idea what the rain would do to the cobbled-together machine.

Then they pulled down the generator, which he and Conley had also covered and put on top of a creeper cart back at the garage. They wheeled both pieces of equipment to the steel door. The lock was a disappointment—just an ordinary, heavy-duty lock that Morgan picked in under a minute.

When he pulled the door open, no alarm sounded. Like the lock, that was a bit of a surprise. However, he assumed that when the locals were afraid of the place and no one on the island was a real threat to you, it was easy to take security for granted.

The door led to a narrow hallway that was tailor-made for Shepard's toy. The corridor was only six feet tall and less than five feet wide. It ran straight for maybe a dozen feet. Morgan followed it to the end, where it made a left turn into a wider and longer hallway that had a more solid-looking door at the other end.

Shep had warned them that his weapon would work best indoors. In fact, it might not work at all in the open. The concrete hallway was the perfect resonant chamber that Shepard had said would give them the best results.

When Morgan came back to the group, they were already setting up the machine and the generator. Morgan started the generator, and then Conley plugged in the device. They kept it in the outer hallway and angled it toward the larger interior corridor. Shepard had assured them the sound waves would reflect, and this kept the machine out of the line of fire from anyone coming from inside the structure.

Dani powered it up and made some adjustments on various panels. That done, she took out her phone and tuned it using some software Shep had developed for the job. Finished, she stepped back and said, "That's it."

"Can we tell if it will work?" Jenny asked.

"Peter and I have some work to do up front, and then I think our friends inside will come this way to give us a demonstration," Morgan said.

* * * *

Alex and her group stepped through the doors from the outside. When they reached the lounge a few feet later, someone came out of the shadows with a weapon. Alex drew her pistol and was about to fire when she recognized him.

"Hold your fire," she called out to her group. She stopped and said, "Michaels?"

"Alex?" he replied. He was holding a large ax in one hand, while his other arm was still in a sling.

The others quickly recognized him.

Alex said, "Shouldn't you be in bed?"

"The doc wasn't happy, but..." he said, not having to finish that sentence.

It was amazing Michaels was on his feet, and he clearly was struggling to hold the heavy ax with one hand.

"Here," Eric said, holding out one of his hatchets. Michaels dropped his ax and took the smaller weapon. "You can have this as well if you know how to use it."

Eric held out the Glock he'd taken from the body of the Ares man Sorina had killed. Eric had also taken the man's AK-47, which he now had strapped across his back.

"I know how to use it, thanks," he said, taking the pistol. "National Guard."

"No kidding. I was Airborne," Eric said.

"We have the last team pinned downstairs, but we have to get there to hold them," Alex said.

Now six, the group moved forward, and Alex put in her ear comm to talk to Schmitt for the first time since this whole business had begun.

"We have a problem, Alex," Schmitt said, filling Alex in as she and the others made their way down the stairwell.

When they reached the cargo hold Alex explained that the Ares fire team was assembling four large and dangerous explosives inside the hold now.

"We have to make sure they don't get out to place them throughout the ship. The reason the *Titanic* sank was not because it had a single large hole, but because it had a long one that ran the length of the ship and cut through most of its watertight sections."

"Would they detonate the bombs with themselves inside?" Sorina asked.

"Yes; they won't hesitate. They always commit suicide to avoid capture, and we think the destruction of the ship is one of their primary objectives," Alex said.

"That will make a pretty big hole in the hull," Michaels said.

"Yes, but the damage will be limited to this area," Alex replied. "We're two decks above sea level. The blast area will probably reach to the waterline and a deck or two beneath, but the watertight doors in this section will close and the ship will stay afloat."

There was a moment of silence while that sunk in.

"Alex, what will happen out here?" Sorina asked.

Pointing to the closed door, Alex said, "That won't be able to contain the explosion from all four devices."

Alex drew her weapon and added, "All of you should leave now. I can do this." She saw the look on Sorina's face and said, "It's my job."

"Excuse me, but aren't you a server on lido?" Michaels asked. "This is my job, and they killed every single one of my team on this ship."

Devan shared a look with Rebecca and said, "We're with you, Alex."

"Eric?" Sorina said.

"Sorina, I want you to get as far forward as you can. Wait in the crew bar near the bow," he said.

"Wait? You're not coming with me?" she said.

"I have to stay. If they get through that door, you won't be safe—no one will," he said.

Looking at the dawning horror on her face, he said, "Nothing is certain. I have training, if I can get in there—"

"Stop!" Sorina said and Alex realized the woman was angry, really angry and that was something Alex had never seen before. "Don't lie to me! Never lie to me!"

Eric looked embarrassed, and then sad. "You're right, I'm sorry. I will never lie to you again. Will you leave now, please?"

Sorina studied Eric, and then the group, and simply said, "No."

That was it. They had all decided and then Eric did something that genuinely surprised Alex. He kissed Sorina. Not a friendly peck. Not the comfortable kiss of lovers. It was a full-on-we-just-won-the-war-and-we're-in-Times-Square kiss.

Alex found that it actually lifted her spirits; she could only imagine what it did for Sorina.

After a full minute, the couple separated and Alex tapped her ear comm. "We're ready down here. There are six of us. They won't get through. Are you able to evacuate the section?"

"It's slow. Watson and the bridge crew are doing what they can, but we shut down the PA when we shut down communications. It will take some time to get everything back up."

Alex could hear the strain in Schmitt's voice. "Alex, I'm sorry..."

"Don't be," Alex replied.

"If there was any other way," Schmitt said.

"There isn't and it's okay. Just let me know when they're coming," Alex said.

\* \* \* \*

"I've got this one," Conley said. He aimed his shotgun at the security camera and fired. It was a direct hit but at twenty feet it would have been hard to miss.

There were two other cameras, but the two men left them alone. If they cut out all the cameras by the front entrance, someone would definitely come in to investigate. As it was, Morgan and Conley waited a full three minutes before they moved.

Staying in the base security's new blind side, they approached the helicopter. When they reached it, Conley pointed to the roll of heavy-duty cable on the side of the copter. "It's an industrial winch, and recently added."

That jibed with the idea that Ares was going to recover something from Alex's cruise ship. "That gives me an idea," Conley said. "You play with the missiles. Let me see what I can do with this."

"What are you thinking?" Morgan asked.

"Don't worry about it. If you get to do what you want with the missiles, I get to dispose of the helicopter," he said.

"Fair enough, just be ready when I am," Morgan said.

He opened up the tool kit he brought and went to work removing the rocket pod that held twenty S-8 80mm rockets. They had been recently loaded and Morgan assumed they were meant to be used against Alex's ship.

Using the tarp he'd pulled off Shepard's weapon, Morgan lowered the pod as gently as he could to the creeper cart that they had borrowed from the hotel garage. It was normally used to allow a mechanic to lie on his back and work under a car.

They had used it to move the generator into position. Now it was holding probably a million dollars of highly advanced and highly destructive missiles. Morgan secured them to the cart.

"Morgan, are you ready?" Conley said. "I have to start the chopper to make this work, so that might draw some attention."

"Putting it into position now," Morgan said as he rolled the rockets to a space between the helicopter and the wide main entrance, which had two large industrial steel doors set back about ten feet into solid concrete. When the rockets were pointed toward doors, Morgan headed back to his and Conley's rally point behind a low concrete rectangle on which Morgan placed his M1

He heard the helicopter's engine start but saw that Conley hadn't engaged the rotors. Then Conley raced around the helicopter to join Morgan as he was taking aim on the back of the rocket pod with his M1.

"Dan, did you really secure twenty rockets to the car mechanic's cart with duct tape?" Conley asked.

"Yes, why?" he replied. "What did you do to the helicopter?"

"You'll see. Just give it a sec for the winch to take up the slack," he said.

Seconds later, the helicopter lurched a few feet toward the edge of the helipad, away from the doors.

"What the hell?" Morgan asked as he watched the helicopter get dragged across the concrete.

"I ran the winch line about two hundred yards into the jungle where there was a nice, strong concrete pylon. Then I just turned it on. And oh, I also wrapped the line around the fuselage so in about a second..."

Morgan watched as the copter started to teeter to one side, then fall over with a loud screech of metal as it continued to drag itself over the chopper pad, following the winch line into the jungle.

Morgan would have like to see what happened, but he had his own job to complete. He took careful aim with the rifle, keeping the rear of the rockets in his sights.

"Something's happening," Conley said. "I see flashlights. The doors are open."

Morgan fired. Then the M1Garand—the rifle that for Morgan's money had won the Second World War—let loose a single round.

The shot was true, and Morgan saw the flash of at least two rocket exhausts. There was a moment when nothing happened, and then the rocket pod started rolling forward slowly. It picked up a little speed and then seemed to jump forward, trailing its signature black smoke.

Disappearing into the entrance, the pod flew on for maybe two or three more seconds, and then the ground under them rumbled and a blast of fire shot out from the front entrance. The flames almost reached the still-moving helicopter, which was now twisted and mangled. The aircraft gained speed when it hit the dirt and then stopped cold when it struck a waist-high concrete structure.

Morgan could hear something in the helicopter strain and then pop. He assumed it was the winch tearing loose. It must have hit something in the chopper because it exploded in a flash as its full load of jet fuel ignited at once. That blast was followed by what Morgan assumed was the explosion of the second rocket pod that had still been attached to the helicopter.

Morgan didn't wait to see what happened. He pulled his head down behind the concrete as the shock wave passed over them, followed by the sound of debris flying overhead.

The men waited half a minute until the sound of the debris falling stopped. Morgan didn't even spare the carnage a look; he turned toward the path that would take them to the back entrance and the women with Conley right next to him.

When they got to the DUKW, they saw Jenny and Dani waiting exactly where the partners had left them.

Jenny ran up to him and pulled him in for a tight hug and a kiss. "What have you boys been doing?"

"Showing off," Morgan replied. "Any visitors from inside?"

"No, no one came out," she replied.

"I'll check," Morgan said.

By then Conley and Dani had separated and the two men stepped into the short corridor. At the end were Shepard's weapon and the generator that was still humming.

Carefully, Morgan peered around the corner.

"Wow," was all that he could say.

"What is it?" Conley said.

Morgan turned into the hallway and then Conley joined him.

At least thirty men in black tactical gear were lying on the floor, their weapons strewn about.

"Yeah, wow," Conley said.

All of the men were in the half of the corridor closest to the machine, as if they had made it about halfway before the sound shattered their suicide teeth. Conley checked a few of them and said what they both already knew. They were dead.

Morgan wondered how many men had been inside. It must have been quite a few, since the explosion in the front had been massive and would have likely killed the majority of the people in the base.

Looking at the thirty trained killers and their weapons, Morgan said a silent thanks to Shepard. If the man's weapon hadn't stopped them, they would have come racing out of the exit and quickly overwhelmed Dani and Jenny.

Morgan took a moment to pull out his phone and send a message to Bloch. **Target neutralized. Tell Shepard his weapon worked.**

When they came out, Morgan said, "There's nobody left inside."

Jenny took a step toward the door and he said, "Don't, Jenny."

She stopped.

Morgan took a minute to top off the generator. It wouldn't hurt to keep it running for a few more hours on the off chance that a survivor from inside tried to get out.

Then they all got back into the DUKW and headed for the beach. The storm still raged all around them, but Morgan wanted to get his wife away from all of that death.

# Chapter 37

Schmitt watched the Ares operatives work. They didn't hurry, which she understood since they were working with nitroglycerin.

Then as she watched, she realized they weren't working with nitroglycerin precisely—at least not yet.

Two of the men guarded the door, with their guns pointed. The other two had moved the bombs behind cover and were working there. They poured the glycerin and the acid into different parts of the bomb casing.

Since nitroglycerin was a contact explosive that would blow if it was shaken too much, it was best to wait as long as possible to mix it. She assumed that was what the electronic and mechanical parts of the bomb were for. Most likely, the casings opened a valve to mix the two liquids and then ignited them.

That meant the devices couldn't be set off instantly.

"Chief, there's no other way in there?" she asked.

"It's all watertight, and reinforced because it opens to the outside," he said.

Of course, it had two large doors that created an opening in the hull so that cargo could be loaded from port. If it wasn't for the storm, maybe they could get in somehow using those doors.

*Wait, because of the storm maybe we don't need to*, Schmitt thought.

She called the chief over and said, "Can you open the double doors while we're underway?"

"Yes, but...the storm," and then he understood. "It's twenty feet above the waterline."

"And we're seeing waves as high as thirty feet," she said.

Navigating a storm like this was an art. You had to keep the ship facing the biggest waves. The problem was that they kept coming from different directions.

A good navigator carefully watched the winds and the wave movements to keep the ship from getting hit on the side.

It was time to stop trying so hard.

"Chief, have your man do his best to make sure we're getting hit broadside. That will slow them up in there a bit. Then open the doors."

The chief actually smiled and said, "It will get rough."

"I'm counting on it," she said.

Then she composed a quick message to Alex that said, **Hold on. We're working on a fix from here.**

At best, a ninety-degree turn was slow for a ship of the *Grandeur*'s size. In a storm like this, it was even slower, but the benefits started before the turn was completed.

The ship was rocked even more roughly than before, and Schmitt enjoyed seeing the fire team bounce around and struggle to keep their bombs in place.

"Whenever you're ready, Chief," she said.

"Done," Chief Cabato said from his station, and then Schmitt could see the door crack open on her monitor. They were slow and it took a full minute for them to swing open.

At first the only difference was some rain pouring in. Then a splash of water.

The Ares men seemed more concerned with keeping to their feet and keeping the bombs in place than they were with the open door.

Schmitt felt the first big wave hit before she saw the result. The ship was rocked, hard—so hard that Schmitt had to hold on just to keep in her seat.

When she took a look at the monitor, the hold looked emptier and she could only count three of the Ares men, two of whom were getting up off the floor. Schmitt couldn't see if they ever got to their feet because the next wave actually knocked her out of her own chair and she felt the ship listing badly—maybe thirty degrees, maybe more.

When the *Grandeur* more or less righted itself, Schmitt scrambled back to her seat. At first, she thought she'd lost the video feed from the camera in the hold. Then she realized that the image on the screen was the hold. It was completely empty, or nearly so, and covered in a foot or two of water, which she saw was slowly draining out.

There were no bombs inside and no black-clad men. There was also very little of the supplies that had been housed there. Pallets of food and other supplies were just gone, washed out into the sea.

"Chief, you can bring us about," Schmitt said. "And you can close the doors— they're gone."

The chief and his men congratulated each other and the ship only took one more strong hit before they were back to the now-normal rocking that they had felt since the storm had started.

Her phone beeped and she saw a message from Alex. Alicia, whatever you're doing, please stop. We'll take our chances with the bombs.

She tapped the phone to call Alex. When the young woman answered, Schmitt said, "How is that, Alex?"

"Better," she replied.

"The bombs and the fire team are neutralized," Schmitt said.

"Seasickness?" Alex asked and Schmitt could hear the smile in her voice.

"No, we opened the door and let them out," Schmitt replied.

"Good," Alex said. Then Schmitt heard Alex giving the news to her team. When Alex came back on the line she said, "Thanks."

"Thank you, Alex," Schmitt said. "Get somewhere comfortable. I'll wrap up down here and see you later."

"Will do," Alex said.

When she got Jack Watson back on the line, she asked him if he was ready to have control passed back to the bridge.

"Not yet, we have a bit of a cleanup to do up here. Tell your friend Alex it's going to come out of her pay," he said. Then he paused and added, "Are you okay, Alicia?"

"I was safe down here the whole time. How are you, Jack?"

"Busy," he said.

* * * *

Alex and Rebecca headed back to their cabin. Alex was surprised by how much better she felt in dry clothes. In fact, she decided that her sweatpants and T-shirt might be the most comfortable things she'd ever worn.

When she got to Schmitt's cabin the woman was in a clean work uniform of khaki slacks and polo shirt, but looked like she'd just gotten up and was ready to attack the day.

Schmitt looked her over and said, "How are you?"

"I feel fine," Alex said. "Actually, I feel lucky."

"Lucky? Do you have any idea of what you did today?" she asked.

"I know I got lucky. I literally dodged two bullets. And then you bailed me out in the end," Alex said.

Schmitt shook her head. "What part of that was luck?"

Alex thought about that and said, "You're right, I also got bailed out by civilians who shouldn't have had to be there. First, two security men and then a girl from the serving staff."

Schmitt actually looked angry. "You have got to be kidding me. All of us are only here because of you. And those civilians are only here because of you. They didn't step in because you failed; they were able to act because you kept them alive long enough to give them the opportunity to help."

"You aren't supposed to do it all by yourself. And you didn't just magically get help—you inspired people to help themselves. I know that for a fact because you did all of the same things for me. Look, you don't have to believe me; you can read all about it in my report. Now come on, you can introduce me to your strike team."

They met up in a quiet corner of the forward crew bar. Rebecca, Devan, Michaels, Sorina, and Eric were already there.

Schmitt spoke to each of them in turn, and then they all sat quietly together to ride out the storm. Sorina sat next to Alex and stayed practically glued to her—almost as much as she was to Eric, who she kept next to her on the other side.

Three or four hours later, the sea started to calm and Alex realized she was tired. Alicia was the first to get up. Her phone buzzed and she said, "That's Jack—I mean, First Officer Watson. I should go check on his, or their, progress upstairs."

"Would you like us to walk you back to your cabin, Alex?" Sorina asked.

"No thanks," Alex replied. Clearly Sorina and Eric wanted to be alone.

Rebecca got up and left without ceremony, saying that she'd see Alex back at the cabin. That felt a little like a setup and Alex was now alone with Devan, who stood up.

"Can I buy you a drink, Alex?" he said, keeping his eyes on hers and giving her a very effective grin.

The look surprised her, and she said, "You have got to be kidding me."

"What? Is it so unthinkable?" he asked.

"Read the room—did you pay attention to anything that happened today?" she said.

"I paid attention to everything. That's why I'm still here, so I could be alone with you," he said.

He was good, very good. And she had no doubt that he was sincere. If things were different, she might have accepted to see where it went. But things hadn't been *different* for a long time now. And Alex wasn't ready to see where anything went.

"Is it because I'm a Scouser?" he asked.

"That's actually what I like most about you," she said. "But how about a rain check?"

Alex headed back to her cabin. She was tired and she'd already gotten a message from Rosa that the staff was expected to report to their workstations tomorrow morning. They were still a day away from port. There was ship-wide cleanup and servers were needed to keep the passengers fed.

Alex checked her watch. She'd get a full eight hours sleep before her shift and that was more sleep than she'd seen in weeks.

# Epilogue

Peter Brown's face appeared on Diana Bloch's screen. For a moment, Bloch couldn't place what was wrong with his appearance. Then she saw it: He didn't look unhappy.

Bloch realized that it had been a number of years since she had seen Brown look like he did now—like someone who wasn't battling four emergencies at once.

"Your people left quite a mess on Savo Island," Brown said, in the tone of someone who was not at all bothered by that state of affairs.

"*Mess* is one word for it," Bloch said. "I prefer to look at Savo as a major step forward in global security."

"These things do depend on your perspective, I suppose," Brown said. "Officially, I am supposed to express my concern with Zeta's extralegal methods and flouting of international norms for cooperation."

"We will have to work on that," Bloch said.

"Unofficially, whatever happened there was amazing work. Was that assault carried out entirely by the two agents I saw in the security footage from Port Moresby?" Brown asked.

"Not at all. They had help. There was another agent on-site. And one of my people brought his wife," Bloch said.

"His wife?" Brown asked.

"Yes, she's an interior decorator...a *very good* interior decorator," Bloch said.

"There's not much left of the Ares facility," Brown said. "And no survivors, of course, thanks to your jury-rigged ray gun. Our tech division is still scratching their heads at that one. It shouldn't have worked, but the only other possibility is that twenty highly trained Ares operatives lost hope and committed mass suicide at the same time."

"You wouldn't rule that out if you knew my team," Bloch said.

"We have a team trying to reverse engineer it, but the software that made it work erased itself and fried a number of components on its way out," Brown said.

"You don't say," Bloch replied.

"We all need this weapon, Diana," Brown said. "This was the first successful strike on an Ares facility, but you know this is only the tip of the iceberg."

Bloch knew it was true. They had dealt the first serious blow against Ares since Zeta had detected the organization. But she'd already seen reports that told her Ares was still out there, and that the base on Savo was one of many—and not even their largest one.

Yet Savo Island would also be a treasure trove of intel on Ares operations. Plus, the sheer number of dead Ares people meant that the good guys might get their first positive identification on one of the Ares operatives. Then there was whatever they would find on the computers and equipment that was left on Savo, to say nothing of what a detailed analysis of the abandoned gold mine on Guadalcanal would reveal.

"You know that I'm always willing to share," Bloch said. "We'll need to combine our efforts if we're going to take the fight to Ares. I can have my tech people work with yours on the specs of the weapon." Bloch took a breath, smiled, and said, "On an unrelated note, my contact at the CIA has told me you are still holding up their forensic and technical teams' access to the site."

"They're your people?"

"Technically they are independent contractors, but I can tell you from personal experience that they are very good."

"I see. I can expedite their access while you set up the meeting between our tech departments," Brown said. Then Peter Brown did something Bloch hadn't seen him do in many years: He smiled. "It will be a genuine pleasure to be working with you again, Diana."

"You as well, Peter," Bloch said.

When Zeta had started, the idea had been to create an independent international security agency that could operate without bureaucracy and without the endless side deals and favor-trading that defined the world of interagency intelligence work.

Now Bloch was faced with a foe that required all of that. The last week had shown her that Zeta needed friends and partners. The stakes in the fight against Ares were too high to pretend any differently.

Bloch had a lot to think about. And she had a lot of calls to make, meetings to attend, and alliances to forge. However, she decided that could wait. She had other, more important, matters to attend to.

She hit the intercom that connected her to her assistant. "Rand, send Alex Morgan her next mission briefing and make her travel arrangements. We need her back here in forty-eight hours."

"Yes, ma'am," Rand's voice replied.

Bloch checked her watch. It was time.

She tapped at her keyboard and her nephew's face appeared on the screen in front of her.

"Hello, Jeffrey," she said.

He looked exasperated and said, "Aunt Diana, we talked about this."

"What's that?"

"Are you going to claim that you know nothing about the cargo drop?" he said.

"What do you mean?"

"I mean the surprise cargo drop that included two commercial mixers, two ovens, more kinds of flour than I could count, and a bunch of other things I didn't even recognize. Basically, we now have a fully outfitted, world-class commercial kitchen—all with the compliments of the US military and Susan O'Keefe," Jeffery said.

"I don't know what you mean," Bloch said. "However, I do understand that besides being an award-winning pastry chef, Ms. O'Keefe is also a patriot. I'm sure she appreciates the service of all of you on the base."

"That's all you have to say about it?" Jeffrey said. "Aunt Diana, do you have any idea of what a cargo drop like that down here costs?"

As a matter of fact, Bloch knew precisely how much it cost: exactly one favor.

"How is the new equipment working out?" she asked.

"Amazing," he replied. "I thought the croissants were great before. Our chef, McMurtry, is over the moon. Do you know what chocolate Pavlova is?"

"No," she replied.

"Me either, but it's amazing," he said. "McMurtry is promising something new every day for a month."

For the next hour, Bloch didn't talk or think about murder, mayhem, or global threats. There was no talk of exotic weapons, conspiracies, or worst-case scenarios.

It was by far the best hour that Bloch had spent in months...years, actually.

\* \* \* \*

When Alex opened the door to her hotel room, Alicia Schmitt was in the hallway. Alex let her in, and they sat on her balcony, overlooking Brisbane.

"I just wanted to catch you before you left," Schmitt said.

"I'm not leaving until tomorrow," Alex replied. "What about you?"

"I'll be staying on through the repair period. And then I still have work to do to bring the new system fully online," Schmitt said.

"What will you do after that?" Alex asked.

"Back to Boston," Schmitt said. "Do you know what Bloch has planned for you?"

"Something is brewing in Japan," Alex replied.

"Well, good luck," Schmitt said.

"What about First Officer Watson—will he be staying with the ship?"

"He wants to, but he doesn't know what the cruise line is going to do. He'll definitely stay for repair and restock...and to get replacement crew settled. A few of the crew had canceled their contracts and left, but almost all were staying on. Most of the replacements were for the lost security and safety team."

"They should promote him. I think he'll make a good captain," Alex said.

"I agree, but he's not sure. He says there's more he needed to learn from Captain Garrett," Schmitt said.

"You can tell him from me that you never feel ready. You just do the job that's handed to you the best you can," Alex said.

Schmitt thought about that and said, "That's good advice. I'll tell him.

"I'll see you on board, Alex," Schmitt said and left.

As Alex was getting her things together for the day, her phone rang. She checked the screen and saw that it was Michaels's fiancée, Jess.

"Please make sure he gets out," she said. "If you let him, he'll stay in his room and play his video games," Jess said.

"How? He's still in a sling," Alex said.

"Trust me," Jess said.

In addition to Michaels, Sorina and Eric were also still in the hotel. Devan was debriefing at the British consulate and would be leaving from there for London. Rebecca stopped in to say goodbye and said she was needed at home.

Right on time, Sorina and Eric were at her door. "Come on, princess, we're late for the beach."

"How can you be late for the beach?" Alex asked.

Eric shrugged and said, "Don't ask me."

"Michaels's fiancée just called. She wants us to take him," Alex said.

"I stopped in earlier to check on him," Eric replied. "He was playing video games. I don't know how—with that sling—but he was doing it."

"Let's go, then—pulling him away from that is going to make us even later," Sorina said.

Grabbing her bag, Alex followed her friends out the door.

\* \* \* \*

Jenny returned with Dani and found Morgan and Conley in the garage. The women had another haul of stone and wood carvings. Apparently, there was a demand in the US and a number of her interior design clients were very interested in the pieces.

Morgan and Conley had their own interests that had kept them pretty busy. They had dived most of the wrecks in the nearby waters. And they had seen countless museums and structures from the Second World War.

But most of Morgan's time had been spent in the garage, which he had basically taken over. His work on the DUKW was finished now. He'd rebuilt the engine, boring out the cylinders to increase both the horsepower and the torque. Then he'd rebuilt the transmission.

He'd also redone most of the suspension, updated the brakes, and welded in a few replacement sections of the frame. The compressor that allowed the driver to inflate and deflate the tires remotely had to be replaced completely. That would come in handy when going from road to sand.

Then he'd set about restoring the shell. He'd started banging out dents, but quickly realized that much of the steel had crystallized, so he simply replaced it. There was a lot of sheet metal work. He and Peter had formed much of it on the vehicle itself, and he'd found a local metal press guy who helped with the more difficult pieces.

For the repaint, he'd considered having his paint guy match the original paint exactly. In the end, he decided to go with something that would work better as a sealer and provide more protection from the salt water. The US Army green color was an exact match, though. He found a good DUKW guy in Chicago who had been able to provide a number of new old-stock replacement parts for some of the missing interior and dashboard pieces. He'd also found a new old-stock gearbox, which would add a number of years to the DUKW's life.

Last, he'd had his convertible guy make a new green canvas canopy. Once that was done, the vehicle looked like it had just rolled off the General Motors assembly line.

"It's time, Dan," Jenny had said. "You can't keep it. You know it was a rental."

"I know," Morgan replied. He'd kept it weeks longer than Jenny's original agreement with the owner/private museum curator. But to be fair, Morgan was returning a much better museum piece.

Handing her the keys, he said, "Just remember to go over the maintenance instructions with him. The weekly lubrication is the most important. And he needs to rinse the bottom with fresh water every time he takes it out in the salt water."

"I will. Remember, he's kept it running for decades. I'm sure it will be fine and I know he'll appreciate what you've done," Jenny said before she climbed in and drove away.

"Come on, Dan, when she gets back we have to move into phase two," Conley said.

"Right," Morgan replied.

They had been on Guadalcanal for weeks now and had all enjoyed it. The next part was a tour of the islands on a sailboat that Jenny had rented. His wife was determined to teach him to sail.

Morgan didn't love the idea of spending that much time on the water, but it was fair enough given what he had asked of her on this trip so far. He was concerned about the fact that there were nine hundred or so islands in the Solomons.

Even if they didn't see them all, Morgan knew they would be out there for a while.

Did you miss the first thriller in the Alex Morgan series? No problem! Keep reading to enjoy the exciting opening pages of **ANGLE OF ATTACK**

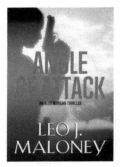

Available from Kensington Publishing Corp.

# Chapter 1

Alex Morgan pulled the long, loose gray tunic over her baggy gray slacks and shapeless gray top. She put the hijab on last, as Lily Randall did the same. They were wearing the more conservative headscarves that covered everything but their faces.

Lily examined Alex, tucking some of her wayward brown hair under the hijab. Strictly speaking, the extra care wasn't necessary. They were already dressed more traditionally than most Iranian women, who were getting increasingly more daring with their colorful hijabs that covered less and less of their hair.

Alex wished those women well, but there was no doubt that they attracted attention. The last thing she and Lily wanted to do was attract attention. Things were tense enough on the streets of Tehran as it was.

"How about me?" Lily asked.

"Perfect," Alex said. She wasn't surprised to see not a hair showing from under Lily's headscarf.

Her friend and fellow agent had dyed her usual blond locks brown, just in case anyone saw under the scarf. Even that wouldn't be catastrophic, but it would attract more attention than they wanted—which was zero attention.

Alex checked the mirror. She wasn't wearing a trace of makeup and though she usually wore very little, she felt surprisingly barefaced and vulnerable without it.

Lily, on the other hand, was wearing subtle makeup to flatten her cheekbones and create dark patches under her eyes. Even with that effort to appear less attractive, Lily was still beautiful.

"Any doubts?" Lily asked in her light London accent. Several years older than Alex herself, Lily was British and had served for years in MI6 before joining Zeta Division.

"None," Alex said. "Though I'll admit it's not what I expected. I always figured our first undercover mission together would involve an underground European nightclub."

"They're overrated," Lily said with smile. "The shoes you have to wear are ridiculous, the wigs are uncomfortable, and nobody ever tells you that those places reek."

"To be fair, these shoes aren't too bad," Alex said. They were wearing track shoes that were reasonably comfortable. She also appreciated that the loose clothing meant they'd be able to move and fight, if they had to. That clearly wasn't the intention of whoever designed this clothing for women, but it was a nice perk.

"First rule of undercover work," Lily said, "it's never what you expect."

That was true, Alex thought. Her first undercover mission had been nothing like she had expected.

"I'm sorry, Alex, that was thoughtless," Lily said.

"Not at all," Alex said. "The mission was a success."

That was true. Zeta had prevented something awful and Alex had helped. Yet there had been losses.

Losses were part of the job, Alex knew. *You never get used to them,* her father had explained. *The day you do is the day you know you've been doing this too long.*

"I want to watch it again," Alex said. Lily checked her watch and opened the laptop. She pressed a button and the video started. It was a press conference at the University of Tehran, where a woman in a green headscarf approached the podium wearing a Western-style business suit.

Maryam Nasiri was an Iranian-American professor who had emigrated from Iran as a small child and was now an American citizen. She was also one of the only two women to win the Fields Medal in mathematics for her work on an algorithm that was so far over Alex's head that her year of A.P. calculus hadn't helped her understand even the Wikipedia entry on Nasiri's work.

The mathematician had made the mistake of accepting an invitation from the University of Tehran for a reception in her honor. After that reception, her family had never heard from her again.

The university released a written public statement signed by Nasiri about her decision to stay on at the university and her excitement about finally being "home."

After a great deal of international pressure, a single public appearance at a press conference was set up and had gone viral. In the video, Nasiri appeared sedated. Standing stiffly at the podium, she spoke in a flat tone. "Thank you all for coming. I want to make it very clear how excited I am to continue my work in the country of my birth. The University of Tehran is my new home and they have given me all the resources I need to continue my work. Thank you."

Then she was ushered away. There had been no questions from the press at this "press conference."

"Let's go," Lily said. "We don't want to be late on our first day of work."

Somehow, while they were watching the video, Lily had executed a physical transformation. The more senior agent usually carried herself with the confidence of an extraordinarily beautiful woman who was also one of the most deadly agents at Zeta. She seemed to occupy a unique space between a catwalk model and an MMA fighter—and carried herself accordingly.

Now Lily's face had sunk into a dull frown. Her shoulders hunched over; her whole body loosened.

Alex did her best to imitate the stance, and the two agents walked out the apartment door. As they left, a woman wearing a heavy, black hijab barked something at them. She was sitting behind a counter at what looked like the front desk in a small hotel.

This *was* a residence hotel of sorts, but the woman wasn't a front desk clerk. She was more like a housemother, a chaperone for the working women who lived there.

Lily replied in Persian. The rough older woman waved them on, averting her eyes.

"How did you do that?" Alex asked when they were outside.

"I added a little Kurdish accent," the agent replied.

That made sense—the Kurds were not exactly a favored minority in Iran. Plus, many were from a territory close to Iraq, which also didn't endear them to the locals. Alex had seen anti-Kurdish feelings firsthand on a recent Zeta mission in Turkey.

"I'll have to remember to do that," Alex said. "Once I learn Persian."

Alex wouldn't need to speak the local language for this mission—the rescue of one Maryam Nasiri from the mathematics department at the University of Tehran, where she and Lily were now part of the crew of cleaning women.

The university was, at best, a low-security environment. A small detail of soldiers guarded the mathematician, but after two months, reports were that they were lax in their approach to the job.

As a mission, this would be the equivalent of a "smash and grab." With any luck, Alex and Lily would have their charge out of the country before nightfall.

The streets of Tehran were bustling, and the air was warm—78 degrees, normal for spring. If it weren't for the covered women, Alex would have thought she was walking the tree-lined streets of any large European city. It was jam-packed with standstill, honking traffic—more than she would have thought even for a city of ten million people.

The cars were mostly European, Peugeot Citroëns and other smallish models with a few more expensive German vehicles. Alex didn't see a single American car on the road; no surprise really, given how the regime felt about America.

There were a fair number of motorcycles, but nothing impressive. Alex noticed smallish Hondas and Italian Benellis. She also glimpsed a few of the locally produced new Saipa electric motorbikes.

It took Alex a moment to figure out what else was missing on the streets of Tehran besides American cars. There wasn't a single sidewalk vendor. She knew that the Iranian authorities didn't approve of them and assumed the city was having one of its periodic crackdowns.

After only a few blocks, Alex was sweating under her heavy hijab.

"You okay?" Lily asked.

"I guess," Alex said. "This thing itches, and it's hot."

"Just like the wigs at the underground nightclubs," Lily said. "They're itchy as hell."

That made Alex smile and they lumbered on, eyes downcast.

And to be fair, the hijab Alex wore as part of her cleaning crew uniform was heavier than many of the ones she saw on the street, where at least half the young women were wearing nearly Western-style clothes and colorful headscarves that showed a fair amount of their hair.

They were all being watched by the green uniformed "Morality Police." This branch of law enforcement was charged with making sure that the population conformed to public morality at all times. Theoretically, men could attract the attention of the Morality Police if their beards were too long or they wore short-sleeved shirts, but as a practical matter, the police reserved their scrutiny for women whose clothing or headscarves were insufficiently "modest."

Women were taking more chances than usual today. It was Wednesday—or White Wednesday—the day that rebellious Iranian women wore white to protest the compulsory wearing of the hijab.

Alex applauded their efforts, but given the number of Morality Police on the streets, she didn't think the day would end well for the women who bent the rules too far. Already, the agents had witnessed more than one heated argument between women and these special police.

The Iranian government's official statements always referred to the mission of the Morality Police as "guidance." Of course, if that were true, Alex wondered why these *guidance officers* were armed.

The agents approached the university's main entrance, on the south side of the campus. The entryway was formed by four twisted concrete arches that were almost like modern art. The academic buildings were surprisingly modern and would not have been out of place in any major European—or even American—city.

Just to the right of the gate Alex could see a crowd forming around a woman wearing a white headscarf and shouting at two of the green-uniformed Morality Police officers. The men were flanked by two female colleagues wearing full black robes. The robed women were shouting back at the woman in white.

Alex could see the problem. The white-clad woman was wearing what would have passed for moderate makeup in the West but was very out of place in Tehran. Also, she wore her white headscarf toward the back of her head, showing fully half of her hair.

Alex supported the women's effort, but she didn't want the commotion to interfere with their mission. She heard a loud yell and watched the woman reach up to grab her white hijab. She glared at the two black-clad women, who were now screaming at her, and then she pulled off her scarf in an act of clear defiance.

There was a moment of shocked silence in the growing crowd. Then one of the men in the green uniforms hurled himself at the young woman—who Alex could now see was the age of a college student.

The girl hit the sidewalk hard, with a nearly two-hundred-pound man slamming down on top of her. Tensing, Alex prepared for action.

She felt Lily's hand on her shoulder. "We can't," the older agent said.

That wasn't true. They could. Yes, the men were armed, but there were only two of them. And the female officers in black didn't seem to have the stomach for anything other than screaming.

Alex had no doubt that she and Lily could handle the four of them before they knew what hit them and get the woman to safety, provided she wasn't badly hurt.

But that wasn't the mission.

It took every ounce of self-restraint Alex had to allow Lily to lead her away and through the university entrance.

The guards at the gate barely noticed them, too busy running outside to the commotion, which was getting louder. The two agents crossed the large campus square, which was humming with college students, about a quarter of whom were women.

At the far end of the campus stood a building that Alex recognized as housing the mathematics, statistics, and computer science departments. That was where Nasiri now "worked."

Outside the entrance was a woman Alex recognized from the mission briefing. She wore the same gray cleaning crew uniform as Alex and Lily.

Lily approached her, speaking quickly in Persian. The woman responded in kind. She then turned her attention to Alex and said in surprisingly good English, "Hello, Alex. My name is Shirin."

"There's a bit of a commotion outside," Lily said.

Shirin shrugged. "It's Wednesday," she said. "There *is* something unusual going on in here, though. They have doubled the guard around Nasiri. These men are fresh and not yet complacent."

That wasn't good, Alex thought. On paper, at least, it was an easy mission with four lazy guards. This change would make it harder.

"Do you think the regime suspects a rescue attempt?" Lily asked.

"No, but there are rumors that she will soon be moved," Shirin said.

That was new. Whatever Nasiri was working on had some sort of technological or military application. If she was moved to a secure facility, Zeta might never get another chance to get her out.

"The extra risk is within our mission parameters," Lily said. "What do you think, Alex?"

"We're prepared for this," Alex said. "Plus, we'd like to meet the woman that everyone is going to so much trouble over."

Shirin smiled approvingly. "We'll start working on the first floor," she said. "We'll reach the fourth floor by lunch, and then you can meet her."

Before they could turn to head inside, Alex heard the distinctive sound of a helicopter's rotors—and not a civilian chopper. It sounded military.

Alex was wrong about one thing, she realized, as *two* large black helicopters flew over the southern entrance. They came in fast and much lower than was normal for an urban center.

In no time the choppers made very quick and very rough landings on the campus square.

Alex and Lily stared at Shirin. "I have no idea," the woman said.

Alex heard gunfire. It sounded as if it came from the guard shack, or outside the entrance. Someone was shooting at the helicopters.

The doors of the choppers opened and men wearing all black filed out. They carried rifles and returned the small arms fire with fully automatic bursts.

"I don't know what this is," Shirin said. "I was told to get you inside and provide assistance, but I can't help you with this."

"You won't have to," Lily said. "I suspect we might not be the only ones who want to get their hands on Nasiri. You've done plenty and we thank you."

Shirin pointed to the all-out firefight that was now going on across the square. In the near-constant gunfire, students were screaming and racing away from the scene. "What will you do?" Shirin asked.

"This development goes way beyond our mission parameters," Lily said, turning to Alex. "We're supposed to abort."

Alex studied the doors to the building. They were so close! A woman, an American citizen who needed their help, was only a few flights of stairs away.

"They don't look so tough. Did you *see* that landing?" she said. "Strictly amateur hour. I say we expand our *mission parameters.*"

"Agreed," Lily replied. Then she turned to Shirin and said, "Thank you again. Get somewhere safe—as far away from us as possible."

Alex and Lily turned to the building, opened the doors, and raced inside.

# ABOUT THE AUTHOR

*Photo by Kippy Goldfarb, Carolle Photography*

**Leo J. Maloney** is the author of the acclaimed Dan Morgan thriller series, which includes *Termination Orders, Silent Assassin, Black Skies, Twelve Hours, Arch Enemy, For Duty and Honor, Rogue Commander, Dark Territory, Threat Level Alpha*, and *The Morgan Files*. He was born in Massachusetts, where he spent his childhood, and graduated from Northeastern University. He spent over thirty years in black ops, accepting highly secretive missions that would put him in the most dangerous hot spots in the world. Since leaving that career, he has acted in independent films and television commercials. He has seven movies to his credit, both as an actor and behind the camera as a producer, technical advisor, and assistant director. He is an avid collector of classic and muscle cars and has won numerous prizes in tenpin bowling. He lives in Venice, Florida.

Visit him at www.leojmaloney.com or on Facebook or Twitter.

# The Dan Morgan Thriller Series

## The Alex Morgan Thriller Series

CPSIA information can be obtained
at www.ICGtesting.com
Printed in the USA
LVHW030319230122
709005LV00003B/295